Angels Tread

Black Angel Saga

Book 4

Rhobin Lee Courtright

A Wings ePress, Inc.
Science Fiction Novel

Wings ePress, Inc.

Edited by: Jeanne Smith
Copy Edited by: Joan C. Powell
Executive Editor: Jeanne Smith
Cover Artist: Rhoobin Lee Courtright

All rights reserved

Wings ePress Books
www.wingsepress.com

ISBN-13: 978-1-61309-575-1
ISBN-10: 1-61309-575-9

Published In the United States Of America

Wings ePress Inc.
3000 N. Rock Road
Newton, KS 67114

Preface

Lieutenant Jezlynn Chambers was an engineering officer aboard the United Planets Alliance's Space Service Corps Embassy Ship the *Constant* when it was destroyed. She woke in the mines of Ezredin as a slave, but she didn't know who she was and had no memory of her previous life. Another slave, Khajarian T'Carta Kar, owned her, his guards having given him his royal due as a prince of Khajari.

Jezlynn had changed. She was no longer one person but became six different individual personalities. May emerged first. She is deaf, mute, and filled with fear. Any event could trigger a terrifying memory. The emotional personality Lynn emerged next. She relieved May's fear and her own grief through song.

T'Carta escaped the mines, taking Jezlynn with him, but he released her once they reached safety. During their trip to freedom, Jesse, the social communicator and perfectionist persona emerged. She could control body time for the others.

Others emerged. Alyss is blind, but that does not hamper her logic, perception, or insightful planning, and predictions. She prefers no one know about her. Nael is a masculine persona who was an inventor and expert investigator. He also avoided recognition—being a man in a woman's body was hard. Jet emerged last. She was a hyperactive, fun-loving and reckless military persona, a soldier and pilot who always protects Jezlynn as a whole.

Once free of the mines, May's unexpected memory of Jezlynn's military status made Jesse return to the Service Corps. She learned she had been deemed a deserter and was transferred to the Rangers to complete her service obligation, a demotion from her former Corps 'elite' status to a common soldier, or Ranger 'meat.' She served during the Alliance-Khajari war, earning distinguished service medals. Once released from the Rangers, she served on several trade ships before joining the crew of Sanker Tricome's pirate ship. On a stopover at a non-allied space station, she found Commander Thomas Langston, another of the *Constant*'s supposed deserters.

When Tom's father disowned him, his aunt gave him her last name of Thorson. Together Jesse and Tom decided to find the other *Constant* crewmembers deemed 'deserters,' but who had been sold into slavery, a dangerous and expensive endeavor. They financed their searches by raids on Space Service Corps drone ships, finding Rafe Dakota and Henry Wakeman, among others. Eventually, Jesse's ability with finances allowed her and Tom to proceed legally with the Pilgrim Shipping Lines.

The head of the Alliance's intelligence department became aware Chambers was the supposedly mythical pirate, the Black Angel. He demanded she use her investigative and discovery talents for his purposes. This brought her to the attention of Undersecretary Corrao, who forced her back into the Space Service Corps with the mission to prevent another conflict with the Khajari. Onboard the Sentinel, she was under the command of Captain Lucien Krayne, the same captain with whom she had fallen in love two years previously while he investigated the Black Angel's supposed misdeeds on the Xanthean inhabited planet Çiro. He is Lu to Jesse, but Krayne to Jet, and Lucien to Alyss.

Jezlynn successfully completed her Service Corps mission, but now finds herself assigned as an ambassador to negotiate a peace treaty with the Khajari.

One

4606:01 Universal Space Calendar, Constellation Station, Earth Sector

"Krayne, it's pathetic how far you got out'a shape since the Nebula." Jet harangued her ship's captain and husband with a mocking laugh while she bounced a few steps back from him.

Lucian Krayne was too out of breath to respond immediately but knew her correct. After the ship's last but turbulent assignment, Jezlynn had endured a competency for duty review. It was now over, but the trial had exposed her multiple personalities despite her desire for secrecy. Now docked, the ship's crew had downtime.

The *Sentinel* would remain at Starbase Constellation, the governmental headquarters for the United Planets Alliance and their military branches, the Space Service Corps, and the Rangers. They waited for their next mission to start, at least until completion of the treaty plans and associated meetings, and of the ship's renovation. Time Jezlynn had decided to remain onboard. Time her athletic persona took to improve her excellent shape.

Jet, the athletic, militaristic personality of his wife, demanded he partner her in training so she could keep her fighting prowess.

Since few onboard could do so, he felt obligated, but he suspected her intent was to improve his physical shape. He now lay on the mat too exhausted to move. Luckily, no crew lingered in the ship's newly enlarged training room to see their captain's humiliating defeat. He huffed a breath while he watched Jet take several dance-like steps to slam her fists and feet in rhythmic order into the stand-alone punching bag. Usually, all crew members showed their captain more respect.

He also knew most of those knowledgeable of her six personalities accepted her the way she was. Perhaps everyone's personality changed with circumstance or time. Perhaps everyone was a different person to everyone who knew them. He knew some of what happened to her, but not all of what had caused her change. However, he knew he loved her the way she was. Except, of course, when she was beating him hands down in a wrestling match.

"Doctor Syms ordered you to take it easy on that ankle," was the best retaliation he had to lessen his defeat. She threw him what he considered an insubordinate smile. He responded with a commanding glare. Jet laughed. While he caught his breath, he wiped sweat from his brow, rubbing his damp palm on the off-duty pullover covering his chest.

Krayne frequently reinforced Syms' orders, but while Jet complained, she wore the brace on the affected ankle, injured after her nemesis Morgan Dachs had abducted her. Dachs was now held in confinement on Constellation. Since her rescue, Krayne had become overly protective, which made his position as her superior officer a good thing. It gave him more power over someone who frequently chose insubordination, and often ignored advice. Jet followed his orders because of her ingrained Ranger training. Yet with her background as a pirate, she frequently flouted authority off duty. Her other personalities were not as aggressive as Jet but just as determined. Strangely, it was the contacts she had made during her pirating and trading background since leaving the Rangers, especially those with the Alliance's former enemy, the Khajari, that forced her back into military service. Now, when they were in private, his enticing but tormenting wife squabbled at all his requests. In public, however, she quietly acquiesced to his orders.

In this instance, Jet's disrespect was correct. Krayne knew he needed to improve physically, not just to better physical shape, but superior shape. Jet stayed in exceptional condition, even while recovering from her recent injuries. He had not realized she had continually trained throughout Jezlynn's exceedingly busy schedule since joining the *Sentinel.* Her shape and condition had impressed Doctor Rae, too. As head of the ship's sickbay, she continued to worry over Jezlynn's mental health.

Jet's laugh answered his taunt. Her startling iridescent-blue eyes were focused on him with humor. She stood bouncing on her feet. "I have been. Order's an order, Krayne. And I promised you to obey orders. I like this new training room you've had developed for the ship."

He gave her an indulgent smile. "You're welcome. With you onboard, its need became apparent. However, the ship is currently undergoing changes for the upcoming mission, so Admiral Wakeman suggested the change." He found her unintentional influence on command fascinating.

"Really? That's unexpected."

Since the review board's findings and her recovery from her abduction by Morgan Dachs, Jezlynn had remained willingly trapped on the ship. He knew Jet's workouts helped relieve Jezlynn's other stresses, especially for Jesse, her social personality. With Alliance President Uebel appointing her as ambassador to the Khajari, her position had changed. She had been appointed to help develop a trade agreement and finalize a treaty between the two former enemies after the recent declaration of peace. In the meantime, chaos continued to surround them. Yet so far, they both waited relatively unaffected, with no meetings, no orders, and no visitors.

It made Krayne Jet's sole entertainment. While they waited for the upper echelons of government to work out the details of the mission, they both had spare time. Jet decided that while they waited, she would involve him in her intense training sessions. He began to wish he had another personality who enjoyed her efforts.

Neither Jet nor any of Jezlynn's other five personalities could leave the ship, not without security guards. Even if she escaped the *Sentinel* without security, the recent exposure of her past had produced an intense public interest and brought her unwanted media attention. While on the *Sentinel*, at least with the minimal staff remaining onboard, few troubled her.

In her current caged status, Jesse, the timekeeper and negotiator, let Jet relieve her stress and anger on him. He knew Jesse hated all the delays and uncertainties, and her public exposure enraged her. It made her edgy, which increased her unpredictability, yet she freely stopped to speak with those working on the refit of several areas in the ship.

From where he lay on the training mat from her last throwdown, Krayne looked at his self-appointed trainer-antagonist. Part of him wanted to argue that gloating-look off her beautiful face. Instead he sought the energy to rise to a sitting position after their vigorous thirty-minute workout followed by a shorter time in hand combat. Part of him agreed with her assessment. That part hoped their mission would begin soon and occupy her other selves more. He pushed his tired, sweaty body to a sitting position, and rubbed his hands along the side of his head.

Jesse, also the social self, flopped down next to him on the mat, leaning back on her arms. She tilted her head to look up at the compartment's overhead. "I need a shower." Her gaze slid toward him and she smiled. "We're healed. Quit holding back on her."

"You still wear a brace and need to be careful until Syms deems otherwise. Besides, I was not holding back." He took a deep breath and stretched-twisted his shoulders. "Well, not too much."

She laughed. "You've trained since the Nebula, but once I rejoined the Corps and your ship, our mission and situations kept you too occupied to maintain Jet's level of training. You'll catch up."

He blew out a deep breath. "It doesn't seem like it."

"Well, since we're all in your pocket, and things have settled down somewhat, I expect your training will be much improved. Jet enjoys testing you."

Lucian aimed a disgusted look at Jesse. "Like you don't?"

She laughed. "You need a shower, too. Let's take one together."

Jumping to his feet at the invitation, Krayne put a hand down to help her up. Jesse rose gracefully, and they left the compartment. Outside the door, two guards waited to escort them through the ship. Undersecretary Corrao demanded the security precautions, even on the ship Krayne captained. He wasn't sure if to prevent Jezlynn escaping from the ship and her assigned duty or to keep her safe from her enemies. Remaining a few steps behind Jesse, Krayne enjoyed watching her move in her tight-fitting workout attire. He guessed the two guards noticed the direction of his attention, but they were behind him, probably watching his wife, too.

Luckily, since in port, most of the crew took advantage of shore leave, leaving the huge embassy class ship largely deserted. One reason Jesse had requested they remain on the ship. Lucian exhaled, feeling what he suspected Jesse felt about security following her everywhere. He nodded to the guards when they reached the door to his quarters. Once in the captain's quarters, the tender's signal flashed, showing it held important messages. He opened the tender, read the notifications, and closed it.

"When?" Jesse asked.

"Day after tomorrow, eight-hundred hours."

She sighed, pulling off her training one-piece. "That timing indicates a lengthy meeting."

He smiled, dropping his own less clingy clothing to the floor, and motioned her toward the rather confined hygiene facilities.

"Did whoever sent you the message mention whether I wear a white or black uniform?" As he gave his head one negative shake, Jesse said, "That means the vacillation is not over. Now I truly need a shower."

"Wear white," he advised.

~*~

Even dressed in pristine white Space Service Corps uniforms like so many SCC officers surrounding them, and even leaving the *Sentinel* at an early hour to enter the station's transport to the meeting, Jesse noted their departure didn't prevent netreps presence. A small crowd of individuals waited, wanting to talk with her. They all watched her departure from the *Sentinel.* For as long as she could remember, an important aspect of her life and work always involved concealment. Her change in circumstance and lack of privacy amplified her anxiety and her temper. She felt furious but also realized a camera picked up her every move and expression. Her alertness brought Jet to ride on her consciousness. This time Jesse welcomed her other's presence.

"Your circumstances have changed," Krayne said, reading her mood. In public, he kept Corps decorum, never touching her, never standing too close, but everyone knew them married. Jesse glanced at him. Shortly after their initial acquaintanceship, he had always known which of them possessed the body. Now he seemed to know how she felt and what she thought. It disconcerted her.

"I never envisioned myself as a public figure," she replied. "Thanks to the Dachs family, a public enemy, yes."

"Now not only a public figure but also a heroic one with an intriguing story that has not been fully told. You present a mystery the public wants to hear."

She huffed softly. "Not heroic to everyone, including me. And I'd just as soon my past remain a mystery." She smiled, but her voice showed her ire. "I can hardly wait to see my visage on the net...again." She felt nervous and edgy but would not show it with Jet overlooking her consciousness, lately a common occurrence whenever she left the ship. To keep her aggressive and defensive alter from taking over, she knew she had to keep her emotions in check, once an easy task, now a difficult one.

Lu, with one glance at her, read her dismay and smiled with a slight twist of his lips. "Get used to it." Inside the transport craft, he took her hand as they settled into their seats and held it even in the presence of four armed guards during the short trip through the starbase. A pack of netreps waited at their destination, meaning that someone had communicated their course.

Amid the noise, one scream stood out, "Major Chambers, are Captain Krayne and Undersecretary Corrao preventing you from talking to the public?"

She ignored the provocation as she had ignored all netreps and any stranger who started asking her questions. Once they entered the governmental headquarters, the noise abated. She looked at Lu. He appeared unperturbed even though the media investigated his past, too. He also ignored the newsrep's question. A young woman wearing government insignia escorted them to a lounge a few floors up. Admiral Teris Wakeman already waited there, looking pensive.

His presence surprised Jesse. His office was in another station sector assigned to the Space Service Corps. As she and Lu sat on the upholstered chairs surrounding a low table, the admiral asked their escort, "Please bring coffee." The wording was polite but the tone an order. Shortly the young woman returned with a tray holding a coffee pitcher and three cups. Lu took the carafe and filled the cups, handing one to her while Admiral Wakeman picked up his.

As the door closed behind the woman, Wakeman looked up at Jesse. She braced herself for his remarks, ignoring Jet's insistence that she could handle the admiral.

"For a long time, I hated you as a failed Corps officer and deplored having to request your services at Undersecretary Corrao's insistence."

::Don't put up with his shit, Jesse.::

Jesse shrugged off Jet's response. *::I'll listen to him first.::*

"Roberre's high esteem of you gave me pause, but all I could think of was that you caused Henry's death." He hesitated and his eyes filled with emotion. "I cannot tell you the grief that brought my family. Then I learned my grandson was alive and involved in what I thought was your criminal organization." He focused on her again. "Did Henry tell you he nearly slugged me when I called you a deserter and traitor?"

Jesse shook her head no, reaffirming her answer, "No, he never told me anything about your encounters."

Wakeman gave a weak chuckle. "He did. Then he yelled at me, told me what you had done to save him. What you had accomplished—not only rescuing him from slavery but also many others. He told me what had happened on the *Constant,* and how you did what the Corps never did—rescued those lost officers. Indeed, your efforts in your mission led to you finding and saving Henry." He took a sip of his coffee and sat back. "I've since seen you in action and witnessed what you can accomplish against unbelievable odds, yet I stayed implacable." He sighed and huffed. "You met my wife, Amish. She has insisted I apologize to you for what I thought about you. I agreed, and not because she ordered me." He gave her a self-deprecating smile and took a deep breath before he added, "but because you deserve it. I wanted to tell you that and to let you know my opinion of you has completely reversed. You saved Henry's life and kept my family safe from Durant Rosche's machinations in the process. For that, you deserve my gratitude and thanks."

"Admiral Wakeman, you don't need to apologize for what you believed about me. It was a habit of mine to encourage such a perception. Your thoughts are yours alone, and you do not need to apologize for them."

Jet mentally interrupted her. *::You should'a reamed him.::*

Jesse shrugged, glad Wakeman couldn't hear her other. "When we met at Corrao's meeting, I taunted you about Henry, reinforcing what you believed even though I saw the pain I caused you." She returned his close regard. "Henry is my friend, but that was a low blow to someone he loved dearly, and I apologize. Yet, even then, I only tried to protect him, and indirectly those he loved, even if it injured you. Henry has helped me in many ways, and I'm glad he has returned to Corps officer status, and even happier he is with his family again."

"Still you noticed what others didn't. Why so many remained unaware of Rosche's conspiracies worried me. It still does."

"Rosche was a master manipulator."

The admiral rose and offered her his hand. She followed his action and shook it. Wakeman smiled, pursed his lips, and said, "I'll go see if the meeting is ready to start.

She looked at Lu, noting his satisfied smile. "Do you know who is attending?" she asked.

"No, I was not informed." He made no mention of the admiral's apology.

She had told him a long time ago about their initial meeting when the admiral coerced her back into the Service Corp. "I didn't expect that."

"I don't suppose you did, but I'm glad it happened." He looked at her. "You deserve high regard from the Corps...and from the Alliance, for that matter."

Jesse shrugged. "I don't want recognition, at least not this sort, but as you mentioned a few weeks ago, we've gone through some troubling times." She turned to him and grinned. "And hopefully, we won't be up against such opposition and odds on our upcoming mission."

Lu returned her grin, "With any luck."

"Captain Krayne, Major Chambers, I've been asked to escort you to the meeting room," the young woman announced, reentering the lounge. She led them down a long hall and opened the door into a large meeting room. Its windows looked out into the Starbase Constellation's open interior. A long table filled the room. Only two chairs were empty at the table, and those were across from each other.

Military Undersecretary Ricars Corrao set at the head of the table. To his right sat General Roberre, Commander of the Rangers. Across the table from Roberre sat Admiral Wakeman. Roberre indicated for Jesse to take the seat next to Roberre. Lu went to the other side of the table to sit between Admiral Wakeman and his son, former lieutenant now Lieutenant Commander Henry Wakeman.

Jesse took her seat, feeling Jet's presence overlooking her mind and for once welcomed it. She took her accustomed attentive but self-assured posture before looking around to see who else attended. Some of her partners in the Pilgrim Shipping Lines had also rejoined the Corps. They sat across the table from her. On Henry's other side sat Tom Thorson. He wore captain's insignia on his shoulder as did Dale Griffith, Biri Detjen, Grzyb-Doulk, and Deb Elkert. All lost crew from the *Constant*, all partners in Pilgrim Lines shipping, and all owners of their ships which the SSC recently conscripted. They sat next to Tom like a wall of white down the other side of the table. Sitting in the last chair at the table's end was Doctor Liz Rae, the *Sentinel*'s chief medical officer.

Nigel Perez, her recent attorney in the military tribunal before a review board and another former member of the *Constant*, sat to her left. He briefly laid his hand on her sleeve, a warning to relax, and smiled. Beyond him sat several upper echelon Ranger officers, a few suits obviously from governmental posts, and the last, a woman Jesse did not recognize who regarded her with inquisitive intent.

"Major Chambers, or is it Major Krayne?" Corrao asked, causing several attendees to laugh.

"Major Chambers," Krayne said with a warning look at the undersecretary.

"Yes," Corrao said grinning at Lu, "Well, let us get this started." Corrao looked at Jesse, his face taking on a serious and worried manner. "I'm sure you will want to know it was determined this morning that Morgan Dachs has escaped. You already know he was not going to stand trial for his stalking and abduction of you, or for his other criminal activity. Instead, the government adjudication offices declared him incompetent. They decided to send him to a mental facility planet-side until he became able to stand trial on those charges, if ever. Somehow during his transfer this morning, he disappeared. We have investigators on the case. He will be found." His gaze turned to Lu. "Captain Krayne, I know you have security measures already in place for the major's protection."

"Indeed," Admiral Wakeman answered the undersecretary, staring furiously at Corrao, "and those protections will be increased."

Lu looked slightly askance at the admiral for assuming control over his answer. Corrao only nodded. "Very good...General Roberre, make sure that all Rangers working with her are also on alert."

Jesse controlled her gut reaction to Corrao's statement, not allowing emotion to show. She focused instead on the man himself, feeling her insides shake. At the same time, she felt Jet slip from overlooking her consciousness to enter and meld into her psyche. Something changed inside her. She felt it but could not define it. She was herself, but then again, she felt different. She did not feel like herself. She could feel Jesse's fear of just the name Morgan, and yet she felt all of Jet's anger at the name, and her desire to support Jesse. She relaxed against her chair's back, feeling her jaw tighten. Who was she? With a quick quirk of imagination and an internal laugh, she called herself Jezet.

Corrao gave her a half-smile as if measuring her response. He seemed pleased with her reaction. "You will make one hell of a fine ambassador."

Jezet took a breath and a quick glance at Lucian. He watched her, his drawn brows and intense gaze indicating close observation and speculation.

Corrao's attention quickly fixed on the group at the table. "Major Chamber's exact position, along with the considerations of the review board and her place in the military, has been settled. Judge Aquilera has appointed the Corps officers Captains Thorson, Detjen, Dale, Grzyb-Doulk, and Elkert, Commander Henry Wakeman, along with Nigel Perez and Margarete Chambers as advisors to Captain Krayne." He glanced at her. "Doctor Rae is your appointed physician. I think you already agreed to that. Captain Krayne, you will find a list of psychiatrists to choose for Major Chamber's treatment. You will keep me, General Roberre, and Admiral Wakeman advised on her progress."

Lu nodded without making a comment.

Jezet sat in astounded silence. The woman who had adopted her, who she had not seen since her father's death, was on the committee? The prospect defied her imagination. "Won't the captains be busy with their own commands?" she finally asked.

Corrao waved a hand in dismissal. "They can still communicate easily. Let's move on."

"This seems like a highly biased group," the woman down the table said. "Of all the people in the galaxy, these are probably the most connected to Miz Chambers, and they all seem to have already benefited from Miz Chambers' assistance."

"Major Chambers," Jezet corrected and noticed Corrao's sly half-smile emerge.

Corrao leaned forward and gave the woman a hard look. "From what I've heard, Miz Silmyn, they earned everything they have, so cannot be accused of the bias apparent at her hearing." He paused before continuing. "Plus, it was a Service Corps board of review, so there was an expectation of Service Corps appointments."

"The Individual Rights Bureau, despite appearances, was not after Miz Chambers..."

"Major Chambers," Jezet inserted with some asperity.

"...Major Chambers," Miz Silmyn repeated slowly, "to benefit from her substantial finances and holdings. The Bureau, will, however, be placing an observer on the *Sentinel*'s Embassy staff."

Krayne replied. "By law, the Individual Rights Bureau always has the prerogative of placing personnel on any Embassy ship."

Quiet filled the room.

Silmyn smiled. "They are representatives, and this individual, while having ties to the embassy's mission, will also have directives about Miz Chambers' welfare. I have documentation for this from President Uebel."

"This person is under the head of the *Sentinel*'s Embassy Ambassador's influence and order?" Corrao asked.

The woman smiled. "Yes."

Corrao looked at Lucian. "Captain Krayne?"

"I have no influence over the embassy staff, except concerning the ship's safety and maintenance. I will advise the Individual Rights Bureau, though, that Doctor Inserra will not be allowed onboard."

Jezet blinked and felt relief at Lu's response. She felt both Jet and Jesse's anger. Inserra had used her authority in Jesse's last mission to further the investigation into Jezlynn's reputed disamine use to nearly thwart the mission. Inserra's actions then lead to her Military Review Board's competency hearing. It ended with public expose of her possible multiple personalities.

The woman looked affronted but nodded her agreement.

"Whoever this representative is, they shall not inject themselves into Major Chambers' situation onboard the *Sentinel*, or involve themselves in her new mission, Miz Silmyn," Corrao said with a hard look at the woman.

He waited briefly before continuing. "All right, then. On to the mission itself. Your ambassadorship is different from that of the embassy side of the *Sentinel*. When you are on ambassadorial business, you have the title of ambassador and the authority of that office. On ship or off, your determination rules in this negotiation, but the *Sentinel*'s embassy Ambassador Nohl will act as an advisor, one whose new mission is to assist you, but not to interfere." He cast a look at Silmyn.

"Am I Meat or Elite on this assignment?"

A few huffed and quickly contained laughs surround the table at the Ranger-Corps quip.

"Major Chambers, you will be changing back to Ranger uniform on the *Sentinel*," Corrao said in his clipped, confident manner, "but you report directly to Captain Krayne. On ship, your duty is the squad of Ranger embassy security guards, and you will report to the ship's captain, although your rank is high for such a command. Will T'Carta Kar be handling the negotiations as a go-between with Kalmona-Rek Kerub?"

Several captains chuckled, disconcerting the undersecretary and the two senior officers.

Henry Wakeman spoke up. "We all assumed you knew."

"Knew what?" Admiral Wakeman asked.

"Supreme Ruler Kalmona-Rek Kerub was, and as far as I know, remains captain of the Pilgrim Lines ship the *Azreal*. Jesse rescued him from slavery at the same time she did me.

Two

Henry's revelation halted Undersecretary Corrao and drew Lucian's attention back to her. The undersecretary swiveled his chair toward her. He slouched against the corner of the armrest and braced an elbow on the chair's arm. His bloodhound likeness stared at her. Jesse's resolve combined with Jet's strength to hold Jezet immobile. After a moment, he asked, "You have an intimate acquaintanceship with the new supreme ruler of the Khajari?"

"Friendship, yeah."

"You provided him a ship? Work?"

She heard the shock in his voice and raised her brows. "Well, yeah. He had to make a living and he couldn't go back to Khajari territory. Even visiting T'Carta put Kar's whole family in danger. Kerub got crew from other Khajari slaves we freed. Most of them were entrapped like T'Carta and Kerub by the old Khajari regime, so his crew feels allied only to him. T'Carta also sent him some crew, anonymously of course, who are now some of Kerub's top advisors."

"Why wasn't this in my report on your contacts?"

Jezet tilted her head slightly as she regarded the undersecretary. "Well, Mr. Corrao, you never told me who or what was in your reports or who was on your list as my contacts. T'Carta you knew, because we stayed in frequent communication, which your investigators discovered. You had previously mentioned Kerub at my hearing, so I thought you knew."

"We had all the names of your Pilgrim Lines captains."

"Kerub didn't transport for Griff...while part of the company, he stayed to more iffy transport lanes on the fringe, mostly in Zeta sector or routes to other non-allied colonies. T'Carta wanted Pilgrim Lines to offer Kerub anonymity, and we did."

"The major designed his ship," Captain Biri Detjen added with an irritated glance at Corrao.

"So...it has all the refinements of all the Pilgrim Lines ships?" Wakeman asked.

Jezet nodded. "Yeah."

Wakeman frowned, asking, "How much does he know about those refinements?"

"The *Azreal* has everything any Pilgrim Line ship has, but the patented work can only be done at Griff Shipyards, or by Griff engineers at Bant Shipyards."

"Do the Khajari have access to how your patents work?"

"I don't know."

"So...you are fairly sure you can knock out a treaty with the Khajari?" Corrao asked, moving into a more relaxed slouch as the tenseness in his face left.

"No. There are no guarantees. The Khajari are hard negotiators, and their loyalty to the Khajari homeland surpasses their loyalty to their leader known now as Kalmona-Rek Kerub, especially with him so new to the office. Nor will Kerub kowtow to anything he doesn't agree to. All you get with me is a measure of trust."

"That, Major Chambers, is more than most negotiators start with." He straightened in his seat.

"Undersecretary Corrao," Jezet said, "before this mission starts, the *Sentinel* must pick up Kar's son T'Carta Kizz from Asedin. He has been stranded there since the closing of Gasch."

Amusement lined Corrao's eyes. "That is interesting, Major Chambers. It seems the Genitor of Asedin contacted Freedom Station, which forwarded her message to President Uebel. The Genitor requested that we allow the Xanthean delegation to visit with you before your mission to Khajari. It seems Asedin's Xantheans also want to join the treaty negotiations. Did you tell them of your mission?"

Krayne answered, drawing Corrao's laser-like attention from her. "The Genitor, like many circle leaders on the Xanthean planets, seems to know whatever interests her people while ignoring much else."

"Can't one of our ships fulfill the assignment?" Thorson asked.

"No, the Genitor asked specifically to speak with Ambassador Chambers, insisted actually, and that was before Major Chambers had even been considered or appointed to the position."

"The Genitor, for someone eschewing modern technology, seems to be well informed on whatever she wants to know," Jezet said, repeating Krayne's comment.

Corrao's fingers thumped the table. "That she does, and she will only accept Major Chambers and Captain Krayne as the Alliance's representatives."

"She ordained both Jezlynn and me as part of her Circle," Krayne said.

"Is that so?" Corrao's glance slid from Krayne back to Jezlynn. "You are certainly embraced in strange places, Major Chambers."

He turned to the former Pilgrim Lines captains. "We will continue with information on Major Chambers' mission, but outside of senior officers, Captain Krayne, Commander Wakeman, the Rangers present, and the representatives from the state department, everyone else is excused. To our new Corps captains, you have received your assignments. You know Captain Krayne will stay in contact with you regarding the major. President Uebel has asked you to attend a short ceremony here at the station at fifteen-hundred hours, followed by a reception and dinner. Before then, you will coordinate with Admiral Zamudo, Head of Fleet Operations, for your orders."

After those excused left, Corrao looked at Jezet. "You are full of surprises, Major, but now we will talk about the terms the Alliance wants to achieve for this treaty, and how you will conduct your Ranger squad on the *Sentinel* while working with the embassy."

It took hours, with lunch served during the meeting. Jezet felt Jesse would be concerned about the meal's contents but knew inspecting it was impolite and felt Jet's humor over the situation. While both were combined in her, touching, or relinquishing to either seemed impossible, so she could not escape her present position. Her sandwich held a concoction of fish and vegetables. It tasted great, so she ate with rare hunger.

She noticed Lu's regard and read his ire at not knowing about Kerub, but she noted something more troubled him. *He knew of her change and could not recognize her.* Jezet felt both sorry and elated at the realization, which also felt odd.

When they finished, Corrao insisted the whole group go with him to President Uebel's meeting. As they left the conference room following the undersecretary, she told Lu, whose tight facial muscles revealed his mood, sotto voice, "It wasn't my secret to keep."

"I understood that," but his voice and expression held an unspoken question and wariness as he regarded her.

Corrao led them to a presidential chamber designed for presentations. A crowd of netreps filled the room along with many high governmental dignitaries, managers, and aides who arranged their superiors' decrees, and large groups of both Ranger and Corps officers. The constant drone of low voices increased as she entered.

"Oh, hell," Jezet said in just as low a voice as before, even as she knew cameras focused on her. Another part of her felt exalted, which left her puzzled.

Lucian touched her arm, urging her forward to where Corrao indicated they should stand. She soon stood next to the other officers of the *Constant,* now uniformed and returned to the Corps, in a line on a low dais. They looked just as uncertain as she felt. She noted others associated with Pilgrim Lines, including Merit, in the audience. Merit's eyes glowed with pleasure as she looked at her Tommy. Captain Tom Thorson returned his wife's regard. Jezet noted Tom's father also stood in the audience. The two had not yet reconciled, and Langston's presence there was the closest proximity the two had shared in years. Jezet thought it might be time for Jesse to interfere.

Within a few minutes, a tall, grey, and somewhat gaunt President Uebel entered. The room quieted. He walked to the podium in front of the audience presenting his usual dignified presence. After a brief pause, during which Uebel looked at the crowd and the row of officers on the podium, he began to speak.

"When an Alliance Ship meets destruction, it always launches public suffering and incurs security concerns, as happened with the *Constant*. The loss of the United Planets Alliance's Embassy Ship was a disaster, and many blamed a group of officers for that tragedy. We now know that the original story was not true. Some of those accused of leaving the ship made the repairs that saved the ship, which allowed the remaining crew to return home. These officers gained the *Constant*'s freedom but lost their own by the gross misconduct of another, who traded them into slavery for the ship's release. As they escaped slavery, they turned to illegal means to make the Space Service Corps pay for betraying them. For these actions, I gave them a full pardon. Many citizens still wonder why.

"I have an ever-growing list, now numbering over a thousand, of Alliance citizens who were freed from slavery with those ill-gotten gains. Certainly a dangerous undertaking, but their bravery did not end there. During this last year's political and inter-galactic uncertainties, they used their ships to protect the Alliance and its allies' space, keeping the Alliance out of another war with the late Khajari regime. Therefore, I, with the legislature's backing, have reclassified their former transgressions into Alliance missions.

"Now they have donned their Corps uniforms again to fill the voids in the service's ranks. For their service, those officers present, and all those unable to attend, will receive this government's highest honor. They have defined courage standards for Corps officers, and it is with gratitude and thankfulness that I pin the Alliance Star of Liberty on these patriots." Turning, Uebel walked toward Tom Thorson, the first in the line, and pinned a gold seven-point star on his uniform's lapel, telling him of his and the Alliance's thankfulness and appreciation. Thorson saluted the president.

It was clear to Jezet how much the honor affected Tom, and looking at those in line, her other comrade officers, too. Uebel moved down the line, accepting their salutes and saying the same until he reached her. She saluted him.

"When you came to my office, Major, I never foresaw this, but I have since learned you are unpredictable in everything but loyalty to your mission. My sincerest thanks."

"You've done something few can accomplish, Mr. President. I am speechless."

"I am glad I could finally impress you." He pinned the star on the lapel of her jacket.

"You'll impress me even more if you can get me out of here without having to talk to any netreps."

Uebel smiled. "That I can do." Before he led them away, he concluded his program with the press. He turned to Lu, "If you would join me and the major," he quickly turned to lead them off the dais.

Despite netreps' vocal requests, the rest of the group, including Corrao, followed him down the steps from the dais and toward the side door through which the president had entered earlier. Assigned security agents had opened the door for the president and prevented anyone outside the group from following him. Uebel walked next to Jezet down a long empty corridor with Lu on her other side.

"Your life is now changed, Jezlynn, may I call you Jezlynn?" At her affirmative reply, he continued, "As my appointed ambassador, your life will necessarily be more public. I am sorry this causes you such distress, but maybe I can help you in that area, too."

Having this conversation on her only second face-to-face contact with the man, caused Jesse hesitation. She realized the strange merging with Jet had ended. Jezet was gone. Unexpected exhaustion gripped her.

He looked at her and smiled. "I've caused you speechlessness again." His smile widened. "You restore my faith in my oratory skills. Our last conversation caused me much the same reaction— speechlessness. However, I am far more familiar with you now, know your story, and background. I am aware you do not want the public's attention for many reasons. From my experience in similar situations, I know netreps can be voracious scythes. Yet any netrep would find an interview with you a treasure beyond imagination. It so happens that I know the names of a few who are true journalists, neither malicious word manipulators nor vicious agents and who do not report for their own glory. You can choose any of these. Each will tell your story in fair and unbiased words with no embellishments. I'll give their names to you."

Jesse knew it was a request bordering on an order. By then they had reached a large and elaborately decorated reception room. President Uebel introduced his group to those in attendance and graciously thanked everyone for coming. His wife joined him. Several servers carrying trays of drinks and hors d'oeuvres for a social hour emerged from a side door.

Jesse fought her fatigue while standing and soon felt Lu's hand on her arm, guiding her to a heavily upholstered bench along the wall. She sank into it gratefully. Lu stood before her looking seriously worried while he observed her.

"You're not handling this so well," he said before sipping some champagne a server delivered.

He gave her a glass and she quickly sipped a small amount. Before looking at him, she looked around the room at an enlarging crowd that was still entering the room. "This doesn't appear impromptu."

"No, I expect it another joint Roberre-Wakeman setup."

"Actually, not entirely," Roberre said, having arrived quickly. He shook Lu's hand and sat on Jesse's right side. She had not noticed him, which was an odd circumstance.

Clearing her throat, she turned to him with a smile. The three of them formed a small group separate from the large crowd of conversing people. Because of Roberre's rank, few had the effrontery to join them.

Roberre spoke with a definite smirk. "It's a Uebel-Corrao-Roberre-Wakeman arrangement. You have done the Rangers proud, Major, even in your position within the Service Corps. You cannot even imagine the number of recruits who have applied since information about you became public. I believe the Corps is also enjoying an increase."

"Glad, sir, that my service could be so useful."

Roberre laughed. "I'm glad to meet your polite self."

His salvo reinforced her new station in life—even he knew about her other selves.

"Don't worry, Major. Wakeman and I have also worked together on a plan to get you back to the *Sentinel* sight unseen." He rose and held a lengthy conversation with Lu on more details of how Jesse's new assignment on the *Sentinel* was to work. She would normally have felt outraged and worry at being left out but instead felt grateful Lu had taken over. As her senior officer, he would inform her. Shortly Roberre moved away to talk to other guests.

Lu sat next to her, and surprisingly, no one approached.

"What happened?" he asked.

A quick side-glance showed his dogged determination to get an answer. Even her short hesitation made his jaw draw tighter.

"When I heard about Morgan's escape—and how was that possible?—Jet was conscious with me. An increasingly frequent occurrence." She looked away from his intent gaze. "I felt, I don't know, alarm maybe, but knew I had to remain calm and in control. Jet knew and seemed to merge with me. I remember everything I said and did, but I didn't feel like me. It was strange." She turned a quick glare on him. "Don't say a thing about my whole existence being strange."

He quirked a smile at her. "I wouldn't dream of it."

She quickly looked away again. "Whoever I was even renamed us—Jezet." A weak laugh escaped her. "Since Jet's and my melding ended, I feel exhausted, shattered even. Nothing like this has ever happened, except, perhaps, when other personalities emerged."

His warm hand covered hers and softly squeezed. "Thank you for telling me. Your captains and I all reacted to the news about Dachs' escape with anger. Your suspicions are accurate. Someone had to have helped him. This time, do not question any protection provided for your safety, all right?"

She nodded as Tom, Henry, and Biri finally came over. "We've talked with both Wakeman and Roberre. Until Morgan is recaptured, and whoever helped him..." Tom began.

"We suspect Austin Dachs," Biri inserted.

"...We've requested you never be left alone on the ground," Tom said, "or in any ship, including the *Sentinel*." He looked at Lu for backup.

"I was just telling Jesse the same thing. Henry, as the newly appointed intelligence officer on the *Sentinel*..."

"... Whether you requested the duty or not, I'd still be checking on Jesse. What happened before will not reoccur."

For once, Jesse did not protest and only vaguely heard Henry inquiring what happened after they left the meeting. Lu explained.

Time passed for her faster than anticipated, and soon Lu told her dinner was ready. Rousing from her strange and unusual lethargy, and still filled with confused thoughts, she rose to accompany him through the stately double doors into the ornate dining room. It was a formal affair, and Jesse sat next to Uebel as the guest of honor. Lu sat at the other end of the exceedingly long table with the first lady. Roberre sat across the table from her, looking pleased as he and Uebel talked. Jesse did her best to provide entertaining conversation, but what had occurred still overwhelmed her.

Later, Wakeman and Roberre saw that she and Lucian, and all the new Corps officers, were able to return to their ships unnoticed.

Krayne watched his wife on the transport back to the *Sentinel*'s berth. Jesse appeared quiet, sitting almost as immobile as Alyss, Jezlynn's blind, analytical alter, and stared out the shuttle's window. He knew she was aware of his regard and ignoring him, which roused his temper. He felt pleased she had confided what had happened in the meeting. It was a big step. Another part of him wondered and worried about what the incident signified. Her fatigue became apparent although she hid it well from everyone else. He recognized the performance, having encountered it before. She had held up admirably while on their short return trip through the president's private exit and various military access ways. Once in the shuttle, she stayed calm but motionless. Even moving through the *Sentinel*, she walked with her normal smooth gait, and like him, nodded at the few crew members they encountered.

Three

Once in the captain's quarters, though, Jesse begged his pardon and went to bed, more like collapsed. Within minutes he knew she had fallen deeply asleep. Turning on the room's observation, he went to his office desk to work. His mind would not let go of what Jesse admitted had happened. He checked if Rae was onboard, picked up his comlink, and left, nodding to the security woman guarding the door, who had already pulled her comlink out to report his movement.

"She is sleeping. I'm watching. No one enters."

The guard nodded. "I've updated T-Omer, and he is already sending a second officer."

With his nod, she said, "She will be safe, Captain."

T-Omer had remained onboard as did nearly half of his security officers, displaying an unexpected dedication to their duty while in port.

Krayne doubted the safe part of the officer's statement. More things were in play than anyone else knew. The guard remained unaware of his uncertainty. He walked directly to sickbay through many darkened corridors where no one currently worked. The ship's doctor had also remained on duty although no patients were aboard. The ship's quiet gave Rae rare privacy and the chance to get caught up on her reports, or so she told him. She didn't sleep there, though. He knew she and Commander Ribberdan were sharing a hotel suite near the docking area.

Liz Rae met him at the entrance to the ship's sickbay.

"Problem?" she asked.

"Not an emergency."

Her serious demeanor persisted. "Let's go to my office. What happened?" Although sickbay held no patients, a few medical personnel performed maintenance and technology updates.

"I'm not sure," he answered, following her.

Once inside her office, she asked, "Where is she?"

"Sleeping."

"In your quarters? Observation on?" At his nod, she said, "Tell me what happened," while she accessed the readings.

He went into detail about what had happened during the meeting and what Jesse told him afterward. "She called their melded personalities Jezet. Whatever happened exhausted her."

"This happened when Morgan's escape was mentioned? That information also upset me, and I have been wondering how it occurred."

"I suspect the Dachs' still hold some power within the Alliance. Can you check on her?"

"The health monitor you insisted she wear should tell something." Her gaze rose to his. "She was very unhappy about its installation. Have any of them reacted?"

"No, they haven't." He gave a huffed laugh. "Her reaction to your health monitor wasn't near as bad as when I had a tracer placed in her," Krayne said.

"Was that the one Morgan Dachs cut out of her?"

"Yes. Your health monitor..."

"...can also act as a tracer." Rae watched the readings on the monitor. "About the Dachs' influence, you could be right. The monitor shows while her cortisol hormone is higher than normal, her melatonin is also high. She is deeply asleep—all of her. I wasn't watching Jesse in the meeting, but whenever she spoke, she sounded a little less formal than Jesse normally speaks, but I didn't sense anything different. Do you think she is changing?"

"It's possible, but why?"

She briefly paused as she watched the monitor, then looked at Krayne. "I would ask her to talk to me, but she will resist. Since Inserra's forced 'therapy' session and her return from Morgan Dachs' abduction, Jesse and the others have evaded any confidences, which has stalled all the previous progress. I stopped the more formal meetings as they were stressing her. You are having her watched now?"

He nodded, raising his observation from his comlink to Rae. "Yes. One of T-Omer's security stands at all entrances to my office and quarters, even the adjoining wardroom."

"Are you still worried about her?"

"Outside of the personality melding, no. Since Jet began taking delight in my physical training, I've noticed all of Jezlynn is more grounded."

"Delighted in your exhaustion?"

"Our encounters amuse her, but she is right. I am not in my best physical shape. Tom told me once I am, I'll beat her...sometimes."

"Thorson?"

"Yes. He has gone through the process and now continues it on his own. Probably all the Pilgrim Line captains do so."

"Did you know Corps' psychology is trying to interview them?"

"Successfully? They are now Corps' officers."

"A little less than successful. The doctor in charge told me his staff has never dealt with such an enigmatic and reticent group. Since the captains fulfilled the minimum requirements, they remain in their positions."

"Plus, the Corps Command wants them."

Rae turned to the monitor's readings. "Well, we don't know what might be happening with the alien organisms in both her system and yours. Medical confirmed all Pilgrim Lines captains have it, too. With her recent use of zenfler on her trips to Asedin, which you know is the herbal base of the illegal drug disamine which shattered her mind after the *Constant*, it might have re-energized the organisms. How are you going to handle this?"

Krayne rubbed the back of his neck. "As best I can. My loyalty feels divided. I do have to thank Roberre for transferring her to the onboard Ranger squad as they are part of the embassy."

Rae laughed. "I noticed Wakeman also promoted all of the *Constant*'s former crew who rejoined the Corps. The local news sites are running the story ad nauseum. Perhaps I can get Alyss to talk to me. She is logical and often detached."

"You've not talked to Nael?"

"No. He, I think, avoids me."

Krayne nodded. "He avoids everyone, even me. Alyss is also reclusive, but I think her blindness drives her desire for isolation. The only other person she has talked to is you."

"She only talks to me reluctantly, probably because you had already introduced us; and you're right—her blindness makes her want to avoid contact. How did you come to recognize her different personalities? You always know who is in control."

"From your research on her, you probably know she kidnapped me and later saved my life after I escaped her ship." He laughed.

"When you escaped and kidnapped her in return?" Rae asked.

Krayne nodded. "My abducting her shocked her. Afterward, I held her in the brig on my former ship, the *Nebula*."

"I read the report. The Xantheans demanded her release and later forced your marriage."

"Before then we had unusual encounters where she just acted differently. Then I noticed odd differences in her behavior. Jesse always touched her hair. Probably to make sure it was in place as she remains somewhat obsessive about neatness."

Rae sputtered a laugh. "Somewhat obsessive?"

"Her graceful movement and conversation first attracted me, which she meant to do. She is exquisitely feminine in appearance. Jet never notices when her hair is bedraggled or covered in grime. She wears drab, inconspicuous, functional-type clothing. She has an aggressive, clipped voice and an intimidating manner. Her movements are more powerful, ultra-quick, and cat-like in stealth, and she frequently stretches her arms and shoulders when she emerges, as if she has been caught in some tight confinement.

"Lynn is overly emotional, buoyant, and sometimes frivolous, but when the others belittle her, she can take vindictive reprisal, including using her time to have her hair bleached blonde or having flashy manicures, which drives Jet berserk.

"It took a long time to recognize Nael, but his low and uninflected voice differed dramatically, and he always looks stiff. Casual conversation makes him clench his fists. Alyss usually clasps her hands and looks downward, almost appearing ethereal, but I noticed she was left-handed..."

"And May looks unusually timid, even fragile. She wraps her arms around herself."

Krayne leaned back in the chair. "Yes."

"I'm amazed others didn't notice these changes."

"Tom Thorson did, but Jesse was careful not to expose her circumstances around most of her closest colleagues, leaving them uninformed once she rescued them. I think Tom kept them, and continues to keep all of them, informed."

They talked a little longer on possible measures to take. Leaving the sickbay, Krayne toured the ship to inspect the changes. With limited personnel aboard and only those with designated duties, few interrupted his journey. He examined the changes in the embassy deck, the Corps offices deck, and in areas associated with other ship functions and defenses. For so new a ship to undergo these changes was remarkable, but Wakeman had demanded them. Krayne guessed at an even higher request, especially after the admiral talked with Jezlynn to discuss the possible use of her patents on the *Sentinel*. Work continued as slated for completion in six weeks. He suspected Wakeman had scheduled another meeting and tour before then. For him and probably for Jezlynn, it seemed disembarkation was too far off, and now another mission with the Xantheans needed completion before approaching the Khajari. Finished with his self-imposed task, he noted two important communications on his office tender, neither of which could take place in a public area. He headed for the captain's office.

His new adjutant, Lieutenant Howard Wakeman, held the front office desk and looked up as Krayne entered. After his previous adjutant had been arrested on charges of treason, Howard had come to him and asked for the position.

"Captain, I have the progress reports you requested on your tender, plus Admiral Wakeman is coming aboard at thirteen-hundred hours tomorrow for a meeting with you and Major Chambers, and Command has sent a new schedule for the *Sentinel*."

Krayne nodded, amused at the number of Wakemans invading his ship. While Howard had been aboard since the ship's first mission, now his older brother Henry would serve on the *Sentinel*, and their grandfather, Admiral Wakeman, had command over all of them. "Are any adjustments needed to any crewperson's current leave?"

"I've already sent the messages for those who are to report early. The Embassy has also updated its staff's assignments and times."

Inside his office, he contacted his first caller, President Uebel. He had to wait through several assorted communication links to finally be connected.

"Captain Krayne, I'm contacting you to reiterate how important Jezlynn's interview has become."

"Sir, she has always valued her privacy..."

"...I am aware, Captain, and I hate to insist, so please encourage her. The names I sent you are reliable. Questions about her reliability have emerged from several government agencies, and, of course, various media sources and public bureaus."

"Miz Silmyn?"

"Among others."

"What about Morgan Dachs?"

"This is also a concern. I know you take all the appropriate measures to protect Major Chambers and will continue to do so when she becomes the ambassador, but the animus and attraction she engenders among the public have become a concern. Corrao has told me about the revelations regarding Kalmona-Rek Kerub during today's meeting. I am most impressed and look forward to a successful mission, but we all need awareness of the forces working against her. Stay in contact."

With the president's distinct demand, the communication ended. The next was from newly promoted Commander Tom Thorson, captain of the *Pole Star*, who, with no deference whatsoever demanded, "What happened during the meeting?"

"Jezlynn? I didn't think anyone else noticed."

Thorson snorted. "Yeah, many of us noticed, and remember, I'm on the committee."

"I haven't forgotten. According to Jesse, she and Jet temporarily melded into a new persona who called herself Jezet."

A moment of silence followed. Thorson looked both disturbed and contemplative. He expelled a deep breath. "Keep me appraised. Remember I'm dealing with Merit, too, who you know will defend Jesse or any of the others to any length."

Krayne knew this and what mayhem Merit could cause, especially for Jezlynn. His lips quirked as he perceived his and Thorson's identical situations. He noticed Thorson saw the movement, his face reflecting his knowledge and awareness.

"We have a lot in common," Thorson said. With a brief "thanks," he ended the conversation.

Even knowing he was dealing in the unknown and unforeseen territory, Krayne said, "A little respect would go a long way."

~ * ~

::He's worried about us.::

Waking from her drowsy state, Jesse opened her eyes and stretched before answering Alyss' mental observation aloud. "I know."

Jet laughed supplanting Alyss. *::Your Jezet freaked him out more than he admits. That felt more like one of my stretches.::*

Jesse shook her head. Two alters at once. *::Does it? My Jezet? You mean our Jezet. Do you think part of you lingers in me? You're not upset with the name?::*

::Nah. It was interesting. Felt different, smarter, and more composed for a few minutes. Gave me more understanding of you.::

Jesse laughed. *::You are smart enough to be cunning. You also saved me from my Morgan memories as you knew how just the mention of his name affected me and how much his escape upset me. How did you do it?::*

::Cunning, yes, when it comes to survival, but not manipulative or political like you. How'd it happen? Don't know, felt your fear. It just happened. Do you mind now?::

::No. How could I? It was an interesting state.::

::Yep. Gotta try it again when I'm training. See if I lose any edge.::

Groaning she said, "Not something to look forward to."

::I do not envy you,:: Alyss said. *::Since you and Jet merged, I can connect with everyone.::*

"What?" Lu asked from the bedroom door. He looked worried but stoic. "I thought I heard you talking in here. You and Jet's melding tired you…to exhaustion."

Completing another stretch, Jesse rolled to a sitting position feeling newly energized. She looked at the timepiece. Twelve hours had passed since her last awareness.

Lu grinned at her. "Yes, you had a long, well-deserved sleep."

"Where did you sleep?"

"You didn't wake when I laid down."

She raised her brows. "Really? What you heard was me talking with Jet about what happened. She thinks we need more experimentation with the…melding…and wants to take me to her training mat."

Lu snorted. "Good luck. Let me know when you do." It wasn't an idle comment but a command.

Jesse smirked a smile, rose, moved to him, and kissed him. "Knowing Jet, she'll have you there as an opponent." She grinned when he wrapped his arms around her.

Before kissing her in return, he smile-frowned, admitting, "You are undoubtedly right."

~ * ~

Once redressed, Jesse headed for the door and let Jet take charge before reaching the corridor. Lu already had returned to duty. Jet headed to the new training facility installed on the *Sentinel* feeling irked Jesse remained in her awareness. She tried to force Jesse to retire, but it didn't happen. While she had body control, Jesse still retained consciousness. Entering the room, Jet met unexpected company. With most personnel off the ship, she thought she would have the generously sized facility to herself.

While any crewmember could use the training room, she kept to the unfrequented hours when few were active. The facility had a wall lined with exercise machines and equipment she often used plus a padded floor for freeform movement. Ceiling lights illuminated the area. As she entered, an awareness emerged as to how rumor spread through the individuals remaining on the ship. She felt Jesse overlooking her time. Those in the gym all stood waiting and looked at her as she entered. She sighed. It seemed many knew about her training sessions with the captain, so now she found three Rangers currently under the command of Major Chambers waiting for her arrival along with two Corps officers. She wondered who had informed them of her destination.

::Probably heard one of my guards telling Krayne I'd left and where I was headed. They want training. I expect the Rangers don't have to ask... probably know what will be expected.:: Jet's smug tone divulged how those men and women would be trained. Jesse sighed internally. Since their melding, she and Jesse seemed to hold a persistent place in each other's consciousness.

::They wonder who we are,:: Jesse said.

::Rumor has spread.:: Jet kept the body's presence.

She knew Jesse saw the speculative looks aimed at her. The Ranger lieutenant walked up to her. Jet quickly read his badge, and Jesse filled in the information for her. *::He served in the embassy squad on Freedom Station, Staff Sergeant Stan Kakowski, newly assigned squad leader to the Sentinel.::*

::Know it. Read the files.::

Kakowski spoke. "Nice to know you're back in the Rangers, Major. We saw you had the fitness room scheduled, so we decided to ask if we could work out with you."

"No need to ask, Stan. Fitness training will soon be a requirement for all Rangers, and we will be on a first name only basis in this facility. In here, I'm Jet."

A broad but subdued grin crossed Kalowski's face. The two Corps officers came to stand next to Kakowski. She recognized them as ensigns who had joined the *Sentinel* when she did just over a year ago.

One spoke. "Ma'am, we'd also like to be included in your practices."

"Not practices but training. Have you done hand combat moves before?" she asked.

"No, ma'am."

::If you agree, there will be more here tomorrow.::

::Good,:: Jet answered Jesse while saying to everyone, "First off, besides first names, no uniforms and no ranks in this training room. Let's get started." She led them through warm-up exercises, after which she paired up her Ranger squad members, learning their names as she did with the Corps personnel. She informed the Rangers they were responsible for showing the Corps officers the basic moves, a rare moment for the Ranger enlisted soldiers. She paired with Kakowski at a more difficult level, flooring him within five minutes. "Stan, you are seriously out of shape." While breathing harder, she was not breathless.

Kakowski jumped to his feet, grinning but gasping for breath. "Yes, Jet."

The others had stopped to watch, so she ordered them back to their training sessions. While her partner gained his breath, she observed the others. The two Corps ensigns knew some moves, but the Rangers were better. However, none were as good as she wanted or expected them to be since embassy ship duty was deemed less dangerous.

"You all need to increase both your strength and endurance. To advance in training, you will need to log two laps around the lower base corridor once daily." Jet noticed movement by the door. Henry Wakeman stood there wearing training gear.

Henry smiled and approached her. "But who is going to keep you in top form?" he asked. "Although you complete six laps daily, don't you?"

Henry calmly walked toward her, but Jet knew he planned to challenge her. His speed and flexibility matched her own, but his size, strength, and weight were greater than hers. She had trained him, so he knew all her moves, but she knew his flaws. She smiled at her friend who would soon be her advisor, if not watchdog. It would be an equal match. "Didn't know you had come aboard, Henry."

"Immediately after our various meetings yesterday, Jet. So, you are a Ranger now." Henry began circling her. Jet turned and backstepped, countering his moves.

"Heard you are a commander, Henry. Bizarre."

"Lieutenant commander; bizarre for both of us. You have a healing ankle. I'll be careful and expect you to be cautious."

Sudden fury filled her. Jet attacked. Henry grinned. He flipped her first, but with a lightning-fast roll and quick jump, she gained her feet. They grappled for a few minutes, but she took him down. He just as quickly regained his feet. She took an incautious step and felt a twinge in her ankle as it twisted.

Henry noticed and immediately back stepped with his hands raised. "Enough. End it."

She took an aggressive step toward him but knew she was limping.

"I said stop. Krayne will space me if you get injured…again."

"Not injured."

"Healing not healed." Henry laughed at her and sank to the mat. They were both out of breath. Jet joined him on the mat.

"Get your ankle checked out."

"Is that a threat?"

"Yep, but more an order." He grinned. "Your health decisions aren't yours to make anymore." He rose to his feet and extended a hand to Jet. "I think I will like, at long last, having some ordering of you."

She huffed in response and rose to her feet without help, but Henry was already looking at their audience.

"You're going to train them?" he asked. "I think you'll need help."

"I think so, too," the *Sentinel*'s captain said. Hearing Krayne's voice, Jet looked toward the door. Krayne stood there looking a little smug. "You forgot your brace."

Jet made no comeback, aware of the trainees watching the byplay.

"What are your plans here?" Krayne asked, strolling in.

"Rangers on the *Sentinel* will be in top form for any and every duty."

Henry looked at Kakowski. "You have an arduous task maker."

"I look forward to increasing my duty fitness, sir."

"We all do," one of the ensigns said.

Krayne's gaze shifted to Henry. "She trained you?"

Henry grinned. "Yes, she did. Demanding work."

"Indeed, it is," the captain agreed. "Until Major Chambers is cleared of all restricted duty, you will oversee and help in these training sessions."

Jet squinted at Krayne. "I look forward to being declared fit."

Krayne smiled at her irritation and made a motion for her to come with him. "Good, then you won't mind seeing Dr. Syms now. He returned to the ship just for this."

Before leaving, she looked at Kakowski. "Stan, I'll set aside time for training—you make the schedule for the Rangers. Henry, you do the same for any other personnel who are interested and continue this session for as long as the participants can handle it, at my guess, thirty minutes."

Once they reached the corridor, Jet asked, "How long does my original promise to follow your orders remain in force?"

"As long as I am a superior Corps officer and captain on the ship where you serve, and as long as you are either a Corps or Ranger officer."

"Two more years?" She swore but knew she was limping on her painful ankle. Before they reached Syms' office, Jet retired, leaving Jesse to face the doctor. She briefly halted at the door. While the smell inside the sickbay assailed her, she felt no violent response reactions as she used to.

Lu watched her.

She returned his look and entered the sickbay. Few worked within the facility and no treatments took place. Lu walked her to Syms' office and entered with her, placing a hand around her upper arm as they entered, earning him another glare. He must have felt her tension, but his charming smile hid the smug arrogance in his eyes, which insinuated he only followed and fulfilled his duty. Her exasperated scowl amused him.

Doctor Syms waited inside his office, but the air felt different, free of any scent. She noticed the lighting dimmed and noise abatement was on.

"Didn't you take the ship holiday?" she asked the doctor, hearing the venom lacing her tone.

Syms smiled and asked her to sit on the end of the examination table. "I only returned this morning as I have some work I need to catch up on. Keeping reports current is annoying." He began asking questions but directed them to Lu, who answered while Syms removed her shoe. The doctor gave Lu a receptor-shield to wrap around her ankle. Reading the results, Syms told Lu, "More healing has taken place than I thought, and while her physical activity probably helps bone regeneration, too much physical usage has caused some stress."

"What are your recommendations?" Lu asked.

Jesse made some movement, and Syms quickly looked at her. She knew her expression indicated her fuming temper. He glanced swiftly at Lu, who also watched her, but otherwise seemed unfazed by her anger.

"Relax, Jesse," Lu ordered.

"You're both acting like I'm insensate."

"While I am sure Dr. Syms would prefer that state, I told him you would not attack him with me here. I am your appointed guardian, your captain, and order you to back down."

Fury engulfed her, rousing Jet, but Jesse pushed her away. Huffing, she flopped onto her back on the table, crossing her arms over her eyes. She felt her jaw tense, but not in fear.

Syms spoke. "You need to remember this ankle was not just broken but crushed. It needs a longer period of healing, continual observation, and care."

She heard Syms, but also sensed the relief in his voice. "She needs to wear the brace whenever physically active, probably for at least six more weeks. I'd like to get another scan of her back."

Jesse groaned, gritted her teeth, and removed her arms from her eyes to stare at Lu. He only smiled and pulled her to a sitting position again.

A little later as they left the office, he said, "Neither Jet nor May roused, so indeed, you did well in there."

"By not attacking Syms? I felt more like assaulting you. Are you now coming to all my doctor appointments?"

He smiled again. She wanted to punch him.

"I'll schedule your appointments."

~ * ~

In the early hours of the morning, Alyss took consciousness while Lucian and her others remained asleep. For the first time, Lynn woke too, and they touched each other's presence.

::Since Jet and Jesse's melding, I can feel and hear you,:: Alyss said. *::I enjoyed hearing your music.::*

::You are so calm,:: Lynn told her. *::But lonely.::*

::Yes. You are lonely, too.::

::You don't see, I do; you have logic, I only have emotion.::

::What are you thinking?::

Lynn mentally giggled, a strange sound to Alyss.

::Can we try melding?:: Lynn's mental voice seemed full of loneliness and longing.

Alyss hesitated, but before she could over-think the proposition, impetuous Lynn moved. It happened. Even in the dark, she could see shadows in the room's low lighting. Turning her head, she saw Lucian for the first time. Tears seeped from her eyes, another thing she had never experienced.

She felt appreciation for the order of her mind, and an urgent desire to play her guitar. *My guitar.* She slowly and quietly rose and walked into Lucian's office, seeing for the first time where she traveled and where her guitar leaned against the couch. Night lighting had begun the transition to daylight, slowly brightening. She looked around the office, out the windows into the large atrium of the central hallway. She picked up the instrument like she always did, but this time she admired its shape and the pattern in the wood and stopped to let her hands ran over its surface. She played as she always did. *::I do not want to go back.::*

Somewhere within her, Angie knew her change was permanent and felt an overwhelming pleasure expressed in her music. Soon she found Lucian sitting on the couch across from her; she had not noticed his entrance. She reluctantly stopped playing.

"Hello, Lucian." Her greeting startled him. She smiled.

"Who are you?" he asked warily.

"I am Angie." She started playing again. She stopped after a few bars of remembered music and looked at him. "Don't worry. Lynn and Alyss melded, as Jet and Jesse did, but they just decided not to separate. I am glad. It is such a pleasure to see you." She put down her guitar and moved to his couch, placed her hands around his head as Alyss always had, and kissed him with Lynn's lust. He pulled her back into his private cabin to actively participate in their new acquaintanceship. Afterward, she fell asleep.

Four

"She called herself Angie and claimed both Lynn and Alyss were gone…or rather they had melded into her, and they wouldn't return." His revelation to Rae made Krayne feel an odd sense of bereavement.

"Certainly, an unpredictable change…" Rae looked at her screen. "Her medical readings show a lot of brain activity, but her body functions remain good," Rae said. "How did this Angie look and sound?"

Krayne swiped his hand over his head and exhaled. "Elated… happy…she was playing her guitar with Lynn's skill, but her voice was different, a little deeper, more precise, more like Alyss, but more mobile than Alyss…sensual and lusty like Lynn."

Rae looked at him, grinning. "What was Jesse's response?"

"She hasn't had awareness since this happened."

"Are you worried?"

"Yes and no…I'm waiting for the others' responses." He sighed. "If this is true, I will miss them."

"They are all the same person, Captain."

Krayne gave her a frustrated look but her interest remained in reading the monitor.

A knock on the door interrupted them. Rather than waiting, the person outside opened the door and came in. It was Jezlynn, but Krayne recognized the new person, Angie, in control. She wore a Ranger khaki duty uniform.

She smiled at him and Rae. "My apologies for interrupting you, but I thought this might be about me." She grinned at him. "Lucian, do you know how remarkable it is to not only be able to navigate from where I was to where you are, but to also see the *Sentinel*? Marvelous."

"You were asleep when I left." While he thought about Lynn's inability to navigate and Alyss' blindness, he felt glad for her.

"I know. Whether you can love me as I am or not, I want you to know I still love you. I think I showed it, too." Another aggravating grin crossed her face with a short laugh, one more reminiscent of Jesse than either Lynn or Alyss. His mind leaped to the fact that Jesse now had competition for control.

Angie talked unabated. "Yes, I am still tired, and yes, Jesse knows about me, as do the others, and Jesse still has time control. They are as dumbfounded as you. But as I explained to Jesse and Jet, they made it happen, and I am not a competitor but a partner." She extended her arm across Rae's desk. "Hello, I am Angie."

Rae briefly took her hand in greeting. Angie took a seat next to Krayne. He noted how Angie looked at Rae in complete control and fearlessness. "So, what do you want to know?"

"You both agreed to do this?"

"It was Lynn's idea, or rather action, a rather spontaneous one. Alyss longed for the freedom of movement, to see things. Lynn wanted order. She did not realize Alyss had such acute hearing or sense of touch. My change is curious and interesting."

"You have their memories?" Rae asked.

Angie's quick smile flashed again. "Yes, I do. Neither of them liked talking with you about all their secrets."

Rae gave a self-mocking smile in return. "None of you do."

"None have been voluntary revelations. That alone colors the interviewee's perception."

"You don't fear this office? The sickbay?"

"Not particularly, not fear at least; dislike, yes. Does it always smell like this?"

"I haven't noticed, what smell?"

"Bitter, astringent, fear, sweat, and stress. No wonder Jesse does not like it."

"You are like Jesse," Rae countered.

"Not really. I already know I do not like confrontation, and I doubt I can negotiate like Jesse. I know the logic behind a topic, but I do not have the combined deviousness, persuasiveness, unpredictability, assertiveness, or spontaneity of Jesse." A frown line formed on her forehead, "and I am not used to talking with people either, other than you or Lucian, although Alyss met you once or twice, Doctor Rae. Lynn had strong emotions, liked to antagonize Jet, but feared any confrontation, unlike Jesse who revels in conquering such."

"You know, then, I am your court-appointed physician."

"Yes, and it seems Lucian has control over Chambers in that area, too, but you probably know she is physically healthy. Jet keeps her, us, that way, and Jezlynn's mental state, while different, is not that much different from many others who have faced trauma. Does your smile mean you agree or have another perception?"

Rae started slightly and settled back in her chair. "Both. My main purpose is to help Jezlynn cope."

Angie laughed. "Duty and purpose help Chambers cope best."

"I realize that, too."

"You are unusually quiet," Angie said looking at Krayne.

He noted the worry behind her direct look.

"I'm adjusting. I loved Alyss and Lynn."

"You will miss them?" She looked downward for a moment.

He put his hand over her hand, which rested on the chair's armrest. "I will, but give me time to adjust to you?"

Her gaze found his, and she nodded. "I can understand that, but I bring Lynn logic and discipline, and Alyss release from exile, things they both fervently desired. I can help Jesse. I will not impose myself on you again, not until you know me better and can accept me for me. Can you tell me why people follow me?"

"Jesse didn't tell you anything?"

"No. Mostly Alyss just advised Jesse, and Jesse tried to ignore Lynn."

"They are to keep you safe. Morgan Dachs escaped and Admiral Wakeman has determined Jezlynn would have more security, not less."

Angie straightened, her gaze locking on his. "So, it is not about any unauthorized action by Jesse or Jet. How did he escape?"

"He was in a secured room at a mental facility. From what I have been told, he was undergoing transport to an Earth facility, but the wrong person was transported. When a check was made on his room, he was gone."

Her eyes seemed to disengage from him while still looking at him. After a few seconds, her gaze re-focused and she simply said, "Interesting." She looked at Rae, "Thank you, Doctor, I imagine I'll meet you again. I will go back to your quarters now, Lucian." She rose and gave him a sudden smile. "I have changed my mind; I am going to the music compartment."

"Do you know the way?" Krayne asked.

"Yes." Her smile widened into a grin as she held up Jesse's comlink. She swiftly left.

Rae gave him a quizzical look. "What will you do?"

He fumed a minute and came to a quick decision. "I'll treat her as Jezlynn Angeline, who she is."

"Before Angie arrived, I was going to tell you, whether the organisms in her body have been there since the *Constant* or not, or have been reactivated, they might be initiating this change. Readings show something works at reducing the amount of the scar tissue in her brain and on her back, but slowly. I'll need you to have a physical since you carry these organisms, too."

"You think this might have instigated Jezet's and Angie's emergence?"

"I cannot say for sure, but perhaps. Have you noticed any changes in your body?"

"No."

"They are happening. Some of your aging factors have stopped. Have you felt more tired than normal?"

"No. I do seem to sleep better, but that could be caused by any number of factors."

"Exactly. It is the same with Jezlynn. You will need to record any changes you perceive. Do you report her condition to anyone else?"

"I have not been assigned any duty to report her medical records to anyone beyond her guardian, and clearly as her guardian, I already know." Relief flooded him. Still, he was unable to guess at any future changes or unexpected events Jezlynn might face. "I will inform Tom and let him tell the rest of the advisory committee."

"Sounds like some upper echelon involvement in the court's decision. Captain, all any of us can do at this point is to watch what happens and help when we can. Are your feelings toward her changing?"

"What? No." He stood. "She continues to surprise me, but she also entertains me, and I treasure both her love and her friendship. I doubt that will ever change." He looked at Rae and smiled. "She can be very entertaining."

"As well as provoking?"

Krayne grinned his response. "It's her specialty," he said as he left Rae. In the corridor approaching the music compartment, he heard the faint sounds of the piano. He nodded to the guards at the door and entered the room. Angie had closed her eyes while she played an ancient piece of music. Within seconds her eyes opened, she smiled at him, and the music changed to one of the pieces Lynn knew he liked. At its conclusion, she rose and walked over to him.

"Enough practice for today, I guess."

"Only if you want to stop. I enjoy listening."

"But you have questions and doubts; want more information, which I do not have, and perhaps you have an interest in interrogating me? I am sorry my presence has caused you such concern."

He looked at her and pulled her into an embrace. "If both Lynn and Alyss wanted you, then I can only welcome you."

She wrapped her arms around him and rested her head against his shoulder. "Could we walk through the gardens?"

"Yes. I thought Jet had time scheduled in the training compartment."

"She does, but we have enough time before then if you have no pressing duties."

Only the chief gardener Laur Schug greeted them. He attended the gardens while the ship docked at Constellation. At Krayne's question about his presence, the long-retired SSC veteran stopped work briefly to say, "No place special I want to be but here." He nodded at Chambers and waved them to move on, so their walk remained relatively private. Once more Krayne watched a part of Jezlynn show her enchantment with the different flowers blooming in the garden.

"I will come here often," Angie said, smiling.

"Did you choose your name?" Krayne asked.

"Yes, a shortening of Jezlynn's middle name."

"Angelina."

"Yes, but I know I will be no angel." She laughed at his expression.

Later, back in his office, he watched one of his monitors display the new training compartment. Jet, wearing her ankle brace, trained her Ranger squad. Along with the eleven members of her Ranger squad, seven Corps officers, and two employees from the embassy side also trained. Henry helped.

His adjutant had reported earlier that most of those training had returned from leave early after hearing about Major Chambers' sessions. Now, Howard watched a monitor showing the training room, saying, "Jezlynn's docking bay crew has asked her if she would allow them to join the sessions."

Krayne recognized most of those with Jezlynn. Their joining amazed him. He noted another surprising applicant—Doctor Liz Rae. He felt astonishment at his crew's commitment and a tinge of jealousy at catching some of the Rangers' looks aimed at his wife. Although Howard said nothing, Krayne discerned he also wanted to train with them. His duties as adjutant ran counter to the timing.

He looked at Howard. "Don't worry. Henry will make sure you get the training. It seems to be a compulsion among Pilgrim Lines personnel, even those in the Corps. Be careful what you wish for." He left his office and went to the training room.

~ * ~

As her trainees and Henry left, Jet walked to him. "I still have an hour a week set aside just for you, Krayne."

"That will take up most of your out time."

"Yeah, but I'm not participating in any mission yet, so it alleviates my boredom and keeps me active." She grinned.

"You don't seem upset by Angie's presence."

"Why should I? Never communicated with either Lynn or Alyss. At least Angie talks to me. You should be prepared, though, Nael's been watching." She laughed at whatever reaction crossed his face.

Krayne put a hand around her arm. Not too long ago she would have pulled away with a defiant look. Now she just turned to him and raised her brows in an inquiring look.

"What do you know and what are you trying to tell me?"

"Well, Captain." She grinned. "As I said, Nael, while not communicating with anyone but Jesse, or occasionally me, knows what Alyss and Lynn did. He has never been comfortable with us, so I expect he is thinking over his options."

"What does Jesse think?"

"Jesse has been remarkably silent about everything."

"Who would Nael want to meld with...you?"

Jet huffed a laugh. "Hell no." She tilted her head in thought. "Not Jesse either, so that leaves May." Her brows squinted in thought. "Or maybe Angie; if she would have him."

"How do you feel about that?"

She briefly glanced at the two guards following their progress and as quickly looked at him. "Well, it would give May speech and hearing, and maybe some courage, which might help tame her fears, and it would give Nael memory, plus, it would give me more time out if I wanted it, so it's not a bad deal." She lifted the front of her sweat-lined shirt. "Come on, the shower waits."

Which he knew was a blatant invitation and turned with her to leave, but he scowled at her. Jet only laughed. He finally grinned. "Tell Henry he needs to get Howard into training."

Jet's grin exceeded his own. "Oh no, I'll do that."

~ * ~

Early the next morning Lu woke her, and Jesse realized she had been asleep for at least ten hours.

"We have a meeting with Admiral Wakeman in two hours," Lu told her.

She groaned and smiled saying, "Plenty of time then," and pulled him down on top of her.

Twenty minutes later he pulled her into the shower. "You are going to wear me out."

"Me and my cohorts? And probably go through our combined water allotment, too. Is that a complaint? Jet says she's going to work you even harder to build up your stamina."

"No complaint, rather satisfying," he answered with a satisfied smile.

All too soon for comfort, Jesse, wearing her new Ranger black formal uniform, and Krayne, dressed in his Corps white formal uniform, entered the captain's conference room to wait for Admiral Wakeman. Lu's adjutant Howard told him the admiral had already boarded the *Sentinel*. Two minutes later Jesse noted Krayne's left eyebrow twitch as Admiral Wakeman entered.

His grandson Henry, General Raul Roberre from the Rangers, and someone Jesse recognized from her first Corps assignment in Engine Design and Development on Constellation Station, Yun Tuen, followed. Tuen wore rear admiral insignia so he was head of the department.

She gave an inner sigh, having an inkling of what Tuen wanted, but also noted Roberre and Wakeman both wore uniforms as tailored as her own. Roberre saluted her, and after a shocked second, she saluted him back. "Your new medal requires it," he said before telling her to take a seat. Henry smiled at the formality before his father started the meeting.

Rear Admiral Tuen spoke first. "Major Chambers, it's been a long time."

"Yes, it has, Rear Admiral Yun Tuen, I'm glad to learn you headed EDD."

"You have made some astounding devices since leaving both military branches, and as you might have guessed, both branches would like access to your patents."

"The Rangers already have some."

"I'm aware of that. The Corps would like to negotiate usage of the ship invisibility covering and the quick repair boxes."

"You know the covering works best on shuttles, and only ships to a certain size?"

"Your Pilgrim Lines ships, even those now assigned to the Service Corps, have that refinement."

Jesse smiled. "They do, but at an exorbitant cost and with a few other added refinements. I'm much afraid, with the technology used on what is now a Khajari ship, the patent may no longer be enforceable."

"Do you have any information on their technology?" Admiral Wakeman asked.

"Yes, through some contacts. I did stop Ranger payments on the patent when Kerub became the Khajari leader, General Roberre. That will last until I can reach agreement with the Khajari government and Rek on what protections my technology has."

"So, you will allow us to use it?" Wakeman asked while Roberre smiled his acknowledgment.

"Yes, for both military branches for both the skin coating and the repair boxes with the caveat that once the patent is protected again, there will be a retroactive per ship cost."

As Tuen nodded, Admiral Wakeman said, "Let's have legal and engineering go over that and fix a fair price, with your agreement, of course. I've also learned you have access to several previously unknown psiroutes we would like to use."

"The Çiro Xantheans gave them to me, and I can only relay them to you, once I receive their permission."

"Can you do this on your stopover at Asedin?"

"Yes, Admiral Wakeman."

Rear Admiral Tuen spoke again. "Major Chambers, I would like to put EDD personnel on the ships recently assigned to the Corps. The captains involved refused without your permission. We know you have instigated some changes on this ship, and we would like closer observation."

"You want to see the changes made to the Class Two engines? You don't need personnel on each ship to do that, and I believe they are acting as hybrid-military ships as their original crews remain on the ships. If you want the redesigned specs on the engines, I will give them to you. Some of those changes are patented, and I'm not sure I will release those patents." She heard some movement in the room. She was unsure whether from discomfort from her answer, or just from sitting.

"Would you be willing to work on another Corps engine group?"

"She is a Ranger," Roberre said, "with an important assignment on this ship, plus another one for the government."

Wakeman spoke up. "What if the engines selected were for those the Rangers currently use?"

"It might be a possible solution, but as I've already stated, Major Chambers already carries a full duty load, plus I understand she has upgrading physical training for Rangers."

"A few Corps officers and even some embassy employees have joined them, too," Henry Wakeman said.

"Rear Admiral Tuen could place some engineers on the *Sentinel* to help her if she would consider such an assignment," Admiral Wakeman said.

Several of those around the table stared at Jesse before Nael finished talking to her. He retired back into her mind before she spoke. "I will work on the United Planet Alliance Rangers SA10 shuttle the *Delve,* currently in the *Sentinel*'s docking bay, as I believe the Corps uses that shuttle type, too. As for help, the *Sentinel*'s crew can help me if needed."

"That wasn't the one I had in mind," Admiral Tuen said.

"It is the one I want to work on, and I will also work on the Embassy's S40 *Crusader.*" She hesitated, staring at Admiral Tuen. "I will, however, have all changes documented for EDD and send the information to you."

Admiral Tuen's brows crunched, and she guessed he had become used to having his requests obeyed, but Nael's interest dictated what he worked on.

"Do you have an idea on how you might change them?" Roberre asked.

"I think I can facilitate their maneuverability while providing greater mobility and speed. The *Sentinel* can perhaps use one or two good designer-mechanics help to complete and record these changes."

"Would the *Sentinel*'s engines interest you?" Admiral Tuen asked, smiling at her acquiescence.

"I have already seen them. Commander Chuck Snyderon showed me the engines."

"By whose order?" Wakeman asked.

Jesse looked at Lu, who as usual listened to the interchange without saying much or giving away his opinion. She knew, though, that he had noted her reaction to the admiral's question. "I've done nothing more than looked at them and studied them a little, Admiral Wakeman, and with Captain Krayne's and Commander Snyderon's permission. Lu even looked on while Commander Snyderon gave me the tour."

"Commander Snyderon has shown her all the engine compartments," Lu said, breaking his silence, "and they have discussed them. She asked him to see the engine's specs, he referred her to me, and I gave permission."

"Are there any changes you would suggest?" Tuen asked her.

"The mains are powerful and well-integrated and seldom have done more than provide forward motion and speed adjustment; yet, after seeing the *Constant*'s engines after the attack, I believe the series of laterals could be improved and might perform back-up drive if needed, but I know the EDD has already been taking their engine designs in this direction. I also think self-propelled escape pods for emergencies could prevent the loss of life suffered in the *Constant*'s destruction. Again, this topic has already been covered by your department."

Rear Admiral Tuen's expression smoothed to an almost preening look, not even questioning her knowledge of his department.

"I think we've heard all we need to for now," Admiral Wakeman said as Tuen opened his mouth to make another request. "I do thank you for your generosity with your patents and shall let legal get back to you on that. As for any other work on any engines, Rear Admiral Tuen and I will first talk to Captain Krayne, who will approve what you work on."

As the meeting ended, they walked their superior officers to the *Sentinel's* main access. Henry waited with her and Lu, watching as the officers left.

"Changes seem inevitable, don't they?" Henry asked rhetorically.

Krayne's comlink chimed and he looked at the message. His serious gaze rose to her. "You have a visitor."

She raised one brow, "Who?"

"Margarete Chambers. Do you want to see her?"

Jesse took a deep breath but hesitated before saying, "Yes. It's time."

"I think Henry and I will join you," Krayne said in his command voice. He spoke into his comlink, "Howard, show her and her companion to one of the meeting rooms." He turned back to her. "Are you sure?"

"Don't worry. I know my own mind, at least, most of the time." She gave one laugh at her lame joke but felt her unease ramp.

It was a short walk down another corridor.

Krayne opened the door, waited for her to enter, and followed her into the small chamber. A long oval table lined with ten chairs dominated the space. Two women sat on the far side of the table's end nearest the door.

Once inside the wardroom, Jesse stared briefly at her mother. Another woman sat with her.

Margarete rose and spoke first. "Hello, Jezlynn." Never demonstrative, Margarete stood looking at her.

Jesse noticed the greyness of Margarete's hair, the wrinkles lining her face. The changes did not match her recollection of her mother. Another memory emerged of Margarete taking her on a walk around her farm and explaining the landscape, its features, and beauty, how her father explored the uninhabited part of the planet Griff, and how the farming techniques worked.

"Hello, Mother, I never expected to see you here. It's a long way from your farm."

Hearing herself called mother softened Margarete's anxious face and warmed her eyes. "A few years ago, you provided me with a wonderful manager although I was unaware of it at the time. Illa is in charge now. She also told me a lot about you." Margarete smiled. "It was a pleasant surprise to learn she knew you and what you had accomplished. Nor would she ever let me make any critical remark about you. Thank you for agreeing to see me, and I must apologize for not arranging a visit long ago, but when Ben told me about you, I thought you wouldn't want to see me." She sighed. "You probably don't have many pleasant memories of me."

<h1 style="text-align:center">Five</h1>

Jesse pulled out a chair across the table from her mother and indicated she should sit. Margarete sat in a stiff, attentive posture with her hands clasped in her lap. Lu sat in the chair next to Jesse. Henry leaned against the wall next to the door.

Jesse spoke first. "When Ben learned what had happened to me, I had few memories at all. Since then memories have filtered back. Yes, you were a strict mother and not overly fond of affectionate displays, but you were a good mother. You taught me much and always encouraged me to try harder. My desire to be one thing and your plans for me turned into something that separated us, but I have no regrets and have considered you family forever."

Margarete kept her usual stiff-looking posture, but her eyes gleamed with emotion. "Ben always called me cantankerous and shortsighted. He was right. I only thought of my own desires and my farm. Since his death, my viewpoint has changed. You are probably wondering how I became one of the committee members with oversight over your health concerns, so I thought you needed to hear from me. I have always believed you were innocent of all the outrageous rumors circulating about you, including the charges made against you, but thought you needed to come to me, not the other way around. After

Ben died, for the first time I was without support other than my few friends...and alone. A strange thing happened. A woman came to me for a job.

"Illa Jakle had heard I was looking for a manager. I learned later that you sent her." She gave Jesse a pleased look. "She sought me out to work on my farm. It was an impossible position to fill on Griff. Although reclusive, her skills were extraordinary. She helped me in many ways. Shortly, we became friends. That was when she told me she was one of those listed as missing on the *Constant* and how you had saved her. She had friends, including Henry Wakeman," she nodded at him, "who also knew you. She became a way for me to learn what you were doing. You did things I would never have had the courage to do. I failed even in finding the courage to face you at Port Griff Station. And despite my thinking you probably hated me, you sent me the help I needed. Before the information about your recent review board had cleared you of all malfeasance, I contacted Admiral Wakeman, who gave me contact to Judge Aquilera."

"I'm glad to hear this. For a long time, I have believed I disappointed you and thought you wanted nothing more to do with me."

"That is a misconception, probably one I fostered. I am not here because you have been cleared of all allegations, but because I have finally found the courage to do what I should have done long ago. I have followed your career, and when you made Griff the home base for your Pilgrim Lines, I believed my strictness and inhospitality kept you away from me, even after I also knew of your generosity to me and to Illa. My only excuse is that I had little knowledge of how to be a mother. You must be wondering about the person I brought with me."

Jesse looked at the other woman, someone older than her mother.

The woman quickly looked at her mother. "Please let me explain this to her, Margarete." The woman's intense regard returned to her. She didn't smile but didn't look threatening or angry, either.

"You have your father's eyes."

Her comment captured Jesse's attention. She stilled and stiffened.

The woman watched her, but her expression remained unreadable before she continued. "When I learned Margarete had left Griff and arrived on Constellation, I came to her and asked her to introduce me to you. She raised many objections, but I am just as obdurate as she is. Frankly, I doubted you would even agree to see her, but I am elated you did. I have information you need to know."

She stopped and exhaled; her eyes brimmed with anguish, but she shed no tears. "When I learned of my daughter Roselynn's death, I discovered she had given birth to a daughter and tracked her. Then I learned Margarete had adopted you. I felt she and Ben would keep you safe. I contacted her many years ago, asking that she not tell anyone of my interest in her daughter. You are my biological granddaughter. I am Isobel Angeline Meitland."

Jesse blinked and felt her body tilt backward and vaguely felt Lu's handclasp over the top of hands, now gripped in a knot of tension in her lap. Her mind raced and it took a moment for her to speak. "You are the daughter of Vanessa Dachs."

Isobel sat straighter and looked at her in speculation. "How..." Whatever she was about to say, she changed her mind. "Yes, I am her illegitimate daughter and only child."

"That makes me..."

"A Dachs descendant from Walter Dachs, my grandfather, yes. I know you probably see this as an ambush, and a Dachs one at that, but it is not. You see, I have tracked you, with good reason, for Durant Rosche hunted me, and ultimately he killed my daughter, your mother."

"Do you want to continue?" Lu asked her. Anger lined his face and voice, but concern filled his eyes.

She looked across the table and saw the same look in Margarete's face as she looked at Isobel. "Yes...yes, I do."

She sounded vulnerable so took a moment to compose herself while Isobel gave her a worried look. As her resolve hardened, Isobel's eyes widened, and she sat back in her chair.

::Expects retribution,:: Jet said, hovering behind her awareness.

"Durant Rosche was out to eliminate all Dachs one way or another. He wanted their power and their wealth. This, of course, is a huge surprise. Do others in the Dachs' family know about me?"

Isobel quirked a smile that swiftly disappeared. "I doubt it, and I want you to know this disclosure is completely my doing. Margarete did not know what I just told you. She only knows of my relationship to Roselynn, whose name was not on the adoption documents." She paused. "Like my daughter. I kept my family heritage hidden. Unfortunately, Durant Rosche discovered it."

Jesse nodded. "He bribed or threatened his informants and had an extensive illegal investigative team."

"My mother never let me go until I married a spacer. She thought I was safe, but while Durant never confronted her directly, he did me. I was illegitimate trash and a tarnish on the family name he planned to remove. He knew my mother knew of his nefarious money laundering and used me to keep her in line."

"He laundered a few Dachs' reputations, too."

Isobel smiled, but it looked sad. "Yes, he did. His stated goal was to protect the Dachs name, but I never believed him."

"Protecting the Dachs name allowed him to hide his disreputable dealings while he handled their investments to his fraudulent advantage."

"Really? Well, he hunted me down and threatened me and my husband with what might happen to my mother if we ever claimed a relationship with the Dachs."

"You didn't go by the Dachs' name, so it didn't count."

"He went after my darling Roselynn, instead. She had settled on Rissilli, but she and your father, Cameron Alston, were killed in a suspicious accident while traveling to the planet Arlon. I have a few good friends, but one lives on Rissilli and has a governmental position. He changed some records, and you became an orphan of space gypsies sent to the Sisters of Mercy orphanage on Rissilli. I asked him to keep me informed of who adopted you, which he did." She looked at Margarete and smiled before returning her stare to Jesse. "Like I said, I have few friends, but they are all trustworthy ones. One informed me of your war against Rosche. I was elated when I learned of his death. My mother knew Roselynn had died, but I kept knowledge of you hidden until Rosche's death. Now she knows you are here, and with your permission, would like to meet you."

"You know Lieutenant Governor Dolf Faute?"

"Yes, but he wasn't my contact. I must add that since meeting you, he has acquired a more diplomatic demeanor and more personal discretion. I will also tell you that he comes to visit with you, too. Rissilli wants to join the treaty. You should also know Morgan and Phelen Dachs are the sons of Vanessa's stepbrother Reed, who married Larkin Nguyen, the daughter of Lacey Nguyen." Isobel looked at Lu. "Lacey was the wife of Alliance President Dickka Vaughn." Her regard returned to Jesse and read her expression, "Yes you've done your own investigations and probably already know, but neither Lacey nor Dickka knew until much later about their close relationship. They were half brother and sister. When they found out, a great cover-up of the facts occurred. You needn't worry about your sanity, however." Isobel's face broke into a quick smile at Jesse's huff of dispute. She quickly continued, "Vanessa was a daughter of Walter Dachs' first marriage. Rosche, who investigated everything, might have discovered the relationship. I don't know."

"So...Morgan's grandfather and my great grandfather are the same person?"

"Yes, but that is the only relation between you and his family."

Jesse took a deep breath and stared at her grandmother. After a long pause, she asked, "Do you think Morgan knew this?"

"I don't know."

Jesse looked at Margarete. "Do you know about me?"

"I do," Margarete said. "Ben told me. You have made a remarkable recovery from the abuse Morgan, and it now seems your family, have inflicted upon you."

"You are my family, and you never inflicted abuse on me; quite the contrary. Self-discipline, yes, and it was a good thing, considering what happened." She turned her attention to Isobel.

"I have only heard the rumors through the news services," Isobel said. "I find it hard to believe."

"It is true, but most of the reports give untrue and unfounded information, yet," she hesitated before admitting, "yes, they are based on truth. I am no longer the Jezlynn Chambers I was when I entered the Space Service Corps, but the rebuilt pieces and parts of her."

"Nonsense," Margarete said. "You are the same body, the same mind, just rearranged. And the many accomplishments you have achieved should only be respected."

Something inside Jesse's chest filled with pleasure, and she remembered Margarete's dictum whenever she had failed a goal as a child. *'You will do it the next time or the time after that.'* She exhaled, saying, "Thank you."

"I will never let anyone declare you incompetent, Jezlynn," Margarete said in what Jesse recognized as her mother's strict voice. "You'll be home on my farm before that could ever happen."

"It won't happen," Krayne spoke for the first time with a warning look at Margarete. Jesse released one tightly clasped fist to grasp his hand which had remained holding hers.

Margarete smiled at him. "I'm glad to hear that."

"Would you like to room here tonight, or remain where you are on Constellation Station?" Krayne asked.

Isobel rose. "I have rooms in the station's hotel and will leave now. I hope what I've told you has not upset you so much you never want to see me again."

Jesse rose as did her mother. "To say that what you've told me has dumbfounded me is an understatement. While part of me is upset, another part is glad to know where I come from, and now, I have family willing to reach out to me. I would like to learn more about my birth mother, and about you. Perhaps we can get together again before the *Sentinel* leaves port."

Isobel reached into a pocket and placed a datawafer on the table. "My contact information is on it, plus some images you might like to see." She nodded to Margarete and left. Henry, who had kept silent, followed her.

Jesse looked at Margarete, who for once looked somewhat lost.

"I, too, have a room at the hotel, so will leave you now." Margarete stood in her stiff and erect manner but expelled a breath in an un-like Margarete way.

"Would you like a tour of the ship?" Jesse asked.

"Maybe another time. I think Isobel and I gave you much to think over."

"You know I will always consider you my mother?"

"Thank you for that. You are my one and only child. In your childhood I believe I was somewhat selfish and driven to reach my desire any way I could, despite your own desires, but that has changed. I've never said the words, but I hope you know I love you."

They walked her to the ship's portal where Isobel waited with Henry. Their conversation abruptly ended at her appearance.

"You will stay in touch?" Jesse asked.

Margarete gave her a hug, the first she could ever remember. "Yes, thank you."

Both women left.

"I think I sense a confrontation coming," Jesse said.

"Deservedly so," Lu said. "And you? How are you with this revelation?"

"Honestly? I'm unsure. I don't seem to have the basic Dachs' appearance or insouciance." She looked at him. "I think I need to do some more investigation."

"Let's go get some dinner. While the manner of discovery was upsetting, I am glad you have found family." He looked down the corridor. She felt his anguish.

Long ago he had told her about his family. His mother, father, and brother had all died during the war. She was thankful it was not one of the battles she had taken part in but recognized the memory still haunted him.

"Thank you...give me a half-hour. I know you have some ship's business to attend to first, and no one is scheduled for the training room, so I'm going there first." She turned and walked away.

Krayne watched her.

"Don't worry, I'll keep an eye on her," Henry said following her.

~ * ~

Ten minutes later Henry watched her enter the facilities wearing her workout attire. She passed him not even noticing his presence, so he knew it was neither Jet nor Jesse, but the one he guessed to be Jezet. Walking directly to the standalone punching bag, she hit the bag four times with vicious blows.

"You need to wear gloves, or our captain will censure me."

She started and turned to look at him, her face wearing an aggravated expression. He expected an argument, but he walked to her, and she let him slip on and secure the gloves.

"Jezet?" he asked.

Giving a quick nod, she turned back to the bag and kicked it before punching it again. She maintained a rapid and powerful attack. Out of breath, with perspiration lining her face, she finally backed off, bent over, and braced her hands against her knees.

Walking over he stopped in front of her. "You okay?"

"Yes, Henry, thank you."

He recognized Jesse's voice.

She straightened and smiled at him. "Now I need a shower."

"Do you feel better?" he asked, undoing her gloves.

"I don't know how I feel, but most of my anger or frustration, or whatever it was, has passed. Jet's idea. I have never felt anything like that. For the rest, I need to think things through. Join Lu and me in the mess hall in ten minutes?"

"Yes, but I'll be walking with you back to the captain's quarters." He spread his arm toward the door in invitation.

Her eyes filled with frustrated mirth, but she started walking. "I seem to have plenty of escorts without your help."

He matched her steps as they quickly started toward Krayne's quarters. "You may have guards in abundance, but I'll act as a safeguard between you and them. You'd have them believing you didn't need their services despite orders."

One brow raised. "They are Rangers..."

"Exactly, and right now you are their superior officer."

"...and you think my just completed performance doesn't prove that?"

He grinned. "An amazing performance, but more of a release than a planned action."

"Has Illa spoken to you about any of this?" she asked, knowing his relationship with their former crew member from the *Constant*.

"She contacted me... yes, about Margarete leaving, but she didn't have more information than that."

Jesse smiled at him, but the slight twist in her lips told him to disbelieve her serene demeanor. "Lu watched me in the training room, didn't he?"

"He didn't say anything, but I'm sure he probably did. So did others," he said looking at the guards. "But the captain likes to keep track of you and is also protective of you."

She sighed. "He doesn't need to be."

"You'll have to convince him, not me, although right now I have my doubts about your opinion." At her look, he added, "Strange happenings have occurred lately."

Once in the mess hall, Jesse found Lu had already ordered their dinner. With so few on the ship due to in-port leave, the galley had been closed. Krayne and Henry had steak, but her plate held a vegetable casserole.

She smiled. "Thank you. Who did the cooking?"

Noting Lu's expression, she asked, "What has happened?"

"One team returns daily to prepare meals. The head chef knows your preferences."

She watched him while he cut his steak; he finally looked up at her.

"What's happened?" she asked again.

He returned to cutting his steak. "We've run into a few glitches with the refit and with our orders. We will most likely remain in port longer than planned."

"May I ask a favor?"

"What?"

"Actually, I would like a few favors. May I take charge of the embassy shuttle *Crusader*'s refit rather than just work on it?"

Lu leaned back in his chair, and she noted Henry hid his grin by looking into his plate. "Will you have time?"

"I will make time, yes."

"You have some refinements you want to add?" She didn't have to answer before he said, "All right, it will free up some workers. What else?"

"I'd like to see the *Sentinel*'s lateral engines."

"So...you are taking Rear Admiral Tu's request to heart. I'll make the arrangements. And?"

"Find out where Isobel Meitland is staying, my mother, too. I'd like to talk to them again, and maybe make a short trip to Earth before we leave port, if possible."

"Why?"

She sighed. "You know I really don't like having to ask permission for everything I do." It was both a statement and a request. Henry made choking sounds as he swallowed his bite of steak. She answered the questions apparent in Lu's arrested demeanor. "I have questions I should have asked but was perhaps in too astonished a state to think about it at the time."

Placing his folded arms on the table before his plate he stared at her for a minute. "Only if I go with you."

"Me, too," Henry said. At his captain's disagreeable look, he added, "I am one of the advisors."

She felt an aggrieved flicker pass over Lu's expression. He aimed a beleaguered look of payback at Henry before he regarded her.

"Now you know what it feels like," she smirked. "I would like to avoid notice if at all possible."

"Do you have a plan? If so, it had better include me," Henry said.

"Do you?" Lu asked.

"No. Not yet."

"Why don't we just have them go to headquarters?" Henry said. "I can make calls to people who will deliver the message. There will be less notice of them traveling there. Also, it prevents any alert to the media if they came to the *Sentinel*. Captain Krayne and you can go to headquarters without much attention...well, more than normal...since you are expected for meetings periodically."

"A good plan," Krayne said. He smiled at Jesse. "And here I thought you were the only devious planner. If you want a visit with Vanessa Dachs, we could have one arranged at headquarters without much comment. After all, her brother Elliot and nephew Walter Elliot still work in Corps Medical. You must be distracted."

Jesse noted their concerned looks and gave a weak laugh that turned into another sigh. *I was out of control. I'm never out of control.* "I must be. Do it, Henry; although I doubt Vanessa Dachs would come or have time to arrive." Then a stray thought entered her mind, and she left them again and walked to the sickbay hearing their steps behind her. She entered the area without thought or emotion. Doctor Liz Rae met her, also wearing a worried look. Jesse asked her, "Is Norma Hughes here?"

"Yes, I am."

Jesse turned to see the nurse assistant standing nearby. "Did you know?" An unusual and aggressive tone filled her voice, and she took a step toward Norma, but a hand grabbed her forearm and stalled her. She glared at Lu in anger.

"Know what?" Norma asked.

Swallowing, Jesse heard the puzzlement in Norma's voice and saw it in her expression. She forced herself to calm. Her actions were so foreign, she felt like someone else. She took a deep breath. "Did you know I was the great-granddaughter of Vanessa Dachs? That we are related?"

Shock struck Norma's face and stiffened her stance. "No! How could I?" A quick grin crossed her face. "Well, at least we're both from the sane side of the family, cousin."

The response stunned Jesse and all she could do was stare. Norma's expression turned doubt-filled and crushed. Unable to help herself, Jesse began laughing, finally clapping her hand over her mouth. A few seconds later she uttered, "There is that, but rumors about me might refute that claim."

"I won't presume this to change our non-existent relationship in any way," Norma said, almost as a promise.

Lu pulled Jesse from the medical compartment, and her mind went blank until he gently shoved her onto the couch in his office. She looked up at his alarmed face. "I know I'm not handling this well."

"It's a huge adjustment, and you need some time to come to terms and accept it."

Henry followed and ordered their unfinished dinners delivered to the captain's office. Within minutes there was a knock on the door and one of the mess crew entered with their food. Lu and Henry talked as they ate. After they finished, Henry left.

Later, in his quarters, Jesse didn't know why it was so hard to call it *their* quarters, Lu had once again guided her to a couch. This time he sat next to her. He said nothing but pulled her against him, his arm wrapped around her.

She told Lu what she knew he wanted to hear. "From the time of the *Constant* until I saw Tom in a slave line on Fortune station, I felt nothing. Lynn and May had all the emotion, and they seldom met anyone. Even after finding Tom, my emotions were nebulous and muted. Then I met you and started my game of hide-and-seek. Pissing you off made me feel, I don't know, pleased. Then I fell in love with you, but I knew, with you tied to the Corps, we could never be together. After that, I felt anger periodically, but today, I felt rage. Jet said to work it off. As Jezet we could do it together—Jet's physical talents and my uncontrollable rage. It has been a strange experience."

"Hearing what you did would probably do that to anyone."

She took a deep breath and smiled at him. "I've discovered rage is not good. It wiped the questions I needed to ask from my mind."

"Henry has already contacted me. The arrangements are made."

"That was quick."

"Tomorrow, fourteen hundred hours you have an appointment in the Space Corps offices."

Six

"You need to wear your black uniform," Lu said as he emerged from his office into his quarters at seven hundred hours.

Arrested in pulling on her casual tunic and pants, Jesse looked at Lu and guessed, "New orders?"

"We have to be at President Uebel's office ASAP." He had already pulled his dress whites out of the closet.

"Do you know what this is about?" she asked.

He uttered a too empathic, frustrated, "No."

"It's okay. I'm good in these situations."

Her comment earned a squint-eyed look from him. "So you are, but maybe not so much recently, and you are all too good at falling into all sorts of trouble."

She grinned. "It's why you love me, and your acceptance is why I love you."

He laughed. "One reason, but not all. Why does this make you love me?"

At his questioning look, she said, "You always help me dig my way out, but it is not the entire reason, as there are many, but the biggest one is for your tolerance and acknowledgment of the real me."

In short order, they left the *Sentinel*. Assigned guards preceded and flanked them with Henry walking on Lu's other side. Early or not, as if receiving notice, a crowd with a few netreps waited, calling "Major Chambers" and screaming questions as they traversed the catwalk to the waiting transport. Jesse kept her focus straight ahead as if unaware of the commotion following their movement. The same scene reoccurred as they left the transport at the governmental offices and walked through the corridors, halls, and galleries to the president's office.

Admiral Wakeman waited in one of the lower galleries with a coterie of officers and moved to join them. Jesse noted with a surreptitious glance that cameras were homed in on the event. She also noticed their guards were on high alert, checking the surrounding area and the galleries above them for anything suspicious. Briefly, she wondered if the other *Constant* survivors suffered this lack of privacy.

"I long for my days of anonymity," Jesse said, looking to the side and noting General Roberre approaching. Someone sniggered behind her, probably Henry.

"Admiral, this is a surprise. What is happening?" Lu asked before his superior even reached them.

"Xantheans," Roberre answered from her left side.

She looked at him, for once utterly astonished. They both knew the sound deadeners in this area prevented any overt overhearing. "Who...few Xantheans travel and never in so public a manner."

Roberre smiled. "A delegation arrived six hours ago requesting a meeting with President Uebel and with the presence of 'Sera Ambassador Major Chambers and Sira Captain Lucian Krayne.' It makes this meeting require the highest levels of protocol and protection."

Opening her mouth to make what she knew an unseemly comment, she quickly closed her lips, exhaling a deep breath. Roberre extended a sweeping arm indicating they should proceed and fell into step next to Wakeman. Jesse sensed a new, more cordial, and cooperative relationship between the two. They talked in low tones behind her, soft enough that sound absorption prevented her from hearing their conversation. A presidential assistant met them at the front doors to the governmental sector and escorted them to a reception room.

Inside the room waited fifteen Xantheans. Few could read their exoskeleton faces but Jesse recognized them as calm but also filled with extreme attentiveness. Their flowing, floor-length robes hid their hard skin-like outer skeleton. Jesse knew an inner system helped hold the body together. They looked somewhat like humans, but they were not human.

President Uebel and a coterie of government officials stood near his office door. Jesse recognized some of the Xantheans, including Sutta from Asedin, whom she had rescued from slavery, and Ahjias from Çiro, who taught her the Çiro Xanthean language. She suspected Lu recognized some, too. Most importantly, Aswenna, the Genitor of the Landwellers on the planet Asedin faced them. For the Genitor to travel indicated a major change in Xanthean culture.

Aswenna sat on a stool rather than squatting on a mat as Xantheans preferred. Her four hands nestled together in a loose clasp. Next to her stood T'Carta Kizz. The rest of the Xantheans crouched in a Xanthean fold on the floor, including Sutta. They all looked up at her in greeting as she moved to welcome Aswenna in proper Xanthean fashion, lowering her stance to her knees with her arms outstretched at ninety-degree angles; her palms toward Aswenna, she held her fingers close together and pointed upward.

She spoke in the Asedin language. "Genitor, my sincerest greetings. My surprise to find you here is unequaled as we planned to travel to Asedin."

Aswenna answered in halting, hard-to-understand space standard rather than her native language, confirming Jesse's opinion that the Asedin leader had always understood space standard. "The Circles met. We come. A delegation to make an accord." She switched to Asedin. "I also brought, as you can see, your stranded Khajari diplomat."

Jesse controlled her desire to smile at the new designation given Kizz. "Hello, Kizz," she said in Khajari. He gave her a brief nod. "Are your other Khajari members with you?" He nodded again, giving nothing of his emotions away.

The observant Aswenna's eyes flickered, but she continued in her native language, "Since you will be meeting with the Khajari as the new ambassador, our arrival saves you travel, which I'm sure will become more important as your mission moves forward."

"How could you, the Genitor, leave Asedin?" Jesse spoke in Asedin.

"Another Genitor has taken my place. I am now a Revered Elder only. We travel to begin a new colony, an un-thought of event before you came to us. Even now one difficult to believe." The lip-like structures on her skull gave a twist Jesse recognized as a Xanthean smile. "We have great hope that you can help us negotiate with your President Uebel to achieve this."

"Why now?"

"You, Sera, and your mate." Aswenna used formal Xanthean address. "Children of my Circle and of dronai, have freed us. Can you introduce me to your president?" She rose with unexpected grace and released the intertwined fingers on her bifurcated right lower arm which when held together gave the appearance of one arm. The six fingers wrapped around Jesse's lower arm. She spoke again in space standard, "Sira Captain Krayne, Lucian, member of my Circle, please..." Her left arm beckoned to Lu.

Lu stepped to Aswenna's left side. They slowly walked toward President Uebel with three of Aswenna's escorts falling into step behind them. Asweena looked back over her shoulder and uttered a few words telling them to remain in place. While Aswenna spoke, Jesse looked at those behind Uebel and recognized both Renny Lebeau and Monica McEntire from the *Sentinel*'s embassy side. Like most embassy personnel, they had remained off the ship since docking at *Constellation*. Their last mission together had resulted in her initial acquaintance with Aswenna, and she knew both rabid to extend their research into the Xanthean culture.

President Uebel stepped forward and bowed in an unexpected gesture, unaffected by his foreign visitors' strange appearance.

Jesse spoke. "Sira President Uebel, I have the great honor of introducing Revered Elder Aswenna, the former Genitor of Circles, the groups which govern Asedin. Revered Elder, this is President Uebel, head of the United Planets Alliance."

Uebel smiled at Aswenna. "It is my greatest pleasure to meet the esteemed matriarch of the Asedin Xantheans."

Aswenna asked Jesse to translate, "so I understand correctly."

Jesse took over translating between the two leaders' words.

"My pleasure, also, Sira President Uebel. From all Xantheans. We appreciate your tolerance and hospitality in our sudden arrival."

"Genitor..." Uebel said, looking at Jesse in question.

"Revered Elder Aswenna," the Xanthean answered, and Jesse advised Uebel to address her as such.

"The ship we arrived on knows our requirements and the captain has generously offered us housing while we are on *Starbase Constellation*. As for any negotiation or other requirements, Sera Major Jezlynn Chambers and Sira Captain Lucian Krayne know our preferences." She turned her head to look at the admiral. "Sira Admiral Wakeman, we gave Major Chambers, better known to us as Jesse, the coordinates you seek. They are for her to give you, as we hold no attachment to them."

Wakeman looked pleased. "Thank you, Revered Elder Aswenna."

"We came unexpectedly, Sira Alliance President Uebel, so appreciate you agreeing to this first meeting with us. We will not stay longer but will wait upon your choice of time to meet again. Thank you, Sira President Uebel. Sera Jesse, stay and make the arrangements. Sira Lucian, will you guide us?"

Aswenna's long drawn-out pronunciation of Lu's name made it sound different to Jesse. Lu nodded to Uebel, glanced at her and at Wakeman before he left. Aswenna's hands grabbed his arm. She turned her head toward her fellow travelers who all immediately rose. One took Jesse's place while Jesse glanced in polite warning at Uebel. The Xantheans turned and left.

Those left in the room all looked somewhat stunned and astounded. Uebel spoke first, dismissing some of those gathered. Jesse noted Lebeau and McEntire remained.

"The ship they arrived on is one of your Pilgrim Lines, isn't it?" Uebel asked.

"I'm a little short on information, Mr. President. Which ship?"

"The *Dark Traveler*, Captain Dakota's ship," Wakeman answered.

Jesse huffed a laugh. "Yes it is, but I had no part in this arrangement, President Uebel. And if Rafe brought the *Dark Traveler* here, you can be assured he had no choice. Currently, he manages Pilgrim Lines' shipping. I will also tell you the Xantheans know whatever they want to know. How they knew Admiral Wakeman asked me for psiroutes is beyond my comprehension."

"About Captain Dakota," Wakeman said, ignoring her last comment, "It sounds like he might be in port for some time. Do you think you can arrange a meeting with us?"

::*Let me,*:: an inner voice said, and Angie emerged.

"He is not under warrant for anything," Wakeman added.

"And he has earned some awards and merits he needs to accept," Uebel added with a smile of collaboration at Wakeman.

"I will try to negotiate with you between both Rafe and the Xantheans," Angie said with a smile.

::*Don't be so smug,*:: Jesse advised.

Uebel turned to those remaining. "Thank you, Mr. Lebeau and Miz McEntire, for your timely advice before this meeting. I will stay in touch and will request your presence again. Admiral Wakeman, General Roberre, Major Chambers, join me in my office."

"Jezlynn, I hope Monica and I will be able to talk with you aboard the *Sentinel*," Lebeau said before they left.

"Certainly, but if it is about joining the *Sentinel*'s mission, I think this turn of events will require both of you." She noted pleasure cover both members of the embassy anthropologists' team.

At a nod from Roberre, three of Major Chambers' assigned guards followed them. One of Uebel's aides was rearranging furniture as they entered the office while the three guards took a stance outside the door.

Angie looked around and asked permission to see the window's view, which Uebel gave. At the window she stared out in wonder, closed her eyes, opening them quickly, and took a deep breath before moving to the one chair left vacant between Wakeman and Roberre.

"Lucian will not be happy with how things have fallen out," she said.

"Who are you?" Roberre asked.

Angie turned to look at him. "Is it that obvious?"

"Not to everyone," President Uebel said.

"I am familiar with both Jesse and Jet," Roberre said, "and you are different in both demeanor and tone from either of them."

"I am relatively new. Alyss and Lynn melded and created me. I am Angie."

"Alyss handled logic and planning, didn't she?" Wakeman asked.

"Yes, and I have her talents. Lynn was the emotional musician, and I have her talents, too." She looked at Uebel, noting his uncertainty. "It is okay, T'Carta Kar knows who and what Jezlynn Chambers is, President Uebel. Nothing will shock or dismay him or Kalmona-Rek Kerub, who no doubt also knows." Alyss then looked at Roberre with a smile. "Nor will Jet allow anyone to usurp what she sees as her duty, especially when wearing a black uniform."

"I take that to mean she doesn't have your negotiating skills?" Wakeman asked.

Her smile widened. "Well, while Jesse is the verbal negotiator, Jet negotiates in a different, more direct manner, as I think you know. But I may understand the situation better than she or Jesse does. Besides, I often advised Jesse during her negotiations."

"What do you think the Xantheans want?" Uebel asked.

"A hint came when Aswenna addressed Jesse as dronai and said they want to form a new colony. Jesse has wondered at the word's meaning for a long time, but I think it is the alien DNA infection that made us what we are. I think reports you already have probably informed you of this."

At Uebel's nod, Angie resumed. "There is only one place that could have happened. The one place that makes Jesse most uncomfortable, so she ignored hints about it. They want Ezredin."

"Why?" Uebel asked.

"Three times, once on Çiro, again on Zeranth Ea, and the last time on Asedin, the elders made claims of dronai about Jesse. This organism is of extreme importance to them, so I deduced that if it entered Jezlynn's body, which Doctor McEntire's research seems to show, it had to have been on Ezredin. I am sure now that the Xantheans want to colonize the planet. I understand that another new human colony has failed there; not surprising, really. While it has atmosphere and water, the oxygen levels are low, and the local life forms are not pliable to human life. However, the Xantheans have many plant-like qualities."

"They do?" Uebel asked.

"Yes. Their skin can absorb certain minerals, and with moisture and light, they can make their own food. They can eat food, too, but their tastes are far different from ours. In the political arena, allowing the Xantheans to claim the planet might help set up a safe zone between Alliance and Khajari space." She grinned. "Plus make Ezredin more inhabitable for humans."

"You will need Khajari acceptance of this new colony," Wakeman said.

"All part of negotiating a treaty." She sighed. "And I'm afraid the Xantheans will want to take part in those negotiations. Since T'Carta Kizz has been on Asedin, the Khajari must already be familiar with Xanthean peculiarities. Their presence on the *Dark Traveler* or on the *Sentinel*, if they decide to transfer ships, will cause either Rafe or Lucian... interesting... problems."

"You, too. Corrao told me I had the best possible ambassador for this mission," Uebel said. "I'm almost envious of the excitement you will engender for everyone on this trip."

Angie laughed, reading more from the voice than the expression. "No, Mr. President. You have no idea of the trouble Jet and Jesse can...engender."

"Closer to provocation," Roberre inserted.

"Well, Major Chambers...Angie, I think I've engendered some problems for you. I've appointed Sal Imada, a journalist I trust, to travel and report on events," Uebel said.

"Devil," Angie said with a direct look at Uebel. "Does he know how dangerous a mission you have assigned him?"

Uebel gave her his rare smile. "Yes, he does. Thank you for your input. Now that my two top officers know the plan, I will wait to hear details from you. Both Admiral Wakeman and General Roberre have direct links to you, to Captain Krayne, and to me."

Dismissed, Angie and the officers rose and left. In the corridor outside the reception area to Uebel's office, Wakeman stopped. "I would greatly appreciate it if you or Jesse can arrange a visit between Rafe and me."

"I will see what I can do, Admiral Wakeman." She saw Lucian walking toward her, checking the messages on his comlink...so did Wakeman. He left them and stopped Lucian to talk briefly. Roberre looked at them while telling her he would be talking to Major Chambers again before he also walked away. Surrounded by guards, Angie was reminded of when Alyss always referred to herself as Chambers, unable to accept herself as an individual. Luckily, Lynn had never had that problem, and now Angie welcomed her emotional reactions.

Lucian stared at her briefly once he stopped in front of her. Angie knew he recognized her and smiled at him. He did not return her smile. He only said, "Let's go get some lunch before we meet your mother and grandmother."

"Here?" Angie asked, unfamiliar with the governmental district.

"They have a good cafeteria two floors down. Let's go. On the way, you can tell me what you suspect about this arrival."

"You knew it was me?"

"Angie, I know all of Jezlynn and how she behaves and responds."

Pleased, she quickly told him what she suspected, knowing they had privacy there with the sound absorbers that would not be available in any cafeteria. Once through the cafeteria doors, she felt excited. Neither Alyss nor Lynn had ever eaten out anywhere. The area was filled with small tables that all seemed to be occupied.

"Let's go to the back where we might have a modicum of privacy," Lucian said guiding her to another section. He selected a booth in a back corner. A simulated voice welcomed them and gave the day's specials. When it was done, Lucian pushed a button and Angie saw all the tiny lights turn off. "Did you hear something you would like?"

"I have no idea. Would you please choose?"

He pushed the button again and ordered two soup and salad specials with two glasses of iced water.

"Coffee, too," Angie said.

When done, he leaned back on his upholstered bench and looked at her. "You haven't noticed, but you are the center of attention here, and I'm afraid some customers have cameras. Certainly, the cafeteria has some aimed at you, too."

"Really? With language translators?" At his nod, she continued, "and Jesse puts up with this? Not even allowed to eat with a measure of privacy in a public dining place?"

He laughed. "No public place is private, but I doubt where we are sitting anyone has clear visuals of either of our lips, so they won't be broadcasting our conversation."

"Jesse never told Alyss about her excursions, and May needed help to navigate, so neither ever visited any eatery. I believe you first introduced Alyss to any food when you made her drink coffee. I think she thought a mouth was only for speaking."

"It was officious of me," he commented staring at her.

Angie smiled. "She came to like it, and I more than like it, so thank you. Please tell me if I look likely to break any social norms. I find this experience exciting but do not want to embarrass you or Jesse."

"Uebel sent me a message about this cafeteria and said to take this booth. He also made sure it was available. It's rare for Jesse to allow anyone this freedom."

"She, most unexpectedly, trusts me. Of course, that is because of Alyss, but she also knew you would be here. Where are your security men?"

Lu looked to his left, and Angie followed the direction of his gaze. The security squad sat at a nearby table.

"I guess I am not as observant as Jesse," Angie said.

A server delivered their meals, ending their conversation. Twenty minutes later, as they left the cafeteria, it was Jesse who walked next to Krayne, in supreme self-control and ignoring the attention she garnered. Once back in the government precinct, Lu asked her, "Are you ready for this?"

Jesse looked at him saying, "Yes, I think so. You never told me how you learned the Xanthean language."

His expression showed a mixture of mirth and frustration. "After you left for the city, Aswenna had me with her daily for long hours of instruction. She enlisted Sutta's help. I understand he knew you."

"I found him with some other slaves as I searched for a crewmember."

"Slavery must have been terribly difficult for him."

"It is for everyone, but yes, even more so for Xantheans. Disrespect is anathema for them, and slaves are always denigrated. He thinks himself weak, so doesn't realize or understand the strength he showed in surviving."

Within minutes they were outside the guest-chamber in the Space Corps Precinct. Margarete opened the door. "I was invited, too," she said, looking at Jesse.

"You are family." She hugged Margarete briefly, knowing she shocked her mother. Their embraces had been infrequent, even when Jezlynn was a child. Two in two days was remarkable.

Another surprise waited inside. Vanessa Dachs sat next to her daughter staring at Jesse as she entered the room.

"My mother arrived here with me, several weeks ago," Isobel said. "She has waited with the hope of meeting you while dissembling with everyone about visiting with her brother."

"Does Dr. Elliot Dachs know about me, too?"

Isobel smiled. "Well, since you confronted Norma, yes. After the unplanned disclosure in my previous visit with you, none of us thought you would seek us out. I have apologized and made peace with Margarete, and mother wanted to meet you, too."

"You have a more generous nature than most..." Vanessa Dachs said at last. She did not look her age of one-hundred-two, but her hair was pure white. She sat as erect as Margarete, watching her great-granddaughter with what Jesse thought hawk-like attention. "...And I'm sure you only came because you have questions and want answers."

Jesse moved to the couch opposite where the mother and daughter sat. Her own mother sat to their left. Lu took the seat on the couch to the right of her.

Vanessa Dachs looked at him and asked, "Do you think she needs your protection, Captain Krayne?"

He gave her a tranquil look as he settled into his seat, crossing his legs. "With three guards on duty outside the door? Not protection, support only. If you have watched any media, you know danger threatens your great-granddaughter."

A flicker of a smile crossed Vanessa's lips. "My apologies. I did not mean to sound so belligerent. I am extremely glad Jezlynn has you." She turned to Jesse. "You might not believe me, but your grandmother and I have been closely watching and trying to protect you since we discovered you survived your parents' murder, right up until the *Constant*. We began again when Isobel heard from Margarete that you had survived. In some instances, our hands were tied. If we made the wrong move, you would have been exposed, even more than you were to Rosche. Although I suspect you will always doubt us."

"He blackmailed my mother," Isobel said, "and me."

"About me?" Jesse asked.

"No, I'm not sure he knew about your relationship to us, at least I don't think so. He didn't know about my granddaughter Roselynn for a long time. I had early experience with his type of slime. He discovered through his wife, my half-sister Laurel, that I had had an affair with President Dickka Vaughn between his marriages." Vanessa smiled and sighed. "Rosche threatened to tell my father, Walter. He eventually did when I stopped kowtowing to his demands." She shrugged her shoulders. "Father deemed me a less-than-deserving Dachs family member, but only after he found out Dickka wasn't Isobel's father. Luckily, by then, I had a friend who claimed Isobel as her own. Later Durant discovered Isobel, too, and much later learned about my granddaughter."

"He had my parents killed?"

"We suspect so, also his wife Laurel, but we never found proof."

"But he didn't know about me?"

"His informants never discovered your birth, or that you survived the planned 'accident' that killed your parents."

"How did that happen?" Jesse asked.

Isobel smiled, but it was a deprecating, sad smile. "I happen to be good friends with Rissilli's Governor, Andrew Faute. He was not only a good friend of your father, Cameron Alston, they were also second cousins. Cameron performed many covert services for Andrew. Andrew also knew about Roselynn's past and where she came from. When my daughter and Cameron died in a transport explosion, Andrew investigated and discovered they had left you in the care of a friend while they were gone. He changed your name from Lauralynn Arella and had anything about you expunged from Rissilli's records, after which he had you placed in an orphanage. He informed me of what he had done. The datawafer I gave you has images of your parents on it..."

"I've seen them."

Isobel smiled. "...And you don't need to think about retribution for your parents. Andrew has already taken it." A real smile crossed her face. "He found it most interesting that you and Dolf crossed paths, and he told me after he met you at the last Governor's Ball, you were as charming as your mother. I think he would like to meet you on a less formal basis."

"Did he tell you about Rosche's death?"

"Yes. He said one of Rosche's associates found out Rosche was playing her all along. Another of his coconspirators had sold her brother into slavery. She took direct retribution. His son Dolf even witnessed it. Whoever it was should be given a medal." Isobel's eyes widened. "You didn't kill him, did you?"

"No, I didn't." Jesse continued without filling in the story. "From this, I understand I am not even who I thought I might be?" She felt Lu's hand squeeze hers, their entwined hands between them.

"You are who you have always been," Margarete said with some asperity. "You—Jezlynn Angeline—are my daughter, but now you know you are Isobel's granddaughter and Vanessa's great-granddaughter."

She looked at Margarete and smiled because she unexpectedly remembered other occasions when her mother had replied in such a tone. The reply was in Margarete's style, straight forward and unambiguous. "And you have always grounded me."

"I didn't punish you that often!" Margarete said.

"I didn't mean as punishment, but as a foundation."

Margarete's lips twitched, and she gave her a somewhat twisted smile. "Thank you."

She looked at the other two women. "Is there anything you would like to know about me?"

Vanessa smiled. "No, I think we already know about you. Both Isobel and I would like the privilege of contacting you."

"Then you know..." Jesse hesitated.

"Yes, they know," Margarete said. "I knew from Ben, which Illa confirmed. I told them when they asked about the rumors."

"We will do nothing to put you in danger and will certainly not share anything you tell us with anyone else," Isobel said.

"She does a good enough job of putting herself in danger," Margarete said. "If it is okay with you, Jezlynn, I will give them some images of you as you were growing up."

"I would like some of those, too, if you would?" Jesse said as she rose, wanting to escape.

Margarete rose and pulled her into a hug. Something Jesse never remembered her doing. "I have missed you."

By then Isobel and Vanessa were also next to her and hugging her too. "Thank you for your generosity in meeting us. Please stay in touch as you can."

Lu didn't touch her as they left the room, which revealed he knew how she felt. They walked in silence for a few minutes before he asked, "Are you okay?"

"Please ask me that again in our quarters because I cannot answer right now."

Seven

Lu was resourceful in returning to the *Sentinel* in the shortest possible time while seeming unhurried. She suspected arriving at certain points with transportation already waiting was not serendipitous, but well planned. Of course, the eight guards surrounding them also helped in speeding their way through a few crowded passageways.

Once inside the *Sentinel* Jesse felt her body relax, but her mind whirled in turmoil. At the door to the captain's quarters, a disembodied voice spoke. *::Margarete was right.::*

Lu opened the door to his quarters, and Jesse passed him, immediately turned, and backed a step to lean against the shorty, closet-lined entrance hall while Angie spoke. *::You are still you...I am still me...we are collectively still Major Jezlynn Angeline Chambers.::*

Somehow her new other's comment stopped her mind's tumult. She let her head fall back against the wall, closed her eyes briefly, opened them, and smiled at Lu. "Another rough day."

His concerned stare disturbed her, but she knew a cure. Reaching a hand behind his head she pulled him forward into a kiss that quickly turned sensual when he finally touched her.

Later, as she lay next to him while he stared at the ceiling, she said, "We need to walk the ship."

He looked at her. "Duty calls, or more dissemblance and distraction?"

Smiling, she kissed him. "Duty, certainly, you are a little behind in your routine, but also interest and distraction, and others want time. I wanted out of Constellation's governmental and Corps Headquarters so much, I forgot about many things, and this encounter was certainly a distraction, yes, but not a dissemblance."

"Unusual, but you were distracted."

She laughed at his comment. "Different type of distraction. I'm debating how much was truth and how much selected vagueness."

"It was a relatively short conversation and I believe they told the truth, but perhaps one altered by time. You do not know all the facts, and they might not either. Plus, while you told the truth about Roache, you dissembled, too, so maybe they did the same. How upset has this made you?"

"I didn't want them to know I witnessed Roche's death. Equal parts upset, sad, content, furious, curious, and disbelieving. The Dachs family...who would believe it?"

"Only five parts of you remain, so listing six parts seems outdated.'

She lightly punched his arm but laughed at his comeback.

Lu smiled. "Get up. Let's go."

~ * ~

By the time they left his quarters, Krayne recognized that Angie walked with him. "Jesse give up?" he asked.

Angie smiled. "No, she is just letting me satisfy my curiosity. She did not notice me, but I was with her during her meeting with our family. The disclosures she heard were difficult for her to accept, but as they learned, she had already investigated the family."

"She just never discovered her own ties to the family."

"True. I have never sensed her stunned before. Has it happened?"

"A few times. And everyone else?"

"I told them. For all her diplomatic capabilities, Jesse tends to internalize the most difficult, personal information. We all deserve to know, though." She gave him a keen look. "You, though, have learned how to handle her."

"Sometimes."

While few had returned to the Corps crew areas, the Ranger quarters were nearly filled and many saluted as they passed. Krayne noted Angie's bewilderment.

She quickly gave way to Jet, who said, "They all want to be here because of the new training requirement."

Lucian wore a smug smile when Angie reclaimed consciousness. "If you want to travel the ship, you better learn both Jesse's and Jets' protocols."

"You mean Elite and Meat greetings?" Angie asked, returning his look. She turned away to look ahead. "It is something I have never had to consider before. It was unique seeing Rangers salute Jet. I expect she salutes those of higher rank first."

"She did until she earned the Star of Liberty. Now they salute her first. Uebel's event was the most Stars of Liberty ever given out at one time. Elite greeting means shaking hands." He held out his to her. She frowned but reached forward. "No, not like that. Use your right hand, clasp hands like this for a count of two before letting go." He freed her hand. "Look at the person's face while you do it. You should look serious but interested and friendly. If it is a senior officer, let them speak first. If the person is lower in rank, you speak first. The same is used for embassy personnel and for general greeting, except you do speak in those cases saying something like, 'Nice to meet you, or good to see you again.'

"How strange." Angie stared briefly at Lucian. "Vision has shown me so much that I never knew happened, including what expressions, postures, and movements say."

"Alyss never encountered anyone until she met me, and Lynn's emotional reactions often isolated her." He waved a hand forward. "Let's continue."

"That is true. Alyss left me with the ability to decipher meaning from words and speaking tones, to even determine if the speaker told truth or lies, but she never knew the nuances of everyday encounters."

Most of the remaining construction work took place on the Embassy deck, but a few worked on reconfiguring a small security cubicle on the side of the corridor where they walked. Lucian stopped, talked to the workers, and inspected their progress.

As they walked away, Angie asked, "Will we need more housing for the Xantheans?"

Lucian frowned. "You think they will move to the *Sentinel*."

"Yes. Jesse hasn't answered the twenty-five messages from Rafe that have accumulated since she left Isobel Meitland's rooms." She sighed. "I'd answer but cannot speak for Jesse."

"Would he notice?"

Angie gave a brief laugh. "Probably not, but Jesse would. I will tell Jesse to contact him and Aswenna to find out what accommodations are needed. Jet already has plans to convert…"

Abruptly Jesse was with him. "The lower deck second cargo compartment needs to be reassigned to the embassy so the Xantheans can inhabit it and still have the protections of embassy protocols."

"It also has docking access. Which might make it the perfect place for meetings with the Khajari, too. Do you want Angie to see it?"

"Yes. Between us, we know how to make it livable for them. Jet decided to use the *Crusader* for negotiations and the *Delve* for transport between ships. I am unsure if Nael or Jet suggested these shuttles first, but she is determined. Since Rafe has arrived and with Aswenna's intervention, the *Dark Traveler* can be used for trade negotiations."

Krayne quashed his first response, and said, "Which is why during negotiations you were adamant to work only on the *Delve* and *Crusader*."

"Yes, and yes Angie is with me, or I am with her, I'm not sure how this goes."

"Did you hear Angie talking about Rafe?"

"Yes." She closed her eyes and took a breath. "He will come here soon." She huffed a laugh. "Make that he is probably already on his way."

Lu opened his link and gave orders to the ship's main access portal. Once he finished, they continued the tour, but Angie was back with him. When they reached his office, he received a call from the main entry portal and relayed it to Angie. "Rafe is here."

It amazed him that Angie stayed out as they approached Rafe, whose annoyance must have buttressed his obvious wariness of standing on the *Sentinel*.

"You no longer answering your contacts?" Rafe asked without any semblance of greeting.

"My apologies, Rafe, it has been a hectic day."

His irritated expression changed to uncertain. "Something go wrong?"

Angie smiled. "Yes. I met my great-grandmother...Vanessa Dachs."

Rafe's demeanor changed like a laser bolt from anger to concern. His expression twisted to doubt, and he frowned. "You're kidding me?"

Angie shook her head, "No. It was a rather disconcerting surprise. One I hope you keep to yourself."

He gave Angie an earnest look. "I will."

"Captain Krayne is having an area converted for the Xantheans to berth here on the *Sentinel*."

Rafe sighed. "Don't know how they bamboozled me into ferrying them here. It's the last thing my crew or I wanted or even expected when we received a message from Asedin." He threw her an aggravated look, "It's been an interesting trip."

Angie laughed. "The Revered Elder Aswenna does tend to have a subtle will you would rather not be enforced."

He snorted. "Experience speaking?"

"Has Aswenna asked you to join her circle?"

Rafe aimed a glare at her. "You do, too, don't you Jesse? And yes, she did. She also finds mirth in my avoidance since her offer."

"You might avoid her plans for you, and at a guess, your crew, at least temporarily by talking to Admiral Wakeman, but if she asked you, it means she already considers you family."

"I'm not rejoining the Corps!" He threw a quick glance at Krayne. "No offense meant."

"None taken," Lucian answered. "Wakeman understands you are overseeing Pilgrim Lines right now."

"You could avoid that, too, by becoming my diplomatic assistant."

Rafe stared at her for a few seconds and looked at Krayne. "My sympathies." His attention returned to the woman he thought to be Jesse. "You are the most manipulative, conniving, and devious boss I've ever encountered. Even Aswenna can't compare."

Angie smiled. "Thank you. Do you want me to return to the *Dark Traveler* with you and invite Aswenna to move to the *Sentinel*?"

"Are you kidding? They are already packing up. She said they will come tomorrow. I'll think about your offer. What about Griff and our contract?"

"Griff has agreed with my request to release the *Dark Traveler* and her crew while we negotiate with the Khajari. They already have a representative in place to join us."

"Who?" He jumped to a conclusion. "Margarete?"

Angie smiled again. "Still perceptive; see why I need you?"

He stared at her again and frowned. "You could have told me you weren't Jesse. Angie?"

"Well-informed, too."

Running a frustrated hand over his head, Rafe spoke to Krayne. "Don't know how you do it. I'll inform Aswenna and make the arrangements."

"For tomorrow, fifteen hundred. That will give me time to prepare."

"Tomorrow, then." He turned and left, again with no farewell greeting.

"Rafe is right. I don't know how you put up with us either,"

"Because I know I'm a lot worse off without you. I have some questions to ask." He indicated they walk back the way they had come. "How will the *Dark Traveler* work into your plans?"

"Since I do not think Jesse would be allowed to travel alone to Khajari to meet with the supreme ruler, it will be important to consider Khajari politics. The Khajari will have more than an embassy ship, probably a whole squad of ships, especially since the supreme ruler himself is taking part in the negotiations, a rare enough event. It is a matter of prestige. It is also a matter of trust. Because of his background, Kerub trusts few. I know Jezlynn, Tom, and Rafe are among those few. The *Dark Traveler*, even to a degree the newly commissioned *Polestar*, will act as neutral territory to Kalmona-Rek Kerub and his representatives. Especially as he knows both ships' captains. Choosing two ships from Pilgrim Lines with whom Rek Kerub, the trader, was associated, will also show goodwill. With the *Polestar* and the *Dark Traveler* traveling with the *Sentinel*, our presence will create greater respect among the Khajari. We will need them. I think more than Alliance negotiators will come. If I am right, Kerub will have trade negotiators with him. Griff is already interested, and from what I heard from Isobel, I'm sure Rissilli representatives will be joining us, too. In which case the changes to the *Crusader* and *Delve* will earn more respect among all representatives."

"You are right. Jezlynn would not be allowed to negotiate alone; Alliance negotiations are not done that way. You now represent the Alliance. Have you chosen any Alliance members to join your delegation?"

She frowned. "Besides which, with her background, many would think her perspective biased. President Uebel has not mentioned any possible negotiators yet, but I think Jesse wants the *Sentinel*'s ambassador to help. She asked my opinion, and I suggested she should leave choosing the delegation members to Ambassador Nohl. She agreed.

"I had not thought about appearances, but you might be right."

"Like the *Sentinel*'s construction, Jesse's plan still needs work. You won't like this, but I think everyone onboard needs to have a security reevaluation for this trip."

He stopped and looked at her. "Why?"

"First, I would suggest traveling with a limited crew and a limited embassy staff as only one operation exists for this trip. Now, with Morgan and Austin loose again, we do not know who their contacts are within the Corps, or the Rangers, for that matter. I think one of their main goals would be preventing Jezlynn, as an Alliance ambassador, from a successful negotiation. Matter of fact, I think they will work with their former cohorts, now the Khajari dissidents, to try and eliminate Kerub."

He stared at her a minute. "We will need to talk with Admiral Wakeman. I expect you or Jesse have already vetted the Rangers."

"Yes, Jet did, and of course I have a list of the *Sentinel*'s crew already cleared, but..." she smiled at him, probably reading his thoughts from his expression, "none of us went into forbidden territory." She grinned at the glare he gave her.

"A good thing, too," Lucian said with his best command voice and look. "I've already been informed the *Sentinel*'s Corps crew will be reduced to essential personal since this isn't a long-range mission, but it will require the highest security."

Angie laughed but a change in the soft but ever prevalent sound of the engines and a slight shift underfoot made her stop. Jet was immediately speaking. "Are teams inspecting or testing the engines?" She took fast steps toward the engine compartment.

"Nothing scheduled." He ran ahead of her, already using his comlink to contact Chief Engineer Snyderon shouting, "Turn off the engines!" Jet ran next to him.

Snyderon yelled back, "Already on it, Captain." The background noise in the engine compartments was increasing.

Krayne used emergency coding to enter the hatch to the engine compartment; both he and Jet quickly slipped on magnetic gravity boots. Krayne yelled at the guards following them to stay at the entry hatch in security mode and to don biosuits. "Warn all crew onboard to do the same." He and Jet rushed, their hands on the ladder's handhold letting them glide down the circular ladder as gravity dissipated. At the final access, Jet charged through the door ahead of him, their boots' catch and release slowing them slightly.

Inside, Commander Snyderon worked at one of the engine-command panels where he punched in shut-down code directives.

He shouted as they entered, "One crew member, Lieutenant Leatha Ottren, is further down the compartment."

Krayne noted Jet had changed to Nael who moved to a second panel and quickly became equally engaged. Krayne found biosuits, giving Nael and Snyderon one, and donned one himself. Finished, he shouted orders through his comlink to the bridge while he began helping Snyderon isolate the *Sentinel's* engine compartment from the rest of the ship.

Several tense minutes passed with Snyderon speaking throughout, "Lieutenant Ottren and I have been going through engine inspection, including trial engine runs. The rest of the crew are all off the ship." He moved to another engine command panel. "Ottren found several chancy things we were looking at when one of the engines stuttered, which made the noise and movement that must have alerted you."

"Dangerous?"

"Very, and uncommon unless someone has perverted engine protocols. I've been in shut-down mode ever since."

Nael had already moved to the last operating engine command panel. Snyderon yelled, "Are you shutting down the laterals, Major?"

"Yes," came the clipped reply. Nael worked quickly, earning an approving look from Snyderon. Krayne and Snyderon both watched all the sensors flickering with shutdown indicators.

Snyderon seemed to relax as he saw the red sensors run across all panels. "All of the major engines and laterals are now shut down, Captain, energy sources contained, and thrusters sealed."

An explosion ended further talk. A wall of sound, heat, and fire punched through the compartment.

The force knocked all three of them off their feet but their biosuits saved their lives. Horror gripped Krayne's heart. Duty called. Before he rose, he connected with the ship's bridge and spoke in fast, loud, and clipped phrases over his comlink with Fournelle. "Keep ship on high alert. Compile all ship and engine readings. Recall all engine crew to duty. And order security to seal the ship." He took a breath before issuing more orders.

Nael rose first and ran further into the compartment, grabbing fire containment equipment and spraying as he moved.

Fournelle responded from the ship's bridge in equally clipped comments before closing communications. Krayne knew his first officer would follow standard protocols.

Snyderon gained his feet and returned to the control panel, but there was nothing more to do. He began to follow Nael, but Krayne called him back, handing him an extinguisher. "Clear a path." They both began picking up equipment and spraying the area around the control panels. In less than two minutes, eight security crew swarmed into the compartment.

He contacted Fournelle again. "Start a ship-wide search for any dangerous substances or situations. Alert sickbay and prepare a verified list of who has had ship access since docking."

"Yes, Captain. Command alerted. Orders are recorded and being sent to command," his first officer replied.

"Collect ship-wide video of this timeframe and have all compartments in this sector sealed until cleared for habitation."

"In process. Security Chief T-Omer already has his crews searching all compartments and one team is inspecting and securing all compartments close to the main engine compartment."

"Let no crew remain onboard except those tied to security, the engine department, or other necessary functions aboard until the *Sentinel* is confirmed secure," Krayne ordered. He took a deep breath. He knew they already knew established protocols, but command also demanded direct orders be given. As he closed his comlink, he heard ventilation start. Waves of floating dust and debris moved toward air shafts showing purification of the compartment's atmosphere had started.

By then he saw Jet returning. Ottren was more pulled along than walking. Jet grasped one of Ottren's arms which was wrapped around her shoulder while her other arm wrapped the woman's waist and held equipment in her hand. Jet reported even as she approached. "Second main thruster engine vent blew. Leatha wore appropriate gear, but she is injured. She helped me seal off the vent before collapsing. I finished securing the section. The area sustained a hole in the hull. In a quick inspection, I saw no other damage to any of the other engines or hull sections."

Two security personnel removed Ottren from Jet's grasp and pulled-carried her up the stairs. As they left the compartment, Krayne heard another security officer contacting sickbay. Jet watched them leave. "Looks like we will be detained a little longer in port, Krayne." She was immediately on her comlink ordering her Rangers to secure the embassy deck.

"I will discover who perpetrated this crime on my ship," Krayne swore, more to himself than Jet.

"I'll assist, Captain," Snyderon said. "Major, could you stay and help me run engine checks? At least until the crew returns?"

"Yes, Chief Engineer," Jet said, grinning at Krayne. "I can tell you the engine shafts and supports remain whole and unimpaired."

"Thank you, Major."

"See you later, then, Captain Krayne."

He fumed at her comment, but she was right...he had other duties to complete, but he noted on his comlink she had already issued orders to her Ranger squad to increase protection on the embassy deck and the embassy arrival position in docking bay. He had much to deal with, for his ship had been attacked, and he had an idea, which he thought Jet shared, on why. "I have ordered Commander T-Omer to keep security in here and outside the hatch." He nodded at Snyderon and left.

<h1 style="text-align:center">Eight</h1>

Krayne immediately went to the bridge where an officer always remained on duty. Only a few staff held ship control positions. "The ship?" he demanded before the access closed behind him.

"Secure." Fournelle showed him the progress already made. Two lieutenants were making a list of everyone's presence on or off board and their activity since docking, including the construction workers, most of whom were Corps, but not all.

"Admiral Wakeman wants to talk to you ASAP. We have cameras dockside and a surge of netreps waiting there. Station security teams are already covering the dock area and Wakeman increased all docking security access points station-wide. How they learned so quickly, I have no idea. We have a list of those already cleared of any possible involvement."

Krayne noted Jezlynn's was at the top of the list, just above his own placement. "Deservedly so," he added, "her efforts helped secure the ship."

"Exactly, sir, as did yours. She has also been and continues to be under constant surveillance," Fournelle said.

"And is usually with me."

"Yes, Captain, so secure, unless you are involved in some type of collusion. Here is a camera replay of events in the engine room." Fournelle touched a few pads.

Krayne watched. "Did anyone unusual enter the engine compartment?"

Fournelle also watched the vid play. "No. An inspector, but we have vid of him during his entire time onboard including in the engine compartment. Any idea for a timeframe about when this bomb might have been planted?"

"Snyderon and Jezlynn are working on it," Krayne answered. "She already has extra Rangers on embassy security detail."

"Her Rangers escorted embassy personnel off the ship," Fournelle informed him. "T-Omer had his security do the same for all construction workers and other crew remaining onboard. They will check everyone allowed back onboard.

"Just before this happened, Jezlynn suggested we have the crew re-vetted for security clearance. She has already done so with her Rangers," Krayne said.

"Although I find it a repugnant idea, I must agree with the need," Fournelle said. "I'll call Ribberdan back to the ship, and we will start."

A call from Snyderon interrupted them. "Captain, Major Chambers has discovered the bomb was planted outside the ship. She has watched the exterior cameras and discovered numerous inspection drones, three of which touched the ship. She is sending you the ship's exterior visuals, including the one of the bomb site. Five engine crewmembers have already returned. Four are working on beginning the restoration of the damaged compartment. The major continues her investigation on the drones."

"What about the *Sentinel*? How much damage, and how much of a delay will it cause in our mission?" Krayne asked.

"Again, with you, the major, and myself, we had the engines shut down ship-wide," Snyderon replied. "Whatever punched through the hull also went through the containment bulwark on engine two. That engine had been under testing just before shut-down. It had shown some problems, but the engine was down, and the fuel connections were removed when the blast went off, so the blast only caused interior damage in that section of the firing tube. The *Sentinel* has not suffered catastrophic damage to the engines or to the compartment. The major thinks a few weeks at most to repair it, and I agree. The hole in the hull needs repair, but she said that should not cause too much further delay, if any. We are now testing all the remaining engines."

"Inspecting them first?"

"Of course, Captain."

Once finished with Snyderon's call, his comlink indicated another call coming in.

"Admiral Wakeman," Krayne answered.

"Any injuries?"

"Minor ones to one engine crewman."

"The major?"

"Helping with the engines."

"Well guarded?"

"Yes."

"I will be onboard in two hours." His comlink closed. The abrupt end gave a good indication the admiral was distressed.

"We will be prepared, sir," Fournelle said. "I'll keep Admiral Wakeman appraised of everything, Captain. I expect Chamber's Pilgrim Line ship captains will call you. I will preemptively call them first."

"Thank you, Joel. I will be in my office."

Howard Wakeman informed him Captain Thomas Thorson, Captain Rafe Dakota, and Lieutenant Commander Henry Wakeman waited inside his office. "Sir, I gave permission for them to come aboard."

I should have expected this. Fournelle was behind in his calls; he probably didn't understand the relationship between the Pilgrim Line captains, even those now officially Corps officers. Krayne nodded to his adjutant. He noted Howard had two screens open and was watching various cameras around the ship's entrances and the passageway outside his office. He also had a third screen up showing he was examining all communication links.

"Very well, thank you." He sighed and smiled as he headed into his office.

All three officers rose as he entered.

"*Sentinel* okay?" Captain Thorson asked.

"Jezlynn okay?" Rafe asked throwing Thorson a shocked look.

"The *Sentinel* has minor damage; and yes, Jezlynn is okay. She is in the engine compartment well protected."

They asked a few more questions but were stopped by Admiral Wakeman, Rear Admiral Tuen of the Ship Design and Development, Admiral Zamudo of Fleet Operations, Ranger General Roberre, and a secretary from President Uebel's office entering the office far ahead of the two hours mentioned.

"Let's move to the conference room," Krayne said, swearing to himself.

Once everyone was seated, Admiral Wakeman asked him to explain the events that had taken place on the *Sentinel*. After giving his report, Krayne explained the measures being taken to discover how it had happened and who might be responsible.

"Your quick actions have saved the ship, and maybe even Starbase Constellation from extensive damage," Wakeman said in approval.

"The major is working in the engine compartment?" Admiral Tuen asked.

"No longer," the major said, entering the conference room, still in her dirty Ranger duty khakis.

Krayne looked at his own disheveled attire before quickly judging Jesse's mood, and looking for any injuries. He saw none.

"Fournelle told me you were all here," Jesse explained, "so I came. Rear Admiral Tuen, do you have an eight-meter section of Class A Engage Engine body readily available?"

Jesse sat in an empty chair. She returned his intense regard inspecting him for any injury as he had her, which gave him an oddly uplifting moment.

Tuen's lips opened to make a comment, but he took a breath before saying, "I'll check." He opened his comlink.

"If not, I have a ship refit going on at Terra Shipyards with an engine section that could be delivered here within forty-eight hours."

Tuen closed his comlink. "How effective would it be?"

"Snyderon and I can convert it here to the specs needed for the *Sentinel*. It will be, at a minimum, a match for the current specs."

"And at a maximum?" Tuen asked.

"Better," Jesse answered.

"Do it. I'll send three engine mechanics to help you with the install."

Jesse looked across the table at Krayne asking, "Have any more situations occurred?"

"Nothing so far," he replied. Krayne glanced at the rear admiral, "Your mechanics' presence will speed up the repair certification."

"Your actions and those of the few crewmembers onboard were remarkable in countering both the danger and preventing even greater damage," Rear Admiral Tuen replied. "If that had gone off while the engines were operating, it would have destroyed the engine compartment and a large section of the ship. Who knew you were testing the engines?"

"We're investigating that. For the rest, duty and experience, sir, plus a known expert in ship engines design and repair onboard," Krayne said, looking at Jezet sitting opposite him.

Admiral Wakeman spoke. "I have approved of all the steps you are taking to secure the ship, Captain Krayne. First Officer Fournelle has kept me informed, and I have advised all those present along with President Uebel. I also agree with limiting the onboard crew to only those necessary for the mission, but before the *Sentinel* can leave port, all possibility of a reoccurrence must be eliminated." Wakeman nodded to Admiral Zamudo.

"I've ordered Corps Security here on *Sentinel* to high alert," Krayne said.

"An attack on one ship could lead to attacks on other ships," Zamudo responded. "I know two Corps security officers are currently in the engine compartment with Chief Engineer Snyderon. He had high praise, Major, for your engine talents and your investigative talents. Others in Constellation's Corps Security Office are currently investigating all drones and have found one anomaly. They will follow all leads. Again, Major, your observations and suggestions to the chief engineer have been found helpful."

"I've also ordered all Ranger contingents to increased security," Roberre said. "Major Chambers had already engaged heightened embassy protections. I've ordered further securities not only on the *Sentinel* but for all embassy ships."

"On another front," Wakeman said, "upper-level embassy administrators are requiring the basic embassy staff to remain onboard during Major-Ambassador Chamber's mission, even though the ship will not be doing established protocols. Major Chambers," he turned to Jesse. "I had a message from President Uebel about some of the refinements you are making to your mission. Would you explain them to us?"

Ignoring formality, Jezet replied. "Certainly. I had briefly discussed them with Lu just before the attack in the engine compartment." She explained about the Khajari expectations and the dangers facing the supreme leader. "Which is why I request the *Polestar* and the *Dark Traveler* to join the mission. Kerub is familiar with both captains and trusts them. I will use the embassy shuttle *Crusader* as a meeting place for negotiations as it is large enough to handle up to sixty passengers so both a Khajari and an Alliance delegation can be onboard. It also serves as a neutral place."

"Dangerous, though," Zamudo said. "A shuttle is an easy target if you are correct about Kalmona-Rek Kerub's enemies."

"True, Admiral, but I believe Kerub will arrive on the *Azreal*, a Pilgrim Lines ship, and unless his enemies know the capabilities of Pilgrim Line ships, what with the *Polestar* and the *Dark Traveler*, along with the *Sentinel*, we will have plenty of firepower, if needed. Plus, six men from Griff with experience in the invisibility covering application currently work at the Terra Shipyards on the *Crusader*."

A silence filled the room. "I did ask Captain Krayne's permission two weeks ago," Jezet said. She just had not told him the shuttles had already left the *Sentinel*, but his next comment showed his knowledge.

"The *Crusader* and the *Delve* have been at the yard six days now," Lu said.

"Gunnerman move them?" Roberre asked and Jezet nodded. His expressionless face matched the admiral's. The other officers wore sober expressions, but mirth lined their eyes in expectation of another imminent explosion, a human one.

"And why did you not inform headquarters?" Wakeman asked.

"Because Major Chambers felt the fewer people who knew about it, the better. I agreed," Lu said in an utterly calm demeanor.

Jezet added, "It was and continues to be a Ranger operation, and I've worked with the Terra Shipyards manager, and with General Roberre's and Gunnerman's, oversight, the change is under tight secrecy and security."

"Since Gunnerman is already in league with you, Jesse," Roberre said, taking up her informality, "I will inform you that I've assigned him to duty on the *Sentinel*. He will continue with the training of the Rangers you've already started and act as the Ranger pilot. He will be second in command while you are engaged in negotiations. Do you expect your negotiations to require more personnel?"

Jezet huffed a soft laugh at Roberre not noticing her change. Krayne noted that her Pilgrim Line associates knew.

"Because of the Xanthean's unexpected inclusion?" Jezet said. "Yes. I also expect representatives from both Griff and Rissilli to join us, and maybe others, but I believe the current Ranger squad on the *Sentinel* is adequate."

"I expect these potential representatives have already asked you?" Roberre inquired.

"Yes, and I've reported their interest to Captain Krayne while the delegates are making arrangements with the Alliance. They are interested in trade negotiations, and both governments know me. Their asking my help is unexpected, but I suppose advantageous for them, and for the Alliance. Of course, the determination on their joining us is not mine to make."

"We can provide further protection, too," Thorson said, speaking for the first time.

"Rafe's ship will need reimbursement for this expedition." Jezet mentioned an enormous sum, but no one flinched. "I'm sure both Rissilli and Griff will share that cost."

"That is true, and I'm sure you want to make sure Supreme Leader Kalmona-Rek Kerub is safe," Rafe said.

"From the miscreants after you?" Admiral Zamudo asked.

"Actually, I think Kerub's and my enemies might be working together."

"Austin Dachs?" Wakeman asked.

"Possibly," Jezet hedged. "They collaborated before, but their contacts within Khajari have far less power, and currently there is no substantive proof of his or Morgan's location, or if Austin is even with Morgan. T'Carta Kar has kept me informed of all situations and actions happening in the Khajari government. My team's goal is to keep Kalmona-Rek Kerub, his Khajari representatives, and all other Alliance and other government representatives safe."

As Jezet talked with the officers, Krayne watched her. He knew as she worked to complete her mission, he would eventually have to release his overwhelming need to protect her, or face losing her.

"Will T'Carta's son help?"

Krayne began listening to the conversation again.

Jezet smiled. "Possibly. He is not particularly fond of me. I have already conversed with T'Carta Kizz in President Uebel's office, and I expect he will soon seek me out. As T'Carta Kar's son, Kizz might become an asset in this mission."

Zamudo looked up from his comlink. "I've already placed all Pilgrim Line ships, whether Corps assigned or not, under heightened security and have prohibited any inspection or governmental drone surveillance without specific permission from the ships' captains. I've given all captains permission to destroy any drone not responding to identification code demands."

Rear Admiral Tuen, who had waited patiently for a pause in the talk, asked, "Major Chambers, may I visit the shuttles under redesign at Terra Shipyards?"

Jezet was quick to respond. "Yes. I cannot go with you because my presence anywhere is reported, and it might expose the ships undergoing change, but Gunnerman will show you the refinements being made. Take all security precautions. Two days hence, thirteen hundred hours?"

Tuen nodded, already updating his comlink. "I've added it to my schedule. I understand secrecy is required. Please know I will not wear a uniform and will have an excuse for visiting the station if I should be recognized."

"May I join you?" Zamudo asked.

"We'll make it a joint excursion," Wakeman said. "I may bring a few more officers with me."

Lu was watching Jezet, who was watching him. She recognized his restrained mirth. She rolled her eyes.

Roberre noticed their exchange and laughed. "So much for secrecy. I will take you there and tell anyone else with authority and curious questions that you want to see the changes made to a Ranger shuttle undergoing renovation, and I will mislead the media about our purpose."

"It's the truth," Jezet said.

"That's the best subterfuge, and I learned that from the master," Roberre answered, his poke earning a few soft laughs.

"Be assured, Major Chambers, we will make arrangements to keep the secrecy of this project paramount. Captain Krayne, let's talk about when the *Sentinel* might be ready to leave Constellation Station," Wakeman said.

Ninety minutes of discussion followed. At the end, Wakeman turned to Jezet. "President Uebel has freed two hours for a discussion tomorrow at fourteen hundred hours. Captain Dakota, you are also expected at this meeting."

Rafe threw an aggravated glance at Jezet.

Krayne rose with the others and was only too glad to see the backs of command officers leaving the *Sentinel* along with Captains Thorson whom Admiral Wakeman engaged in conversation, or orders. Rafe Dakota said he wanted to talk to Jesse... privately. Jezet became Jesse and stood next to him, looking like she expected another explosion. Henry stood next to Rafe.

"Were you injured in the blast?" Krayne asked.

She looked at him. "Perhaps some bruises. You?"

"Perhaps some bruises." He looked at Rafe. "Let's go to my office; you can talk there, and we have to make some plans."

Jesse nodded but stepped back to lean against the wall as she fell into a sudden mental abyss. She closed her eyes. Images of a blast flashed in front of her, and she felt her body slide down into a crouching position hearing shouting and a wailing hum. The horrible images persisted.

"Jesse." She heard Krayne calling to her as she experienced the mayhem in the engine compartment but could not respond. He yelled her name again and she felt a swift pain on her cheek. Her eyes opened, but she didn't attack her assailant. Realization came. She was on the *Sentinel*. The hum was coming from her like a whine. She stopped it, but adjusting her fast, hard breathing was difficult. She looked at Lu. "The *Constant*."

With her declaration, sanity returned, but she was shaking. She looked at Krayne. Henry and Rafe squatted next to him, surrounding and watching her. "Its engines. No attack. What just happened was a repeat of then. I remember. Its engines showed the same problems. They imploded." She looked at Rafe. "You weren't on duty at the time, were you?"

"No, I only returned when the warning came, but I arrived after the detonation. Only helped to get the wreckage back together enough to allow the ship to move."

She looked at Krayne. "You slapped me." His expression only turned grimmer.

Doctor Rae approached. She tried to skitter aside in panic, saying, "I'm okay." Lu's grip tightened and held her in place. Rae quickly gave her an applied spray.

The drug took effect quickly.

"Yes, you are, just somewhat stressed," Rae said, looking at her comlink.

"Did May send you memories?" Henry asked.

"I don't know. She might have, but maybe it was just imagination." Jesse looked at Lu. "Jet did not break any of your protocols," she said. "I knew two shuttles leaving the ship's docking bay would be reported."

He shook his head at the sudden change in topic but smiled at her deflection. She thought it was a twisted, cranky-looking smile. "I know, but that's not important right now."

Rafe seemed to ignore everything. His gaze locked on Jezlynn. "I remember Chernov saying something like what was described in the meeting," Rafe said referring to the *Constant*'s chief engineer. "But in all the chaos after the explosion, it was ignored. I'll contact Illa Jakle and Biri Detjen. See if they remember anything. I'm not sure they were on duty at that time either."

~ * ~

While within the Space Service Corps Headquarters section of Constellation Station, Jesse knew she had less exposure to netreps, and the corridors reached into the government sector without entering any public areas. She and her party still garnered many speculative looks as they walked through the government offices. Inside the assigned meeting rooms, she saw Tom and Rafe were already present. Tom looked spectacular in formal uniform, and while Rafe only wore formal attire, he looked handsome and clearly uncomfortable. They both gave her worried looks. She assumed Rafe had duly reported her episode on the *Sentinel*. Like her, they were probably unsure if she had remembered what happened on the *Constant* or only imagined it from what happened on the *Sentinel*. It left her shaky and for once, unsure.

Within minutes Corrao, Wakeman, and Roberre entered, followed shortly by the *Sentinel*'s Ambassador Ang Nohl. Jesse had met him at a few ship get-togethers, but until now had generally avoided the embassy side of the ship. It was hard to believe she had to work with the embassy personnel now, but Angie had recommended it. Nohl gave her an unreadable look, but Jesse guessed him unhappy or resentful of her position.

A few minutes passed and Jesse began wondering who they were waiting for when Dolf Faute, the Lieutenant Governor of Rissilli and the son of the governor, walked in with her upset-looking mother. He gave Jesse a beaming smile and moved to greet her.

"Jezlynn, I'm glad to know of your mission. I've already asked President Uebel to join your negotiations on behalf of Rissilli." She gave him a welcoming accord and he moved to stand next to Thorson. All the time she wondered if he had given Margarete a true account of what had happened to Rosche since he had been present and involved.

Margarete nodded in greeting and walked over to say in a soft voice, "Griff's governing board thought as long as I'm already here and related to you, I could represent them best. I hope this doesn't upset you."

Jesse smiled. "I'm the one who suggested you."

The shocked look of pleasure on Margarete's face made Jesse smile. "I mentioned it when I requested the shuttle technicians who also came with you."

Margarete nearly expanded in pleasure. "That long ago?"

"Yes."

Margarete paused before saying, "Thank you."

Jesse was shocked to see her mother's eyes water.

A scent recognizable to Jesse, and she assumed to Lu, drew her attention from Margarete as the tread of Xantheans entered the room. One of President Uebel's assistants quickly asked them into the conference room. The assistant looked vaguely familiar to Jesse, but she couldn't place where she had met her.

Uebel already stood at the far end of the table. At the near end of the table, a low, wide, and well-padded bench replaced the chair, indicating a place reserved for Aswenna. Everyone sat, Uebel's assistant indicating a chair midway down the table to Jesse, while she indicated Krayne should sit, saying with a wide smile, "Luke, sit opposite Major Chambers, please." The assistant calling Lu by Luke indicated they knew each other. He gave the woman a look Jesse failed to read, and with his annoyance came recognition. Jesse had never met her, only seen her once, with Lu. Her hair was platinum now rather than the strawberry blonde when Jesse first saw her. Jesse recognized the woman Lu had told her was his former wife. Jesse raised a brow at Lu as she took her seat. He remained unruffled. Roberre and Wakeman took the chairs on either side of him. Once everyone was seated, two attendants took typical folded-up kneeling positions behind Aswenna, their eyes closing.

Nine

From across the table, Krayne gave Jesse a brief, supportive smile. Her gaze lingered on him for a few seconds while she kept perfect meeting composure. Her gaze shifted to inspect the others in the room. She knew of Jet's disinterest in negotiation, so Jezet would not take over.

"Before we start," President Uebel said, "There have been some developments. Xanthean Revered Elder Aswenna has requested that the Alliance allow the establishment of a Xanthean colony on the planet Ezredin. The Alliance Legislature met yesterday, and not only agreed to this but also turned the planet over to Xanthean control as one of their homeworlds. In return, Revered Elder Aswenna made a generous offer which I also accepted. Ezredin is now neutral space between Khajari and Alliance space. Space where the negotiations can take place. I know, Major Chambers, this contravenes many of the ideas you have presented and worked on, but I believe it a safer option and the governing body agreed."

Krayne noted the many gazes turn in his wife's direction. Jesse kept her regard on Uebel and her expression inviolate. She flicked Krayne a glance and must have read the humor in his eyes. She gave him an ephemeral smile although he kept his expression fixed. She looked down the table at Aswenna, meeting the Xanthean leader's gaze. "Although I have no love for Ezredin, it is only a somewhat minor change. However, I will not go groundside. All meetings will still be held in the *Crusader*."

A quiet stillness filled the room. Krayne heard a familiar sound of a croak of Xanthean laughter behind Aswenna. He recognized Sutta's distinct voice. Aswenna nodded her head once in acquiescence at Jesse.

Lu spoke in Xanthean, surprising many at the table. "May I know why Ezredin?"

Aswenna croaked and answered in that language. "Child of my Circle, your skill in our language increases. I assume from your mate. It is simple. Dronai. Sira Sutta, speak for the others."

"Dronai?" Uebel asked when Sutta finished in understandable space standard.

Aswenna spoke, and Sutta quickly translated. "During Sera Major Chambers' visit to Çiro she helped the local Circle with a problem of illegal trade. The Çiro Circle Elder learned she was dronai. It generated great shock. We believed dronai extinct since it has disappeared from our selected homeworlds. We believed dronai no longer found our relationship worthy. When Captain Krayne married Jezlynn on Zeranth Ea, their sacred Leader echoed the Çiro truth. Then I discovered it in her and in Captain Krane on Asedin. We investigated her past and discovered the only place this might have happened was Ezredin."

"That is the infection in her?" Lu asked, hearing Sutta's translation.

"Not an infection, a joining of lifeforms," Aswenna answered, "Dronai choose who they join, but zenfler is always involved. Now it has reemerged in some of our Circles, a gift Sera Jezlynn has given us. The dronai have accepted our bodies again. It means we will not die out altogether."

"While this is valuable information, it is more of a medical development, and I'm sure they will be interested in it," Uebel said. "But we need to get back to our purpose. Ezredin's transfer of ownership is completed. It has had a sad history with human habitation. We hope the Xantheans can make it into a viable colony. Major Chambers has stated her boundaries, but I see no reason why this negotiation cannot go on as she has already suggested."

Lu watched his love gather her composure after another public exposure. "While trade relationships are important," Jesse said, "the most urgent topic is to establish space boundaries, what is neutral space and what routes will be acceptable for trade routes. I have spoken with T'Carta Kar on this.

"Here are the initial ideas we discussed." She showed the maps on the table devices in front of each person. "Any ship engaged in trade would be safe if following one of these routes. Those using the routes must record their travel intentions with both governments who will coordinate information. When in Khajari space, there would be acknowledgments from Khajari authorities for Alliance ships following any route. The same diligence would be followed on the Alliance side."

"These go beyond the Xanthean psiroutes," Wakeman said.

"The Xanthean routes you have already learned about, but I knew of a few others from tracking slave traders," Jesse said.

"Does T'Carta Kar have the authority to help in making such decisions?" Ambassador Ang Nohl asked.

"Since T'Carta Kar helped keep him safe during the previous T'Kalz rein, Prince Kalmona-Rek Kerub trusts T'Carta Kar implicitly, something rare among Khajari," Jesse replied in the same detached tone as the ambassador.

"As he does you," Undersecretary Corrao said.

"I presume that is why he chose her specifically," Uebel said.

"Will this implicit trust impair your ability to negotiate?" Nohl asked.

"No," Jesse said without explanation.

Another brief silence prevailed before the meeting's members began discussing the plan. The planet representatives quickly claimed certain routes as their own but agreed before Uebel to a joint set of mandated rules for usage.

When the topic turned to trade, Jesse quickly said, "Because Captain Thorson and Captain Dakota are both adept traders, they will oversee those negotiations. Griff and Rissilli have already joined the trade negotiation team, and while I've have heard nothing from the Tarkians, I suspect they might join the negotiations. I will be tied up with other details for the treaty—mostly for regulations between the Khajari and the Alliance, as I have already explained. T'Carta and Prince Kalmona-Rek Kerub have already appointed representatives to participate in both the regulatory and trade negotiations."

"You have already predicted and prepared for many of the unexpected changes to the plan," Corrao said.

"It was not that difficult to realize what planets would be interested in this change to travel and the relationships between two former enemies."

"Do you have any ideas of any who will actively work against it?" General Roberre asked.

"Certainly, all slave traders, a group not exclusively Visekan. There are other traders in all known territories, who if not active in slave trading themselves, deal with them. Another group will be the Khajari T'Kalz family and their adherents. While now out of power and without a leader, they remain a strong presence in Khajari politics. Both T'Carta Kar and I expect subversive attacks from the T'Kalz. T'Carta Kar has arranged for the R'Kalmona family and their adherents to protect Kerub."

"And while you act as an ambassador, your Ranger squad provides you protection," Corrao said, "which will include protection from your known Alliance enemies."

Krayne knew he was not the only one aware of her annoyance at Corrao's statement. For once it was hard to prevent a smile, glad he was not alone in concern for her safety.

"There is another problem. When the Individual Rights Bureau learns of the dronai and how it has changed my body, they will carp to be allowed on Ezredin." She looked at Uebel. "I'm sure you are aware of this, but I think you should set regulations for access to Ezredin with the Xantheans now."

Uebel smiled. "I've already been speaking with Revered Elder Aswenna about this topic. And you will need to be aware, also, that the *Sentinel*'s ambassador and his core embassy staff will remain on the *Sentinel*."

Uebel gave a brief grin at Jesse's look, alerting Krayne others suspected her attitude. "Do not take umbrage, Jesse," Umbel said. "You are no longer a free-ranging anonymous spacer, suspected traitor, or rebel, but an important diplomat, trade partner, friend, and family to many. Your safety is of utmost concern, not only to General Roberre, or your husband, or your Pilgrim Lines captains but also to me and many others."

"I do not take umbrage at Ambassador Nohl's participation, for I expect I will need his help, nor to anyone necessary to help him carry out his duties, but not all embassy agencies are needed, and I hope you don't mean their family members. This could turn into a dangerous mission, as already explained."

"Noted. The Alliance Embassy Department will be notified." Uebel resumed the meeting. "Admiral Wakeman, please take these plans to your senior officers and discuss their viability. Also, planetary representatives here should discuss their trade routes and the protections needed. Our delegation meetings will alert them about trade negotiations and what to expect. General Roberre, work with Major Chambers on issues of her safety and what duty you expect from her on the *Sentinel*. Revered Elder Aswenna, I have appreciated your input and hope we can continue our discussion on plans for Ezredin as neutral space with port availability there." In short order the meeting was over.

Krayne walked Jesse back to the *Sentinel*. "Are you sure you don't want to stop at one of the restaurants along the way?"

She glared at him. He controlled his laugh. "I take that as a no."

"Your ex-wife works for Uebel?"

"You recognized her? I haven't seen her in three years, not since when she demanded my help and recommendation for a job." He read her expression correctly. "I didn't give it. Listen, we were married all of six months. The marriage was a major mistake I made twelve years ago. I was...naïve...thought good sex meant love. I quickly learned she was more interested in me as a business arrangement to further her own career. She never loved me. Let it go, Jesse. I only love one woman, and that's you."

She looked at him and finally smiled. "All the more reason to forego a restaurant."

They entered deck two's main access to the *Sentinel*. Looking down the corridor, Jesse noted the many security offices which lined the entry corridor, a few lighted, showing someone occupied and worked within. To their left was a small, empty waiting area for guests, to the right two security officers manned a console, waiting and watching for anyone entering the ship. While an attractive area, it was more functional than welcoming, almost presenting a warning. For her the docking bay gave a warmer welcome.

Regulation required everyone from the station had to report entry into the ship. Even now one of the on-duty officers logged them in. At the security console, another surprise awaited. Lieutenant Howard Wakeman stood behind the console next to one of the seated security officers, far from his third deck adjutant's office next to the captain's office.

He spoke as Krayne approached. "Captain, T'Carta Kizz and his entourage arrived as you expected he might. I've given them quarters on the embassy decks, a suite on the embassy side for T'Carta Kizz, and seven separate rooms for his entourage. Also, Dolf Faute, the Lieutenant Governor of Rissilli, will be coming aboard as a negotiator for his home planet."

Krayne nodded. "Good, thank you, Howard."

"T'Carta Kizz asked to speak with Major Chambers when she returned. I've made arrangements for use of one of the embassy meeting rooms."

Krayne turned to her. "Are you up to it or would you like to put it off until tomorrow?"

"Now is okay."

Howard named the suites assigned. "There is more," Howard said. "A journalist, Sal Imada, came aboard."

Jesse's groan interrupted him. She uttered an invective against the president that made Krayne grin. "You did not hear that, Lieutenant Wakeman."

"Hear what, sir? Imada came aboard with presidential permission. I've also given him a room in the embassy suites, but far away from any place Major Chambers might travel."

Jesse smiled. "Thank you, Howard. I doubt that will thwart him, however."

"Maybe you should just meet him head-on," Krayne suggested.

"Maybe. Can we meet with Kizz in one hour?" she asked Howard.

"I'll arrange it, Major."

"Jesse."

Howard nodded and smiled as he headed back to his office.

"Let's get something to eat first," Krayne said, leading her to the mess hall. As they walked away, he spoke. "Don't get too informal with my crew."

"I'm a Ranger now. I have no control in ordering your crew around nor am I undermining your authority. My friendship with his brother overrides protocol formality."

Deck two held most of the public areas and services including the gardens and the mess hall, so more ship personnel traveled its corridors. They entered the mess hall and found more crew at lunch than normal for an in-port ship.

Within minutes they were seated, eating, and mostly silent, until Krayne received several messages. With one he looked at her. "Your mother has come aboard. Howard gave her a private suite in the embassy, too. She has company."

Jesse looked at him. "Let me guess, Isobel Meitland." Being the communication and social personality, Jesse was unusually quiet, which told Krayne how upset she remained.

"Yes. I can have that changed if you want."

"No. If she is here, Margarete asked her. Did Vanessa Dachs come, too?"

"Yes. Howard gave them private apartments. At this rate, the embassy deck will be full. I haven't seen much of Angie today," Krayne said.

She eyed him with mockery. "That's funny. She has been in near-constant communication with me. And although I like hearing her music, she doesn't have Alyss's strictly objective outlook."

"How so?"

"Alyss's thoughts were always linear and objective, although she considered lateral ideas that could impinge on her analysis. Angie, however, seems to look at everything at once and develop two or three or more outcomes. She can be emotional and a bit scattered at times."

"Like Lynn?"

"In a different, coherent, but hard to decipher way."

"Are you upset with what Alyss and Lynn did?"

She looked over his shoulder in thought for a brief pause. "Not really. I miss them, and though I find Angie's scattered thoughts less straightforward, she has predicted several outcomes I had not considered, like Dolf showing up. She is more talkative than Alyss. She is also more sensible in her talk than Lynn ever was, and she keeps May calm and entertained."

"I haven't seen May for several days," he said in inquiry. It had been longer.

"Nael has been talking with her."

He changed the topic, thinking some in the mess hall might overhear them. "How are your deck one offices?"

Deck one was the lowest deck just above the cargo holds at the bottom of the ship and held Ranger and Corps personnel quarters and housing services, and her Ranger office.

"It's adequate, although a long way from the refinement of the embassy deck where most Rangers serve." She laughed. "That might prove a benefit. It's not as elegant as the Corps offices or the captain's quarters on deck three, but I've lived there."

"That you have; just don't take up residency again."

She smirked at him. "My office is closer to the Xanthean quarters, so that is good. The embassy quarters up on deck four are far superior, almost all of them better than your quarters."

He gave her an equally deprecating look. "Topdeck has more elegant offices, meeting rooms, housing, services and entertainments often not allowed to other ship personnel. They bring family, though, and most families are often unused to or unfamiliar with usual ship facilities and functions."

"Big, elegant offices often impress colonial leaders, too," she replied.

Somewhere nearby Krayne heard a muffled laugh, informing him his assumption correct. He noted Jesse noticed too.

"I wonder if they know most ship's crew know the top deck is the most vulnerable to damage?" she asked.

Krayne gave her a warning look while seeing the smugness on the faces of those at surrounding tables.

"What? Why the warning? It's true, and most of those housed on deck four hate looking out their view panels. Give me deck one or three any day. Far more secure."

"More embassy personnel survived the *Constant* than crew personnel."

A brief glare entered her face at his reminder of her first ship and its disaster, but Rae advised him since the recent recall incident to keep bringing it up. She smiled. "Yes, they did, but that might have been planned, so was different, although embassies can be targets, too. And few Corps crew survived the *Constant* because they did their duty. I sent Rear Admiral Tuen one of my suggestions yesterday. One for stronger hull panels on non-military decks."

"They do have security practices in place and run exercises for those practices at least once a month. Did you send him any other suggestions?"

"With Margarete there, I'm glad to hear it. Yes, several. I suggested ways to strengthen the hull materials. But I doubt it will happen as it significantly increases construction costs."

"I'm guessing Pilgrim Lines ships already have these improvements?"

"Pilgrim Lines ships are also homes. It was necessary."

~ * ~

Stepping onto the embassy's deck four, or topdeck as most crew called it, seemed strange. Jesse seldom went to the embassy level, not liking the superior attitude held by many of the staff and their family members. They all thought their mission more important than the ship's Rangers' and Space Service Corps' jobs, which they thought were to serve them. The embassy worked with Alliance colonies on different planets and sometimes with non-allied colonies. While onboard, the ambassador had a strong say in what happened as far as destinations and any change, although the captain could override his decisions. Ambassador Nohl had a distinguished career as an ambassador. Jesse also knew his requests occasionally exasperated Lu.

Embassy deck security was a Ranger duty, which held certain protocols the ambassador could not override, not without the captain's permission. While the corridor bulwarks and doors looked the same as those on the rest of the ship, they somehow felt different to Jesse. Quieter, and right now, empty as all families were off ship.

Outside the designated wardroom, four Rangers stood as security. Inside the sumptuously decorated meeting room, T'Carta Kizz waited with his seven staff. The two guards constantly following her also entered the meeting room behind her. Jesse recognized the Khajari woman she knew had entertained Kizz on his sojourn at Asedin. She judged Kizz lacked his normal harassing look as their gazes met. He nodded his head once, "Major Chambers."

She returned his greeting in his own language. "Ambassador T'Carta Kizz." His start of reaction at her address caused his mouth to twitch in negation.

"I have not received that designation."

"Until the *Sentinel* encounters the treaty negotiation team, you are, indeed, the Khajari ambassador on this ship. I have already received the notification from Supreme Leader Prince Kalmona-Rek Kerub."

Kizz stared at her. "My father only notified me minutes ago of the possibility."

Jesse returned his regard. "I hope your facilities here on the *Sentinel* are adequate for you. If you have any requests for services, you only need to contact Ambassador Ang Nohl. Let me introduce you to Captain Krayne."

Lu immediately made clarifications which Jesse translated. "Since Ambassador Nohl is currently off ship, speak with my adjutant, Lieutenant Howard Wakeman, for any of your needs," Krayne said. "Until the ambassador is aboard, you have access to all the amenities on this deck, the mess hall, and to the training room on deck one."

"Rangers, of course, will guide you there," Jesse said.

Kizz didn't respond to her jibe but merely nodded his head. "I've heard you follow a rigorous training schedule."

She nodded, answering, "Yes."

Krayne broke in, and Jesse translated. "The T'Carta family shuttle is also onboard. I will have Major Chambers guide you to it so you can see it remains undamaged."

"Thank you, Captain," Kizz replied in Space Standard.

Jesse still replied in his own language. "Be prepared, Kizz. Kar has asked me to include you in some of the pre-meetings for trading negotiations planned during this journey. Has Aswenna adopted you?"

He looked both exasperated and relieved. "Not exactly. I don't wear the tattoo like you and your captain do. I've found her a hard negotiator."

"Kar will notify you of this and of the Khajari positions on these plans. He wants to know exactly who to include in the finalization of the meetings at Ezredin."

"Ezredin?" he asked looking bewildered.

"Well, by now you are familiar with Xanthean tactics. They have requested Ezredin from the Alliance President for a new colony, received it, and plan to take part in the negotiations."

A quirky Khajarian smile crossed Kizz's face and his demeanor relaxed. "I now begin to understand my father's attraction and trust in you."

"I hope so. It seems we might be working together."

Kizz turned to Krayne. "Thank you, Captain Krayne, for your hospitality and acceptance of your former enemies on your ship. You have my promise to cause no trouble. I have another ten members of my team on the *Dark Traveler*."

"They are welcome on the *Sentinel*," Krayne said. "I'll have rooms arranged near your own. You must be aware the ship has some damage. Major Chambers and my chief engineer will make the repairs, but we will remain in port longer than expected."

Jesse, looking at the Khajari present, realized the Khajari officer who had physically assaulted her after capturing her on Asedin would be one of the remaining ten. She wondered what expectations the man had and quashed her thought.

Kizz nodded again at Lu and grinned. "After the amenities available at my last posting, I can assure you both my team and I find those we have already enjoyed on the *Sentinel* far superior." He gave a signal, and he and his seven team members left the wardroom. The four Ranger security followed them down the corridor.

"Strange," Jesse said. "He was actually agreeable."

Krayne laughed. "Either he has learned from his mistakes and misassumptions, or his father has spoken with him. Let's go see your family."

"Yes, and we will need to visit the *Dark Traveler* and see what the Xantheans want for quarters. They might not want the cargo hold." Jesse replied.

As a trade negotiator for Griff, Margarete's apartment was more spacious than any crew personnel's quarters, but Jesse knew much smaller than her home on Griff. Yet Margarete seemed satisfied. Isobel and Vanessa stood next to her.

Margarete graciously invited them in, smiling at Jesse, saying, "I am glad you came, Jesse. Welcome, Captain."

Jesse's mind briefly stalled at her mother using her persona name. Her smile must have shown her response, but Margarete gave her a brief hug.

"Lucian, please, Margarete."

"Except when you are on duty," Margarete added. She invited them to sit down. The large sitting area had access to the adjoining bedrooms with a small closet kitchen.

"You are you whatever name you go by," Isobel whispered to Jesse before she could move, hugging her again. Jesse swallowed and controlled her impulse to bolt and escape.

Isobel explained, "Margarete had asked my mother and me to visit her on *Constellation*. When we learned she was a trade delegate, well, we asked to join her."

"And you joined the mission as?" Jesse asked.

The three women laughed. Vanessa answered. "Influence peddling. Isobel is a between-colony administrator for several of the representatives here with the Alliance trade department. I'm here because she is my caretaker." She smiled, looking slightly abashed. "Not that I need it, but it was a plausible situation and solution."

Lu looked at her from under his crinkled brows. "You have admitted a falsehood to the ship's commander, you know."

Vanessa gave him an unworried look. "At my age, it is hardly a falsehood. Will you report me in my delusional state?"

He took the cup Margarete handed him. "Probably not but stay out of any influence-peddling or other trouble. Besides, Margarete is a trade delegate which entitles her to have family with her. At least you are over seventeen."

"So the age of the child limits which family can join the embassy?" Vanessa asked with a grin.

"These are small quarters compared to what you have lived in," Jesse said. "Are you comfortable?"

"Very," Isobel said.

"We came aboard as family. The *Sentinel*'s crew quickly and effectively changed two separate apartments into this quartering configuration," Margarete said. "We had been getting together daily after your visit on the starbase and have been sharing meals and tea-time, so we decided to move in together. Your adjutant gave permission for our bedrooms to be adjoined and a sitting room enlarged. My daughter seems to have great influence on this ship's personnel."

Jesse looked at her smiling husband. She hoped he couldn't read her mind.

Isobel said, "Margarete invited me to come with her."

"We have become friends," Margarete said, smiling at Isobel.

Isobel smiled back. "Good friends."

Jesse never remembered Margarete having friends...friendly acquaintances, yes, friends, no.

"I am glad you came to visit so soon," Margarete said, pleasure filling her voice. "We've barely settled in."

"I am your daughter. I will attempt to visit every day."

"Well, your numerous duties might prevent that, but you will always be welcomed. Have some coffee with us."

Isobel looked at Lu. "Is it possible, Lucian, to get a tour of the *Sentinel*?"

Ten

Rafe greeted them at the Dark Traveler's access. He looked frustrated and glad to see them.

"You come to relocate my guests?"

Several of his crew were nearby and looked like they wanted to laugh but also like they were caught in a quagmire.

Jesse greeted them by name, smiled, and gave Rafe a knowing look. "Too much for you to handle?"

"No, just neither I nor my crew like all the delving into our past. Our passengers are obsessive and insistent that my crew and I learn their language. Why, I'm unsure. Enough of them speak Space Standard." He glared at her. "Thank you."

"We just came to find out their desires for travel to Ezredin," Krayne said.

Rafe's eyes hardened in worry, but he waved them a gracious entry into his ship. "Please, invite them to the *Sentinel* in your best no-nonsense, do-it-now way."

Jesse muffled a laugh as Rafe obviously was speaking to Krayne. He led them to one of the ship's cargo holds.

Twenty-six Xantheans occupied one cargo hold remade into livable quarters. Each Xanthean had its own sleeping mats which were rolled up next to them along with bags Jesse assumed held clothing and the minimal necessities Xantheans required. Nearby containers with lights grew their food.

Aswenna crouched in a Xanthean manner in the middle of the bay with others meditating around her. Her eyes opened to stare at Jesse. She blinked and gave the Xanthean hand motion of approach. Ahjias from Çiro rose from her position next to Aswenna wearing the floor-length draping garment common to all Xantheans. She tipped her head in greeting, her large luminescent eyes prominent in her otherwise calm face.

"It is good to again see you," the acolyte Ahjias said in very slow Space Standard, "and now I learn your words." She wrapped her arms around Jesse in an embrace, but when Jesse moved, Ahjias quickly released her.

"You've changed your safety zone," Jesse replied, implying they had left their homes.

"My sister Jezlynn Angeline has led the way," Ahjias replied.

Aswenna spoke. "Greetings, my children Jezlynn and Lucian. Yes, we will come to the *Sentinel*. You see, simple fits us. Harmony." With her words and a hand motion, Sutta helped Aswenna rise. All the other Xantheans rose and slung pack straps crosswise over their shoulders.

Exiting from the *Dark Traveler* was arduous as each Xanthean stopped before each crewmember giving them thankfulness and farewells until they met again. Unexpectedly one crew member threw her arms around Ahjias, saying, "Thank you and I look forward to seeing you." Other crew members offered their hands in farewell greeting, even Rafe.

Jesse watched with some amusement. The Xantheans welcomed the human rituals and followed them in their own way.

At last the protracted goodbye ended. Aswenna stopped before Rafe and spoke in her slow Space Standard. "Reluctant friend, good host, brother to my child Jezlynn, you are now a child of the Ezredin Circle."

As Jesse passed Rafe, he threw her an almost panicked glare. Jesse smiled in commiseration but followed the Xantheans out. Lu stayed behind in a brief conversation with Rafe. Jesse, though, knew her duty, even with the outrageous attention waiting on the decks outside the *Dark Travel*. The Xantheans had also earned the media's attention. Both media and curious humans watched the Xantheans' move to the *Sentinel*. The last she heard from Rafe was, "That was easier than I thought, thanks."

Jesse walked next to Aswenna with Ahjias on the Revered Elder's other side. Immediately, Jet's Rangers dogged the group's every move, two falling in behind her as well. She heard one call for more security.

Within a few minutes, Lu passed her to move forward to the leading Xantheans just as *Sentinel* Corp's security arrived and helped clear their way. The Xantheans all seemed impervious to the attention they gathered, but the attention troubled Jesse.

"Use it to your advantage," Aswenna's soft voice advised.

Looking at all the netreps and cameras, Jesse said, "We could have called a transport."

"We wanted to see your space city," Ahjias answered. "Most amazing."

A few Xantheans croaked a laugh at Jesse's coarse reply "I'm guessing you had them at one time," Jesse answered.

"Too far and long ago to remember. Even travel on ship differs... exciting."

Several crew members waited at the *Sentinel's* main access. Surprisingly, each Xanthean stopped at the security console and gave their name, their Circle's name, and voice verification.

"It is standard here. We adjust," Aswenna said, answering what she must have recognized as Jesse's surprise.

Once inside the cargo hold, all the Xantheans stood and stared at their new temporary home. On the floor were organic oval mats placed in a specific design, sleep cushions arranged along one bulkhead, and lighted plant environment cabinets along another.

"It was the common placement of seating of every circle I've attended," Jesse said. "I hope I have not exceeded bounds."

"An unexpected honor to our practices and to our circle. I did not realize you noticed," Aswenna said. "You always see more." She bowed and moved to one of the mats, folding her body into typical Xanthean meditating position.

"If you have any needs, just ask," Jesse said.

No one seemed to notice. Soon all the Xantheans followed their leader in settling into deep, folded positions, their sleep mats and packs left by the entrance. They seemed insensible to everything else.

"I think we've been excused." Jesse grinned at Lu. "I'll check back later," she assured him. As they stepped out of the cargo bay, her comlink and Krayne's both vibrated at the same time. Jesse said, "Ambassador Nohl wants me to come to his office." She sighed. "I'll meet with him in one hour, no sooner."

"I've a notice from the admiral, and I'll come with you. Rafe seemed relieved to see his passengers leave."

"No one prizes privacy and self-rule more than Rafe. His crew is the only exception he makes, and they all shared his experiences in slavery. He has never talked about those to me or Tom. You don't have to come with me to Nohl's office. I am capable of meeting with him alone."

"I am aware, but even as a Ranger in command of the embassy squad, I am still your commanding officer and I have some qualms about his request." He smiled at her. "I want my authority present."

~ * ~

Ambassador Ang Nohl rose from behind his desk and extended his hand to Lu and to Jesse. He was tall and thin, his face rather contained and immobile but lined with creases. His gaze was measuring while his tone sounded pleasantly calm. Jesse had redressed in formal Ranger uniform. Nohl inspected her regalia. She discreetly observed the bare but highly polished desktop, the room's somber but elegant camel and emerald details, and she observed its expensive décor. She guessed he had a desk in another compartment for his diplomacy work.

"Please sit," Nohl said, his hand inviting as his arm swept the area before his desk graciously

She found the cushions luxurious and soft, but too deep and far beyond the Corps' usual comfortable but utilitarian designed seating.

"I understand while on the ship you are in charge of the Ranger squad securing the embassy and its inhabitants' safety."

"Yes," Jesse replied.

"So you will follow my requests for placements and…"

"No, you request them from me," Lu said, "as general embassy ship protocols determine. Major Chambers reports to me and I make the orders."

"Sorry, all these changes are somewhat confusing. And I will tell you quite frankly, I'm not used to being superseded in my own embassy."

"Presidential order," Krayne said.

"It is a strange situation; normally someone of…"

"Ambassador Nohl," Jesse said, knowing why he broke off. He knew her background, knew much about her from her service since joining the *Sentinel* nearly a year ago. While she felt her own umbrage at his preconception and presumption of her, she refused to show it. "I suspect you are informed about my somewhat sullied reputation, but I am only ambassador for the actual negotiations with the Khajari."

"Yes, the head of the Diplomatic Division, Miz Fyed, has given me information on you. She talked quite at length. I find your position rather unusual and astonishing, but yours is the only current mission for the *Sentinel*. Miz Fyed ordered the embassy to remain in place, which puts my own position in limbo." For a diplomat, his expression showed a stern and upset demeanor.

"That is true, but President Uebel and Mister Corrao wanted my knowledge of the Khajari involved, my understanding of the dangers of the mission, and my knowledge of all the languages of those who will be involved in the negotiations, which seem to be growing in scope. It now includes the Xantheans currently onboard. On the other side of this unusual equation is your knowledge of the embassy's Diplomatic Division's responsibilities and mission scope is superior to mine. It is far different from either the Corps or Ranger procedures I am familiar with. You have all the knowledge of diplomatic protocols, of the Alliance's aims in treaties, and what the government will vote to pass and what they won't."

As she finished, Nohl looked pleased and finally relaxed into his chair. "What are you suggesting, Major Chambers?"

"I suggest a collaboration between us. You know much of what I need to learn, and I need help with all the trade negotiations this treaty seems to be generating."

"Trade negotiations between the Alliance and the Khajari?"

"Yes, and with the Xantheans, who as you know, have been given the planet Ezredin to colonize; and with the representatives from Griff, and Rissilli, and maybe others. I suspect Tarkia will also attend."

"I had not heard of these changes."

"They've developed within the last few days and are causing chaos in President Uebel's plans. The Xantheans are already onboard, as are Ambassador T'Carta Kizz of the Khajari, Lieutenant Governor Dolf from Rissilli, and Margarete Chambers from Griff."

"They've all been assigned housing here on the embassy deck," Krayne said.

"This suggests some negotiations can start while we wait as well as when we travel?"

"Yes, but we must work together. I can assist you with any language difficulties," Jesse said, "while you can teach me standard negotiation approaches and the regulations involved." Nohl then did something Jesse didn't expect.

"My apologies for any umbrage I may have presented, Major Chambers and Captain Krayne. I thought your appointment a dismissal of me, so did my superior, who it now seems knew little about what Uebel planned. Our department has been kept somewhat in the dark about this situation."

He looked at her, Jesse guessed for elaboration. He didn't trust her and probably listened to the news reports on her to back up his department head's information. "I can assure you, despite all the bizarre news circulating about me, the assertions are not all true. However, I do have a direct connection with all persons involved in these negotiations, including all the Khajari. Further, I will tell you the displaced Khajari faction of the T'Kalz family will make attempts not only on the current Khajari government leaders but also on us and our mission. Which was one reason I asked for the embassy's delegation to be limited here on the *Sentinel*."

A crease showed between the ambassador's brows. "Miz Fyed objected to exclusion of families and extended embassy departments, but like I said, I do not think she had all the information needed to make that decision. Do you think our families will be put in danger?"

"I hope not. Captain Krayne and I, along with many others, are trying to minimize any danger, but there are no guarantees, so we must be prepared."

"Due to some situations," Lu said, "Major Chambers is the most endangered."

"Morgan Dachs?" Nohl asked. At Lu's nod, Nohl turned his attention back to her. "Can you schedule time with me for us to meet and work on the many aspects of this mission? As well as handle your Ranger duties onboard?"

"Yes."

"I will do what I can to only have necessary personnel onboard, but many will object to leaving their families on Constellation for months on end, and others will be most unhappy, including my superior."

"If employees sign documentation that they know of the mission's danger, their families can remain," Lu said.

Nohl looked at him, showing his awareness of the recent attack on the *Sentinel*. "How dangerous is this mission?"

"Due to Major Chamber's ship-safety precautions, the *Sentinel* should be safer than one might expect." Lu continued with the basics of all the ships included and their abilities and securities.

Nohl's gaze often shifted to her, but Jesse kept her expression Ranger inviolate.

Once outside the ambassador's office, Lu remained silent until they entered the lift to deck three. "Who is Fyed?" he asked.

"Did I react?"

"Yes. Nohl noticed, too."

"Laura Astra Fyed is a relative of Reed Dachs."

Lu swore.

Jesse laughed. "The Dachs are everywhere, aren't they?"

~ * ~

The next morning as she approached her level one office, Jesse stopped. Ranger Colonel Gunnerman, wearing what she considered a blatant Ranger smirk, stood outside the door with several Ranger security officers. Sutta stood with them. She entered her office, guessing that someone was there.

Ambassador Nohl waited inside. She had no outer office with an adjutant or secretary. "Good morning, Ambassador Nohl."

"Good morning, Major." He smiled at her and took the seat before her desk. "I came to set up a schedule with you and to, out of curiosity, see your workstation."

"It is not as...welcoming...as your office."

"I expected an actual duty office to look more severe. You do not have to impress any visitors and are most likely to give orders rather than negotiate."

Jesse laughed but noted that her reaction shocked her guest. Within seconds her tender sounded. She read the message and pressed a button. "Howard, has Terra Shipyards contacted you about the delivery of the engine section?"

"Yes, Major Chambers. I've advised Captain Krayne and Chief Engineer Snyderon."

"Advise me when it arrives. I want to inspect it with Snyderon."

"Yes, Major, you are already on the list." The communication ended.

"Engine section?" Nohl asked.

"Part of one of the main engines was destroyed in the recent attack on the *Sentinel*."

"How does this concern you?"

"The engine section technically belongs to me and I will be helping to install it. You didn't know I'm an engine expert?"

"No." He looked surprised. "Somehow that information is lacking in your files, other than you began your career in the Corps at the Engine Design and Development department, but the report never mentioned your position."

"Certain details of my background have been classified." *Or deleted*, she thought with perfect composure. "It will only take a week, at most two, to have the ship back to operational."

"I had heard it would be much longer."

She smiled but added nothing else. "I, like you, have a busy schedule, but I can probably rearrange mine more easily. How often and at what time would you like to meet?" She readily agreed to what he asked. "I hate to cut this short, but I have a newly assigned Ranger and a Xanthean waiting for me, plus I have a training session scheduled in thirty minutes. I would, however, like to introduce you to the Xantheans, perhaps tomorrow?"

"Yes," he smiled. "I also wanted to ask about your training sessions, too. Several from the embassy department have mentioned they are training with you. Might others join?"

"Certainly. The only rules are a willingness to work out, and use of first names only, no ranks or titles."

"Thank you, Major, I will take you up on that, and I look forward to working with you."

She laughed again. "That sounds like a change in viewpoint, Ambassador."

"Yes; a surprise, but a pleasant one for me." As he left, Jesse made sure he had an escort back to the embassy just as Gunnerman came in.

"Came to tell you Roberre ordered me to help with training and wherever I can help. Saw your schedule. It seems the captain's adjutant will keep me informed. Just alerting you to my presence, and I'll talk to you about my duties later." He saluted and walked away.

Sutta entered but like Gunnerman, he did not sit down.

"How can I help you, Sutta?"

"I wish to assist you. Aswenna agrees, if you accept my offer," he said in his heavy Xanthean-accented Space Standard.

"Assist me how?"

"Train you in Xanthean skills while you train me in human skills. I will act as your guide, liaison, and guard."

Unsure of Aswenna's and Sutta's intent, she said, "It sounds like a good idea since we will be working so close together at the negotiation site."

"I need to learn such defense skills as you possess. Aswenna knows our presence will bring danger to you, so we need to lessen it to be successful on our new colony. She asked me. I agreed. You rescued me from slavery. After my many years of living in fear, you bring me strength to take back me as I was."

"Do you know what Aswenna sees?"

"No."

"You know I don't need your help on this ship?"

He gave her the grimace of a Xanthean's grin. "Not among Rangers. Not among Service Corps. Yes among all others. Others here on this ship."

Jesse laughed and heard Sutta's croaks of laughter.

"You also will give me strength to become more on Ezredin," Sutta added.

"Do Xantheans practice self-defense?"

"Not for a long time, but I will. I will not stop any of your endeavors but help keep danger from you and learn from you. Ezredin will attract humans. Xantheans need to know more to act correctly."

"Let me talk to Captain Krayne. You will need to be put on the payroll and given specific duties in accordance with ship law."

He nodded, his features wearing the smile grimace. His eyes glowed with pleasure.

"Don't be too happy. I've heard I'm a hard boss, and you will have to keep up with me."

Krayne's reply to her message was instantaneous. *Come now.*

In the corridor outside his office, three Xantheans were already folded into their seated form. Sutta did not follow suit but took the stance of the Rangers on the protection duty Roberre had ordered. Jesse knew immediately what was happening and sighed. Sutta heard the soft sound and croaked once in response.

Inside Aswenna sat on the floor before the low table in the informal seating portion of the office. The upholstered loungers were repositioned but still locked to the floor. Lu sat on the floor opposite Aswenna and waved Jesse to a place on the low table's end, where no chair had ever existed. She gracefully lowered herself to the floor.

"Aswenna has already told me about Sutta's desires, and I have agreed. His new position is as diplomat's liaison and guard. I've received a message from Admiral Wakeman with his approval. He is contacting President Uebel about the arrangement's details."

"So glad I didn't have to haggle the details," Jesse quipped throwing Lu an aggravated look. He just flashed a smile. A decanter of coffee sat on the table. Aswenna held a cup.

"Is this your first coffee?"

"No. I asked Lucian for it. My new child Rafe introduced me to it."

While she poured herself a cup, Jesse briefly wondered about Rafe's acceptance of his acquisition into a Xanthean circle. She felt she might need it. "How do you think Sutta will handle physical training?"

Aswenna's smile was more practiced so not so grimace-like. "Xantheans are agile when necessary and can change their body's formation. Lucian was asking me about dronai when you contacted him." She looked at Lu. "I will explain now that Jezlynn is here."

Lu nodded and leaned back against the base of the lounger.

"Dronai are what helped cure you from your injuries. A long time ago, most Xantheans held dronai in their bodies. They live in peaceful coexistence in the bodies they select for their housing."

"Not just anybody?" Lu asked.

"They choose their host and provide good health for their host while living off that body's benefits of food and safety. While they prolong life only through good health, they do not overly elongate life. Our legends claim they even communicated with some of their hosts. Sometimes they abandon a host. We do not know why. When we lost their presence, we stopped our explorations. We held guilt that we had committed some sin the dronai felt irredeemable. Now, thanks to you, we know where they still exist. They are willing to exist within us again, as well as the Xanthean living on the planets Ciro, Asedin, and Zeranth Ea. All who came already share some of Jezlynn's dronai. We now feel we can resurrect our explorations of space, plus the Circles have pledged to protect the dronai on Ezredin."

"The dronai speak to you?" Lu asked.

"Not yet, or maybe only indirectly, but Xantheans have made the pledge, so many believe the dronai guide us. The number who have volunteered to come amazed the genitors on all of our home planets."

"More than those who have accompanied you?" Jesse asked.

"Yes. They will come when the initiators have developed the colony."

"Humans have never successfully colonized on Ezredin." It was clear Lu's comment amused Aswenna.

"Dronai would never let it happen if they rejected the bodies on the planet. They do not fear danger but have strong desires to protect their own. The dronai renewing their integration with Xantheans is both a gift and a challenge. That they have inhabited humans, and Khajari, gives us hope for a future existence of peace."

"You think T'Carta Kar has dronai?" Jesse asked.

"Assuredly. His son does. So do my children Rafe and his entire crew. Dronai live independently on his ship, and we expect on all your Pilgrim ships. Yet the Circle knows this knowledge will cause much trouble."

Surprisingly, Aswenna rose in a strong fluid motion. "The dronai will not accept all humans, nor all Xantheans. We know not why. I will leave you now as your together time approaches." She left the room in an easy but slow walk.

"Dinner first?" Jesse asked with a grin.

Lu's tender sounded. He checked the message and answered, "In my adjutant's office." He turned to her. "Just notification that remaining Khajari from the *Dark Traveler* have joined the *Sentinel*. One has asked to meet with you before going any further."

Jesse, with Jet's help, recognized the Khajari who entered. He bowed to her and immediately began an apology in Khajari.

"Well," Jesse answered him in his language. "Thank you, but I must admit I provoked you and your squad to get where I wanted to be.

His face finally rose to hers. He looked surprised both by her response and that it was in his language. She extended her hand in Khajari greeting and accord. He responded and seemed pleased.

At Lu's nod, she added, "We will walk you to your onboard quarters."

Eleven

While Krayne worked in his office he listened and intermittently watched the feed of the *Sentinel*'s engine renovation being sent to Rear Admiral Tuen's office. Nael worked with the engineers sent to help rebuild the second main thruster in the engine compartment. The feed frequently interrupted the work he wanted to complete on crew assignments for the upcoming mission. Fournelle was leaving, elated to earn the captaincy of a ship. Ribberdan had been promoted to the *Sentinel*'s executive officer and was back onboard. Engine staff and Ranger staff were the only departments with a full staff.

On this trip, they would have far fewer crew and embassy personnel, and while the Ranger embassy squad would stay at eleven, he decided to adjust some other ship duties.

All departments had been reduced to minimal levels, or what Admiral Wakeman, Henry, and he deemed adequate for all normal ship's function duties or for any emergency. A few crew members were transferred, some to other ships, or to temporary duty on the *Constellation* because this flight had one specific purpose. Some remaining staff were working two different duties. Howard was now not only his adjutant but also head of the communications staff. Rather than being disconcerted at longer duty hours, Howard radiated elation. He huffed. Jezlynn served in several positions besides head of the Ranger staff.

Ambassador Nohl had already reduced the embassy staff by a third, which only allowed more delegation members to join the *Sentinel* and meant shuttles would be necessary to the different ships conducting negotiations.

One voice from the feed continually disturbed him as he listened to the audio. It drew him from his contemplation of the ship's staff. He heard Chief Engineer Snyderon's response to that voice, "We'll need to adjust the other engines to meld with the power of this one."

"Plans are already underway." It was not Nael's flat voice. "I've adjusted the power surges to blend, but to get the best efficiency, it will need an ongoing modification to blend with the other engines. The good news is this thruster alone could power the *Sentinel*."

Krayne noted whoever was working on the engines was just as efficient as Jezlynn's engineering self, but not Nael. This personality talked with ease and even courtesy to the EDD engineers and to the *Sentinel*'s crew who helped with the engine and hull repair. Something Jezlynn's reticent male and tech design mechanic personality found impossible. Another change, he decided. What more would come? He listened to the back and forth of comments as the work was finalized and the crew began leaving the compartment. The feed ended as the team finalized the overhaul. That his duty required him to observe certain ongoing procedures on his ship filled him with satisfaction. It felt less like spying.

He worried about Jezlynn, about her changes, and how her initial coercion into the Service Corps and its continued demands on her affected her. Would all of this destroy their marriage? He knew she struggled with those changes not only in her selves but also with the media's obsession. He also knew he needed to let her control her own life, which meant he needed to reclaim his own direction. His steps to adjust his duty accomplished some of the changes he wanted in the ship's command structure.

This would leave Jezlynn and him far less time together, which created an obsessive urge for him to watch her whenever he could. In this case, his fixation was a good thing as he needed to find out what had changed. He suspected May and Nael had melded. He had an uncomfortable feeling about these changes and wondered how they would affect their relationship. If she could let go of her other selves, those closest to her, could she do the same to him? Again? Refusing to speculate further, he turned his attention back to his current work.

Ninety minutes later, a bleep interrupted him. He responded to his adjutant's communication. Howard told him T-Omer was coming in. Within seconds, his Tarkian head of security stood before the captain's workstation. While his short, muscular body showed stiff hesitancy, his golden-skinned face remained void of emotion.

"Problem?" Krayne asked and nodded for T-Omer to take the chair before his desk. He guessed from the man's demeanor this was about Jezlynn. And his chief of security seemed unsure of his captain's response.

"Maybe. My office has intercepted some messages coming into not only your wife's personal communications but also into the Ranger's office."

"Threatening ones?" Krayne guessed. He had given his security permission to breach privacy standards in his wife's case, and General Roberre had given his approval of breaking Ranger communication protocols.

"Yes." He handed Krayne a comlink with some of the messages on it.

Krayne immediately sent a message to the *Sentinel*'s Ranger's office and asked for the immediate presence of Major Chambers in his office. While he waited for her to arrive, T-Omer updated him on how his crew and the Ranger embassy security team worked together and coordinated their duties.

Howard informed him Major Chambers was entering. From her expression at noting T-Omer's presence, he judged she knew what was coming. She took the chair next to his security officer as he indicated. As always, her blue eyes drew his attention.

He handed her the comlink, saying, "Would you explain these?"

He recognized her inscrutable expression as she flipped through the list and handed the comlink back to T-Omer.

"I have dealt with threats for a long time. I have before I was assigned to the *Sentinel*, while I was on it as a Corps officer, and now as a Ranger officer. There is nothing new here."

"You did not report them. That is the problem," T-Omer said.

"No, I didn't. I keep track of them and investigate where they come from. It often gives me information on where my enemies hide." She watched Krayne, but he kept his command mien firmly in place.

T-Omer answered. "The situation has changed. You are now not just a Ranger officer aboard an embassy ship, but one of its ambassadors, one with known enemies. You are supposed to report issues to me, and this is an issue. My team should also be tracking this information."

"Sometimes too many investigative probes alert the senders," Jesse answered.

Krayne fastened an intense glare on Major Chambers. "Regardless, you will now report any and all threats from any communication, personal or professional, media or personal interactions, to T-Omer. This negligence incident will be entered into your duty assessment."

She had difficulty containing her mirth, which he noted T-Omer also recognized. "Well, sir, it seems your crew already has access to all my messages."

"They do so by my order and that of Commander Roberre's because of your known reluctance to reveal threats. Did you find out what you wanted to about Sal Imada?"

"I thought it prudent to know something about the reporter assigned to this ship, one whose goals include interviewing me."

"Does he have valid qualifications?"

She reluctantly admitted he had written some good and timely reports.

"Then desist that investigation. Dismissed."

"Yes, sir." She rose in clear and abrupt annoyance and left the office.

"Good luck," T-Omer said as he rose to leave.

"My order remains: you and your team are to continue investigating and to watch for any threats to Major Chambers."

T-Omer grunted a laugh. "Security investigating security, strange circumstances."

"Indeed."

~ * ~

Henry Wakeman stood in formal dress uniform in his brother Howard's office. He smiled at Jesse's fuming exit from the captain's office. He had obviously heard the curse she uttered under her breath. With one glance she knew he already knew about her reprimand. Despite her enforced calmness, she knew he noted and recognized her irate state.

"None of us has much privacy anymore," he said. "What's up?"

"You knew? That he's having my private communications scanned?"

"More like ordering it so? Yes, I was questioned about what I knew. You've been threatened and never reported it."

"I'm threatened every time I leave the ship—who knows what the media pick up?"

"Everyone known to have served on the *Constant* receives the same attention. We all try to escape it, but do not have the protection you do."

Her ire increased and she aimed an effective glare at him. "Maybe I should see that you do. Besides, you know I've received threats forever."

Howard looked at Henry and then at Jesse. Henry answered his brother's unasked question. "It's okay, Howard, we're not going to come to blows." He looked at Jesse. "Well, yes, you have received them forever... or almost, at least from when you began your own investigations."

"I'd beat him," Jesse said to Howard.

"Jet might but not you," Henry challenged. "Did you know Merit had an exhibit arranged from Tom's drawings and paintings?"

Jesse stopped short, shock threading through her. "No. Did Tom know?"

Henry laughed. "No, this is a Merit-arranged extravaganza. It opens tomorrow and from what I've heard has already attracted viewers. Would you like to see it?"

"What? Expose myself more to save Merit's ass?"

"We've all been exposed and hounded more than we like, Jesse."

"You didn't tell me that," Howard said, sounding incensed.

Henry looked at him. "Nothing you could do about it, Howard. No more than Jesse can escape notice. The *Constant* and our notoriety have left us a long-lasting legacy."

"What do you want to do?" Jesse asked.

"I suggest we, meaning those from the *Constant*, present a spectacle."

Jesse looked at him, her face blank of any emotion, while her mind filled with speculation. At last, she swore and said, "You've become awfully devious."

He grinned. "We need to support Tom. He and Merit will both need it." He laughed. "May providence keep me from falling so hard for a woman that I'd do anything for her."

"Though you had already done that with Illa Jakle."

"True, but Illa hates any type of trouble. You and Merit revel in it."

"I've made sure Griff protects her from any unwelcome visitors."

"I know. Illa and I talk every day."

"When do you want to take this unplanned outing?"

"We will all meet at the *Sentinel*'s front entrance at eight hundred hours tomorrow. Go finish your day's duty."

~ * ~

A few hours later Jesse entered Lu's quarters. He waited for her, dressed for duty on the bridge. He looked annoyed, and she guessed why.

She smiled, "Our duty times are conflicting." She didn't have to ask why. He loved the bridge operations, even when the ship was in dock, plus with Fournelle leaving and other crew being assigned to other ships, only he and Ribberdan were qualified for the duty.

He walked to stand in front of her, his eyes filled with fury, but said nothing for a long moment. She didn't expect his question. "Who was in the engine compartment?"

She hesitated, looking at him before speaking, "Melany. When May and Nael melded I don't know. It's an anagram of their names... go figure, but it happened sometime after I left this compartment this morning." She saw the anger drain from him. "You don't trust me," she said. He noted her own mounting anger.

"Usually, yes, but sometimes you cross lines. Whether spontaneously or purposefully, I'm not sure."

"Only if something like Melany takes place when I cannot contact you, or if I need to protect you." She wondered if some of his anger was a result of their earlier meeting in his office. "Nael researched all the threats, and you know he excels at discovering sender identities without becoming identified himself. I expect Melany shares his skills. However, I apologize if this has caused you trouble."

"It caused mostly worry. I need to get to the bridge." He took several steps toward the door, stopped, and looked back at her. "If I need protection, you warn me, you don't just take steps on your own, especially if it puts you in harm's way."

Once he left, the quarters felt too empty. *::I need to practice,::* Jet demanded. *::And no, I don't want to meld permanently with you or anyone else. Jezet lacks my drive.::*

"And my persistence. A workout sounds splendid." Jesse said as she changed clothes.

::And your persuasiveness,:: Angie said, *::You don't work out, Jet does.::.*

"Yes, but everyone gets to enjoy the benefits of her physical activity." As she stepped from the captain's quarters, security fell in behind her as she made her way to the training room.

As Jet took over, Jesse felt her anger and gave her warning, *::Control your temper, Jet. Our melding into Jezet is useful in certain situations.::*

The spacious training room had three sessions running. Henry trained a group of Corps officers and Embassy officials while

Gunnerman trained the Ranger platoon, including a group of six Xantheans. They tried to copy the human exercises and moves but sometimes had to change the moves as their bodies differ.

Gunnerman saw her. "About time you showed up."

Jet laughed to herself. ::*Keep my temper? Better to release it.*::

~ * ~

At eight-hundred hours Jesse approached the entrance to the *Sentinel*. Sutta trailed her. A large group of formally uniformed officers stood there. She was the only one wearing black. Her former crewmembers from the *Constant* and now newly reappointed Corps officers greeted her. Lu stood there along with Ribberdan, Rae, and more *Sentinel* Corps and other embassy personnel than Jesse expected, including Ambassador Nohl and Sal Imada. Lu moved to her side as they left the *Sentinel*. Outside netreps lined the decks but numerous transports were lined up for transporting their group to the gallery which was on the business deck of the starbase. The crowded corridor had been cordoned off in front of the gallery where visitors were checked for entry credentials. Their group was politely given access to enter.

Inside the gallery, Jesse immediately recognized Tom's works framed and lining the walls. Digital screens presented more images, many showing portraits of her. She looked around and spotted Tom standing with his hands clasped behind him looking uncomfortable. Walking to where he stood, she smiled. "Quite a surprise."

"Yes, it is," he answered, but he did not look pleased. "She invited my father, too."

"Are you on the outs with Merit?"

He sighed, "No."

"He was under duress, Tom." She looked across the room and noticed Sutta stopping before every artwork, scrutinizing each one as if memorizing it. Surprisingly, Ambassador Nohl along with his wife stood next to the Xanthean. They gained as much attention as the artwork.

Tom flashed a grin-frown. "Yeah, I've heard all about forgiveness from Merit."

"And?"

He glared at her. She smiled at him, but her gaze returned to look at the artwork decorating the walls. Some were of her, some of Merit, a few of his son, and a few landscapes. She could see his improvement over the years of his hobby. When he didn't answer her, she said, "Life's full of surprises. After all, I've just discovered I'm a Dachs."

He huffed but a glimmer of humor escaped. "I guess it is time for reconciliation, huh? Quite a few of these have sold. I told Merit to donate the profits. I don't need them. Don't need this exposure, either. Thanks for coming to support me, though."

Crewmates from the *Constant* approached and started conversations with Tom. Jesse took part for a while before she eased away.

Sal Imada approached her with a friendly but detached demeanor. "Can you please introduce me to Captain Thorson?"

She called Rafe over. "This is journalist Sal Imada. Would you please introduce him to Tom?"

She read Rafe's slight squint-eyed look at the man, which Imada noticed, too, but Rafe politely acquiesced. Imada nodded his head at her.

"Well handled," Lu said from behind her. "Tom has some amazing artwork."

"He was always drawing in his off-duty time, not that he had much. Have you forgiven me?"

He raised a brow without looking at her. "I thought you realized I did last night."

She smiled at him. "You look tired. I switched my duty time to your bridge shift." Her smile grew into a grin of expectation until she read his frozen look.

"Well, guess I made a mistake. I'll prepare myself for your anger." She then realized he was looking elsewhere. She looked at what held his attention. His former wife approached.

"Hello, Luke."

"Hello, Fleur."

"You must be Jesse," Fleur said with a friendly smile holding out her hand. "I'm Fleur Paliva, Luke's former wife."

Jesse took her hand in a brief greeting-shake.

"You are lucky to have Luke. You beat me to the punch there, as I was going to try and win him back."

"I'm aware of my great blessing in attracting a man like Lu," Jesse smiled in a friendly manner.

Fleur looked around the gallery. "This exhibit is quite extraordinary. No one expects a Service Corps captain to be so artistic. He has quite a few drawings of you."

"Yes, he does. He is talented in many areas."

"Would you mind if I had a few minutes to talk with...Lu?"

"Not at all. I have some friends I need to greet." She smiled a Lu. "It looks like Sutta has introduced Rafe to Ambassador Nohl. I better go rescue him."

As she approached Rafe, he threw her a beseeching look, but Sal Imada stepped before her. "Thank you, Major Chambers, for allowing me to be introduced to not only Captain Thorson but also to Captain Dakota."

"You are welcome. Is this so you can learn more about me for a story?"

The tall man grinned. "While I would love to have an interview with you, no. I think a story exposing what actually happened on the *Constant* would create great public interest. Your compatriots seem as reluctant to talk to me as you are. You all might find that the release of some truth will stop some of the salacious lies abounding in the media."

"Perhaps. I'll think about it and let you know."

Imada nodded and moved away. She suspected he was a keen observer of all that went on. She went to Rafe. He was trying to translate Sutta's comments to Nohl.

"Here's Jesse, Ambassador Nohl. She speaks the language far better than I do." He abruptly left.

Nohl laughed. "That's what I call a rapid retreat. Usually, I am far more astute in such situations."

"Jesse!" Merit shouted, interrupting them and hugging Jesse. "I miss having you onboard so much! Isn't this great?"

"Are you ready to face Tom's ire?"

"Oh poo...we had it out last night. Guess what? After you talked with him a few minutes ago, Tom spoke with his dad. His dad told me afterward he has hope of resurrecting their relationship. Thank you!" She hugged Jesse again.

"Mostly as a favor to you. Try a little harder to stay out of trouble?"

Merit punched her in the arm. "Only following your lead."

"Let me introduce you to Ambassador Nohl and Sutta. They are going to help Tom and me on our next assignment."

Merit became chatty with Nohl before moving off to talk with others.

Sutta spoke, "Interesting human, like you."

Nohl asked for a translation. She gave it. Nohl smiled. "He told me I will need to learn their language. I'm glad I'll have time with you to learn some of it."

Jesse noted that even though he earned much interest, Sutta ignored everyone's scrutiny.

After conversing a bit longer, she found Lu beside her. "I've arranged for transport for us back to the *Sentinel*."

"Great, let's go say goodbye to Tom and Merit." She had a feeling no matter how tired Lu was, he would be meeting Melany before he went to sleep. She felt an inner smile. It worked both ways. If he didn't freely disclose his conversation with his ex, he would face her duress.

Entering his quarters, Jesse called up Melany.

Krayne noticed the change immediately as Melany was unsure where she was and looked around the room with wide eyes. Recognizing him, she smiled, saying, "Hi."

Her voice was lower and softer than Jesse, Jet, or Angie. "Melany?"

She gave him May's smile. "Yes. I learned from Jesse you were upset at Nael and May melding, but together I am much more comfortable than either of them, especially in public. As a benefit, it feels nice to be in public. I can speak to others. May couldn't speak or hear at all, and Nael hated talking to any stranger, which was everyone but you. It was interesting working with other engineers on the main engine compartment. Now I am looking forward to finishing work on the *Crusader*. Jesse dropped me off most unexpectedly, and I know she wants to know what your former wife requested."

"They had been considering melding for quite a while. Why now?"

"Nael wanted May's memories. May wanted stability. Nael insisted they be equals. May was indecisive. They were both lonely, but I don't have to be. I may have lost a little of his technical and engineering proficiency, but I also lost much of May's fear, and while her memories may not be as complete, they are more than adequate."

"Tell Jesse Fleur just wanted to be part of the negotiation team. She would love to attract Jezlynn's media attention and suggested she could deflect it from her. I refused her offer."

Twelve

A few weeks later, Jesse stood in her Ranger office watching the departing view of *Starbase Constellation* on the wall's viewscreens as the *Sentinel* left dock. She had invaded Lu's office through his living quarters so she could watch the *Sentinel*'s departure but decided to move to her own office. While her office lacked a window, it had a viewing screen.

The station's dimensions dwarfed the ship. Such sights always induced awe.

Sutta crouched in his duty pose inside her office, but she noted he, too, seemed enthralled with the viewscreen's images.

Lu was on the bridge as the flight crew operated the ship's departure. She knew he loved bridge duty, both the management and control of flight operations, more than all his other duties as ship's captain, except maybe walking the ship and inspecting it. Although the maintenance crew did that regularly, he found it a calming activity. When she was with him, he found Melany's opinion on the ship enlightening, probably due to Nael's experience in ship renovation with Pilgrim Lines. Melany seemed to nearly intuit when an area needed additional maintenance.

The new engine was secure, all mission personnel and all the delegates were onboard, and the mission had begun.

Miz Silmyn from the Bureau of Individual Rights had boarded, too, good luck to her. Already the woman sought to visit the Xantheans, but Aswenna refused access, which rankled Silmyn. Silmyn was raging at Nohl, but Jesse knew the ambassador held an unwavering position to the woman's rants.

Nohl told her after his last meeting with Silmyn, "Her presence has nothing to do with our negotiations. She chose to come onboard knowing what the mission was. Law says this is permissible, but it doesn't say I need to address her issues. Nor do you have to speak with her, although you might encounter her on the embassy deck." Jesse knew his estimation of her had taken a drastic turnabout.

Roberre had informed her the woman also tried to influence President Uebel, Wakeman, and himself, but all involved refused her requests. She then threatened to take the issue to the courts. Uebel informed the Individual Rights Bureau that Aswenna had talked to him about Major Jezlynn Chambers, and he had overruled the court's decision on the major.

The woman had tried to approach her, but it was either herself or Jet in control when traveling the ship's corridors, and they evaded her very successfully. Especially with Sutta acting as a personal guard. The one time she had welcomed such protection. Jesse guessed she would still have to prepare for an eventual confrontation, knowing dronai were of extreme interest to the bureau. She smiled to herself. *Maybe she should convince Aswenna to talk to Silmyn.*

Jesse wondered...what did she love? Certainly, they all loved Lu and her Pilgrim Lines' captains, but also, a brief grin emerged, all four of them had come to love Jezlynn's new family members as they were all feisty women. Beyond that, she knew Melany loved working on engines and creating new adaptations. Jet loved being a warrior and a pilot. Angie loved contemplation and music and even enjoyed logic-based argumentation with the delegates. She had enjoyed being her others' manager, controlling their conscious-body time, but somehow that had disappeared. She possessed more social talent and tact than any of Chambers' others, but Angie, except for confrontational arguments, had taken over negotiations. So now she handled the difficult interactions and the finances, but those seemed just tasks.

She knew many of those who knew her condition considered hers a strange existence, but it was the only one she knew. With the appearance of Jezet, Angie, and Melany, existence had changed yet again. Did she want to disappear, too?

::No, you do not,:: Jet said, interrupting her reverie.

Watching the entirety of Starbase Constellation coming into view as the bridge crew carefully guided the *Sentinel* away meant change was approaching. Perhaps her last mission. It was a hundred and forty days to Sigma Sector. Days full of work and basic negotiations among delegates with perhaps some confrontation, plus work on the shuttles involved, and Ranger patrol duties. Lu was engaged in a duty he loved. Did she have any purpose or even duty?

Since Melany's appearance, the Nael-May meld insisted she have time to work on the *Crusader* and the *Delve*. Lu would not take that assignment away from her as it was important to their mission. Melany also liked working with Snyderon in engineering, and John Olson, the transport chief, gladly let her inspect and work on any of the shuttles in the docking bay area. His crew's eager assistance endorsed his decision. The shuttle bay was a strange place Jesse avoided. As a shuttle pilot, Jet felt comfortable there, and although piloting was different from working on a shuttle, it still brought Jet and Melany closer.

Sighing, Jesse knew Melany had changes she wanted to install on the shuttles, many of them from Nael's patented mechanisms and processes, others of her own creation. She also worked on ideas for the lateral engines that both Lu and Snyderon thought promising. Somehow May and Nael's melding had developed into a more demanding personality.

Melany interrupted Jesse's reverie. *::The new coating mirrors what is on the other side of the shuttle, so the ship looks invisible.::* She continued, explaining that the shuttles' new coverings tended to make them disappear in their berths, which had initially created a bit of chaos with docking bay personnel. Jesse knew Melany wanted to coat all the *Sentinel*'s shuttles despite Jesse's recommendations not to. Jesse began to think her opinion would be overlooked as Melany ignored financial ramifications.

::Not so; finances are your area, and I'm not oblivious to your opinion or costs…just considering. I have more plans.::

Jesse smiled. Melany had also brought an overall serenity to all of them. May's fears had often overwhelmed everyone, even Jet. Now in Melany, Nael's impassiveness calmed May's over-reaction and fearfulness.

Jet made a change to her duty, too. With Gunnerman onboard, she had contacted General Roberre and made a request. Gunnerman was pleased to be in command of the Ranger squad in charge of embassy security, although Major Chambers kept her office and oversight of the Ranger's mission. While Jet remained in the Rangers and in overall command of those serving on the *Sentinel*, Melany's work on the shuttles, and now Angie's ambassadorial duties, took much of the physical time available.

::I needed more time for my duties,:: Jet interrupted her again, showing she even listened to her thoughts.

"You didn't have to speak with each on-duty Ranger every day." When alone, speaking aloud to her others had become more normal.

::It builds trust and increases their sense of duty. We might need it.:: Jesse heard Jet's continued exasperation.

President Uebel, Admiral Wakeman, and General Roberre had cavalierly made decisions for her. Liz Rae, Henry, and Aswenna also liked to 'guide' her. Lu ordered her. While it all provoked her, at least with Lu she often felt pleased afterward rather than the continual aggravation she did with everyone else. However, she felt it was time to regain control over her and her others' lives. Angie and Melany agreed.

::As you've noted, we've changed, become more integrated,:: Angie observed.

Angie liked helping her make plans and even liked interviewing difficult delegates for specifics in the negotiations. Some of the trade negotiation preliminaries had already taken place, but that was between specific delegates.

Angie interrupted her. *::You must lead the actual negotiations as you are far more manipulative than I am,::* Angie said, showing she listened to Jesse's thoughts, too. *::And Melany wants to work on 'her' shuttles. Our work is a necessary part of the mission.::*

"Lord, not even my mind is inviolate now."

::You've known before now that we could hear you.::

"I cannot overhear you, though."

::I know. A strange situation. What's new? Tuen misjudged you,:: Angie said.

"You mean he misjudged Melany." Jesse laughed, then quieted, knowing Sutta, while still watching the screen, heard her talking to herself.

After Rear Admiral Tuen's engine mechanics and the *Sentinel's* engine crew had efficiently repaired the engine and bulkhead, Tuen had contacted Jesse, telling her of the high praise he received from his personnel who had helped with the engines and inspected the shuttles. He also told her that her duty stint in the engine compartment was over.

::Not quite, as I will continue to help Snyderon test the engines, and with the chief engineer's help, I have reconfigured two of the lateral engines,:: Melany said. *::I did more than that, but no one knows.::*

"What?" Jesse asked.

::I've searched every engine, connection, and compartment for any glitch, fault, or change in patterns or coding. After your memory I thought it a worthwhile inspection.::

"And no one noticed?"

::I'm known for my obsessive compulsions. No one thought it out of the ordinary.::

"Did you find anything?"

::Yes, like in the first incident, but I've corrected everything.::

Jesse knew Snyderon had informed Vice Admiral Tuen of her ongoing assistance and the unique changes made as he remained unaware Tuen had dismissed her. Jesse wondered how Tuen had taken Melany's breach of orders.

"Thank you, Melany. You were not his to order, anyway. You do need to report this to Lu."

::No she wasn't under Tuen's command, but Roberre probably heard an earful,:: Jet said.

"Probably, but I'm sure he ignored it with subtle humor." Catching herself answering in speech rather than thought again, Jesse shrugged. No one else was in her office and Melany had made a few changes in the office's surveillance.

::I have other things I wish to do,:: Jet said, practically reading Jesse's mind before she made a thought. Gunnerman had also taken over and kept the physical training of Rangers a priority, and the Xantheans continued to train with him. He reported to Jet how they became increasingly aggressive with the training, also lither and quicker than he had believed they could be. Henry continued to train the Corps crew and embassy personnel who had requested it.

She heard Jet laugh in her mind. *::He took over training Krayne, too, which leaves me free to continue my own training, although he has interfered there, too. Gunnerman, the meat, told me I was the one who contacted Roberre about him taking over training, and Krayne will work harder with him than me.::*

"I contacted Roberre, and he had his own ideas for change. You always told Lu he was holding back." Realizing she talked aloud again, she gave up. It probably made no difference to Sutta.

::Sutta has taken over. He wants me to learn meditation. Who would'a thought that?::

"It makes you less angry."

::I know. It's relaxing. He insisted on showing me how Xantheans use the technique during battle. Empty the mind, react.::

"Xantheans have battle techniques?"

::Yep. Surprised me too. Anyway, learning some more gymnastic moves. Told Krayne to turn the cameras off. Got'a nuff guards watching me.::

"I know. He ignored you."

Jet made an amusing obscene comment.

Jesse thought of her own work. Several weeks ago, Nohl had begun discussing the process of embassy negotiations. Angie listened with her. More work was needed.

::*Much more work,*:: Angie inserted.

"I took the ambassador to talk with Kizz. T'Carta's son is now friendlier toward Jezlynn, but I don't know if he knows about me."

::*Probably. T'Carta talks to him.*::

"He told me he had discovered not all of his mother's opinions were valid. In that moment he looked more like Kar."

::*I could teach the pup a lot more about not disrespecting you... us. We have more to investigate,*:: Jet said. ::*We all shared that memory that took you down.*::

::*May did not have that memory,*:: Melany inserted, ::*but it might be true, which is why I checked all the engines. Angie needs to investigate. I'll help her.*::

:: *Me, too,*:: Jet said.

"Investigate what? All information on the *Constant* is gone."

::*Not necessarily,*:: Angie said.

Gunnerman entered her office, nodded at Sutta who rose and left the room. Gunnerman gave her a run-down on the day's progress. "They find it easy duty, but boring just standing at watch, or traversing corridors on security checks. One thing your physical training does is relieve their boredom. Kind'a like bootcamp. They're worn out so glad to stand around and not have to move too much." He grinned. "I've sent a list of all communications, those directed to the squad members, and those overheard. It's surprising how embassy residents forget a Ranger is on duty as they walk the corridors."

Jesse realized her squads were more vocal with Gunnerman than her.

"Good. I've sent a list of the negotiation rooms and times to your comlink. Be sure to have security posted."

"Yes, Major." He saluted and left.

Aggravated, Jesse left her office. Sutta followed her. Fewer walked the corridors once out of the Ranger area. She took the long way up to the embassy deck. Nohl had excused those on his staff who had young children from the mission, as he didn't want them endangered. This led to him dismissing the childcare personnel. Many of the entertainment and businesses that served the embassy staff and families' needs were also gone. The embassy had always had a store providing some clothing, gifts, and other products the entire ship's residents used. He had also dismissed the sociologist and linguistics departments and limited the number of legal and protocol experts to those who would be involved in negotiations. Like SSC crew, Nohl had promoted or transferred some personnel to other ships or station positions. They would not be replaced until this mission was finished. It all meant that with little other entertainment available, many crew members took longer work shifts. Jesse or Angie had to go through many meetings listening while Nohl conducted business.

As she entered the captain's quarters, she wondered if Lu was on the bridge. She saw less of him, often only in their quarters in the ship's evening or in the early morning before duty. It felt strange. With fewer meetings with the embassy, Lu reclaimed his duty on the bridge, sometimes taking the night shift. It left her wondering if he was avoiding her.

::He is the ship's captain and will do his duty,:: Angie said, showing she shared awareness. *::You have time, go see Margarete.::*

Jesse picked up her comlink. Margarete messaged back saying they were having a tea. Jesse passed many crew wearing Corps duty blues, but they no longer gave her double-takes upon seeing her in the khaki duty attire as had frequently happened when the ship's crew first returned to duty. Embassy personnel always noted her arrival on the embassy deck.

Whenever she entered the embassy deck, Silmyn always appeared. Silmyn had introduced herself once, but Sutta trailed her, and whenever Silymn neared her, his presence made the woman back off. She still watched.

Jesse went to Margarete's quarters and pressed the announcement button. The door quickly opened. Margarete smiled and let her enter. Isobel, Vanessa, and Norma Hughes sat in the main room.

Since learning Norma was her cousin, Jesse had invited her to have coffee together twice in the Corps' mess hall. It was a fragile relationship, but one that Norma seemed committed to making.

"We are all so glad we came." Isobel looked joyous as she spoke. "We have found we all share many interests."

"Such as?" Jesse asked.

"The major thing is you," Vanessa said with a polite smirk. "But we have all felt isolated, and now I have my daughter back, plus my brother's granddaughter," she said smiling at Norma.

"And I have my daughter back," Margarete said.

Isobel resumed. "We all had so few trustworthy friends or even family until now. We've learned we all enjoy friendly conversation. It has been a pleasure and learning my niece Norma onboard is another benefit."

"You were informed of the dangers this mission might face?" Jesse asked in a controlled voice.

They all smiled at her. Margarete waved her to a seat while Isobel said, "Since we are living together, we've explored so many topics and found many shared interests."

Vanessa, who looked surprisingly young and fit for her age, spoke. "We enjoy being with each other. We have also received frequent visits from Norma, and now Aswenna. The first time Aswenna came was a bit startling. It is hard to understand her, but she attempts to teach us her language. Do you believe they are precognitive?"

"I don't know. I doubt it."

"Well I believe it," Isobel said. "And we all look forward to a bit of adventure, something else lacking in our pasts, which I believe both you and your mission provide."

"We are also keeping track on all media for any falsehoods being published about you..." Isobel started only to be interrupted by Margarete, "...or anything too invasive."

"...Plus we look for any information about Morgan or Austin. My brother Reed didn't know I had some knowledge about their communication channels. He always tended to be incredibly old fashioned and somewhat misogynistic. I find it hard to believe he was so evil." Sadness crossed Vanessa's face at her admission.

Jesse took a breath and sat down. "I do not want any of you to put yourselves in dangerous positions, especially one of trying to track Morgan or Austin. It is too dangerous, so please give up any attempts in that area. Plus, my reputation was in tatters for a long time and some people will never give up their impression of me. I will warn you now, my enemies are depraved and dangerous. They keep track of some of my channels of communication, so do not try to follow them and stop all this now. I am what I am."

"You use them to dissimulate!" Isobel said, her eyes opening wider and brightening.

"How…Who are you after?" Vanessa asked.

"I have more enemies and more pursuits than you can imagine. Please stop your investigations and defense of me."

"Does Lucian know what you do?" Margarete asked.

Jesse began to speak and closed her mouth, remembering Margarete's astute awareness of all transgressions when she was a child. She might recognize any half-truth.

"I thought so," her mother said.

"Mostly, he does. He also has Chief of Security T-Omer watching all my messages." She took a deep breath, exhaling slowly while staring at her mother. "I have vast experience in protecting my back, and I have many associates who do the same. While I will admit to not telling Lu everything, you must understand, I communicate with some people whom I must protect from any Alliance, Corps, or Ranger notice. They give me valuable information not easily come by. I will not betray them. The same is true of Lu. I will protect him and never put him in a situation where he must choose between his oath to the Space Service Corps or his desire to protect me from myself. I must insist you end these endeavors on my behalf."

"Thank you for your honesty," Margarete said, who looked at her two friends before adding, "we will not betray you, either. However, I will plead with you to be extra careful."

"You are our only progeny," Isobel said, "and my mother and I agree with Margarete."

"Do you want some entertainment accesses?"

"We already have them," Vanessa said, looking too complacent.

"Good. I need to resume my duty." She squinted back at her great-grandmother, who only smiled. She noticed they did not agree to disengage from all interference.

Norma walked out the door with her. "I want you to know, Vanessa asks me to come quite frequently, but I do not tell them anything that is in your medical file."

Jesse nodded and left hearing Norma reenter the apartment. She spent ten minutes walking off her anger at her interfering, busybody relatives.

~ * ~

"I think we broke her show-no-inadvertent-emotion protocol," Vanessa said at Jesse's rapid departure.

"We certainly caused irritation," Isobel said.

"We have not met any of her others," Margarete said. "While she visits us, she doesn't trust us."

"Small steps, Margarete," Vanessa said. "I understand her performance and some of her precautions well enough, having had to use them myself. Now that I've found her, I will protect her."

"Be careful," Norma said. "She has endured horrendous things none of us have, and she has the physical power and training to make her dangerous."

~ * ~

After stopping to talk with every Ranger on the embassy deck, Jesse went back to her office. Within minutes of sitting down, Lu walked in and sat across the desk. As senior ship's officer, he always wore a formal white uniform when on duty. She sighed.

"Is this a duty call or a personal visit?"

"Both. You probably know we will reach the psiroute to Sigma Sector in a few days. You haven't said much about returning to your old stomping ground."

Smiling she asked, "Do you expect me to attempt escaping my captivity?"

His expression turned serious. "I don't want you to feel like I'm holding you captive."

"With you aboard? It's voluntary captivity." She laughed. He saw through her ruse, and she gave him the answer he wanted. "I don't, not entirely at least. Get the tracer out of me, and I won't feel it at all." She read his face. "Not likely, I know. I want to achieve the goal set for this mission. And yes, Ezredin is in Sigma Sector, which is also the sector for the planet Griff, the home of Pilgrim Lines, and for the planet Arlon, where I have used the Bant Shipyard."

He didn't look relieved.

"Lu, you are my husband. The number of people I love is growing, friends and family, some I never knew I had, but I have only one lover, you. I'm not likely to want to escape you." As an expression of pleasure crossed his face, she added. "At least, not yet. Are you trying to avoid me?" She laughed at his grin.

"Avoid you?" he looked puzzled.

"With night duty."

"No, I am not. I'm trying to become a more proactive captain. I'm sorry you thought that. Believe me, I miss our frequent encounters." He smiled at her evocative smile. "And how many of those you love do you trust?"

She felt the jolt of his rejoinder and his recognition of her reaction as he laughed at her. She let a note of drollery enter her voice. "Well, I've been talking with my family. A more conniving collection of women is hard to imagine." Lu smiled at her snarky comment. "I know what you're thinking."

"Like mother, like daughter?"

She laughed.

Lu returned to duty demeanor. "T-Omer mentioned he liked your promptness in filing reports and that together you have integrated your assigned duties."

"Cooperation works better than obstructionism. It is easier when the two security component heads are well acquainted. I've introduced Gunnerman into the association, too. He likes T-Omer and sees him as another superior officer. As captain, you are privy to all my dealings with the Xantheans and the Khajari onboard."

"T-Omer said Kizz was very polite when he took him to his father's shuttle, never made any moves to reclaim the controls, only stating his father would be glad to have it back."

"He has been amenable since onboard. I'm not sure what changed his opinion of me, but I've talked with him every day."

"T-Omer said Kizz even made some complimentary remarks about you." He ignored her subtle snort. "And he commented about Aswenna. The Xantheans are interested in learning all human ways, including those of the Khajari."

"Yes, they seem determined to rejoin the world of today."

He nodded and rose. "Meet me for dinner in our quarters; I've ordered it delivered."

"I have something to tell my commanding officer." Whatever he read in her expression made him stand in front of her.

She faced him. "I'm always confused on how to behave in such situations, salute you or kiss you."

"It's private here. A kiss is treasured."

She took his response as an order, took a step toward him and passed out.

~ * ~

Jesse heard Doctor Rae. "She's coming around." Opening her eyes, she saw the doctor looking down at her. She leaned against Lu who sat on the floor holding her hand. They were in her office. Sutta stood at the door. Puzzlement flooded her. Jesse spoke. "What..."

Rae smiled. "You passed out due to your early pregnancy."

"What?"

"You're pregnant."

"Can't be..."

"Yes, you are, about four weeks. I think the surgeries Doctor Syms performed on you to repair the damage of Morgan's beating made it possible. His notes said he did some reconstruction."

Jesse looked at Lu. "Help me up." His expression looked like a combination of anxiety and elation.

He helped her not only stand but also got her back to her chair. She felt shaky.

He looked at her. "If you go through with this pregnancy, it changes things."

::A baby forms inside of us!:: Angie's ecstatic voice emerged in her mind. *::Part of Lucian!::*

Melany chimed in, *::Another reason Nael was glad to meld with May, but I am excited about this development.::*

::You knew?:: Jesse asked.

::Yes, but suspected or wished more than knew.::

::Tell Krayne I won't change my training schedule,:: Jet warned. *::How soon can a child start training?::*

Jesse swiped her hand across her brow. *::What child would want a such disjointed mother?::*

::Every child only wants a good mother,:: Angie said. *::We will be better than good.::*

"So, what is everyone saying?" Lu asked.

"How did you know?" Jesse asked.

"I only needed to look at you to know everyone was communicating. What's the verdict?"

"I have my doubts about what type of mother I'll be, but everyone else seems overwhelmingly elated and looking forward to it."

His lips formed a broad smile and his eyes glowed with euphoric emotion. "Good."

"You will need to come to medical," Rae said. A glance showed the doctor watching her with intent interest.

"I will come, but not right now. I do not want to be paraded to medical in front of my Ranger squad and would prefer no ship-wide spread of this news before I come to terms with it."

Rae smiled. "Good enough. I'll send some information to your comlink." She turned and left and Sutta closed the door behind him as he stepped out.

"If Sutta knows, the Xantheans will know. He will report to his circle." Lu said.

"Some secret."

"I think with Rae rushing here, questions are already being asked. I doubt she will spread the word, and certainly, no one could guess. Lucky for you, your cousin Norma is a pediatric nurse."

She looked at him. "You aren't going to rearrange my duties, are you?"

"I can't see how your condition would change your ambassadorial or Ranger duties, but I'd prefer you didn't practice hand combat moves."

"Jet punching a bag remains all right?"

"And her running and other strength exercises," Lu said.

::Not to worry,:: Jet replied. *::Henry and Gunnerman have already taken over that aspect of my training.::* She sounded exasperated.

Jesse relayed Jet's comment. "And what about you? Are you ready for fatherhood?"

"I'm surprised and overjoyed. I think you have reservations, though."

"Yes, I do." She sighed. "I suppose I should tell Margarete, Isobel, and Vanessa before any leak happens."

"Let's go together. When the crew finds out is not a problem."

She gave him a droll look. "Maybe for you. With Henry and Gunnerman? I'll be on a major protective detail. Mine."

Lu grinned. "That's my detail, too."

At that moment, her three female family members entered. Isobel looked frantic. "We heard the doctor was called to your office."

Lu smiled. "We were just on our way to your rooms."

"We were not there but in the embassy canteen," Margarete said.

Jesse felt dumbfounded. Lu's hand, which clasped hers, tightened. "You should understand ship gossip by now—it moves at the speed of light. Do you want to tell them or allow me?"

At her look, he turned to the three women. "Jesse fainted. A most unusual circumstance. I was already here and called Doctor Rae. Jesse just found out she is pregnant."

All three faces turned from distressed to overjoyed.

"Oh, how wonderful!" Isobel said.

Jesse looked beyond them. The door was open, and Henry and several Rangers stood there, including Gunnerman. He grinned in a maniacal manner. She sighed. General Roberre would know almost as soon as the rest of the crew, which included the embassy, and included the journalist Imada. She closed her eyes and groaned.

"Before current circumstances occurred, you were about to tell me something," Lu said.

"It's only going to change your euphoria to anger."

"You have more contacts that you think T-Omer doesn't know about." He gave her his commander's smile. "But Henry knew, so yes, T-Omer knows."

"Did he tell T-Omer how important it was to not divulge anything about those contacts?"

"Yes, he did, but I'd like you to explain them to me," adding as he looked at her, "no report, no recording."

Thirteen

The next day Jet burst into the captain's office interrupting a meeting between Lu and his adjutant. She crossed the room shouting, "I don't need any solicitous concern, Krayne."

Jet's anger and frustration had overwhelmed Jesse's caution and her presence.

Lu rose from behind his desk, strode to Jet, grabbed her arms, and stared at her in obvious captain's mode, glaring a message of 'control yourself.' Jesse tried to intervene, feeling Jet's shock that Lu could stop her from yanking her arms free of his grip. *::His conditioning has improved,::* she told her furious other with a hint of humor, *::and he wants to stop you from making a serious mistake.::*

"I did not make any such order," he told Jet in livid, clipped words. Contained fury lined his eyes. He nodded to his adjutant Howard Wakeman, who quickly left the office. Sutta, who had followed Jet into the office, nodded and stepped out as well.

"Everyone knows!" Jesse said with less belligerence, finally able to push a still seething Jet aside. A brief struggle for awareness stilled her, while she felt the same exasperation. Matter of fact, she and Jet were switching back and forth in quick sequence, which had never happened before. Believing Lu knew what was happening, Jesse closed her eyes and took several calming breaths. He spoke before she could.

"I didn't need to tell anyone. If you remember several people, including Gunnerman and Henry, heard the news outside your office when you learned of your condition." His face looked livid but his voice while stiff was controlled. "Hell, Jesse, your captains probably know."

Before Jesse could answer, Jet took over, renewing her fury and still unable to shake off Krayne's grip. "Gunnerman ordered his platoon not to engage with me in hand-combat training. Henry did the same."

::Shut up, Jet, and back down.:: Jesse exerted her power and took over, something she had never done before, realizing she probably glared at Lu as ferociously as Jet. "Moreover, all the Rangers and many Service Corps crew now see me as their self-imposed protection duty."

"I gave you the same order, and you are everyone's protection duty," Krayne said. A hint of humor broke through his irritation. "You are the key person in our current mission, as you were in the last one, which ran into near disaster with so few knowing your assignment. What just happened? You couldn't handle Jet's outrage and ended up here?"

Jesse exhaled. She never imagined herself in her current situation. Not with her others, not with her body. "Yes, and now she will be pissed off with me. I just told her to shut up. Gunnerman now treats Sutta as a Ranger, one whose duty, either self-imposed or by Aswenna's request, already entails trailing me whenever outside your quarters."

"Our quarters." His lips twitched in both exasperation and humor.

She took another deep breath. "While onboard this ship, Sutta has changed into an annoying and intimidating presence from the browbeaten slave Jet rescued and returned to Asedin years ago. He's lucky Jet hasn't turned on him!"

Lu ignored her complaint and a concerned expression crossed his face. "That was an alarming thing you just did."

She shrugged. "Jet exploded. She hasn't done that since her wartime duty. When she feels threatened or enraged, she can overcome my awareness, it just doesn't happen that often and hasn't happened in this manner before. Denying her training will only increase her frustration."

"Hand-to-hand combat is risky at the best of times. I agree with Gunnerman and will reinforce his order of hands-off. Jet knows basic exercises and she can run the track for as long as your pregnancy allows such movement. You both must understand your body will change."

"I know." She shrugged. "I keep wondering how it will affect my negotiations, and I'm worried about what kind of mother I'll make."

Henry entered the office. "Howard called me." He looked at Krayne. "Is everything all right?"

"No, it isn't!" Jesse said with a seldom shown belligerence. At Henry's alarm, she calmed down. "I don't need a committee to oversee my health, my psyche, or my job. What the court decreed about my 'condition' has proven incorrect and Uebel has officially dismissed the court's findings."

Lu's hand closed around her upper arm again. She glared at his presumption. *::Control yourself,::* Angie advised. Just what she needed, another intruder. "I am not Jet and not about to wallop Henry."

"Calm down, Jesse," Henry said. "I know what you think..."

"No, you don't."

"...But those appointed have a different viewpoint. Since dronai exist in all of us, we think you do need some protection, just for a slightly different reason. I agree with Captain Krayne. Jet needs to change to basic fitness exercises. It will give her the same release as hand combat training and keep your body fit, and relieve some of her angst and anger. She can also continue punching the bags."

Jesse closed her eyes and took more deep breaths. Lu's hand dropped from her arm. "I'll talk to her."

::I and Melany are already talking with Jet,:: Angie said in an overly calm tone. It gave Jesse pause at her change as Lynn had always been so emotional.

Jesse uttered, "This is a losing battle."

"Yes, it is," Lu answered.

"You could help all of us by requesting information from Aswenna," Henry said. "They accept the dronai, even want them. They can teach us a lot."

"And maybe not," Jesse said. "They've lacked it for centuries."

"Only one way to find out, isn't there?" Henry asked. He smiled and his brows rose, recognizing her irritation.

Lu spoke, perhaps to prevent Jet's appearance. "It's time for dinner. You are probably cranky from hunger. Do you want to join us Henry, Howard?"

Since Lu arranged their time together, which was usually breakfast and dinner, she thought he did so only to make sure she followed Rae's recommended diet. She expelled an exasperated sigh.

~ * ~

The next morning, Jesse dressed in her Ranger khakis as she had for all her embassy meetings. The duty uniform informed all those she negotiated with exactly who she was, and who she represented. She left Lu's quarters to go to the embassy deck.

Sutta fell into step behind her as soon as she left. "Don't you sleep?" she asked.

Sutta croaked a laugh and straightened. "Xanthean rest is different from human oblivion in sleep. You seem in better serenity."

She glared at him and he croaked a laugh. He seldom engaged her in talk, so she stopped and turned to him, asking, "You have something to say?"

He looked blank for a moment.

She noticed he stood well over her height and his limbs seemed thicker. "Have you grown?"

"Xantheans change to face their new mission, their first in this era." His gaze aimed forward, watching something. "When you found me, returned me to Asedin, knowledge told me I'd never be the same. I gave up. Then you returned into my life. We have both been in the same bad place. You gave me courage I lacked for a long time. Now I have joined a new mission, and I change again, more into the Xanthean I was before capture, but more, too, than I ever was." His gaze focused on her. "Thank you."

She placed a hand on his arm in a Xanthean gesture learned long ago. "You did it, not me. Now you inspire those in your group."

She looked and saw Ella Murray and Liz Rae waiting near the ship command deck's exit for the embassy. *::A group attack,::* Jet said with an expletive.

"Ma'am..." Ella said, looking uncomfortable.

"Jesse, Ella—as I'm sure you've found out about Jezlynn."

Ella looked delighted at Jesse's admission. "Thank you, Jesse. Even after apologizing to you, I didn't think you would..."

"But you did apologize, Ella. How can I help you?"

"I've heard you might start some general exercise classes and I wanted to know if you would let me attend."

"Of course, if it happens."

"I wanted to ask to join, too," Rae said. "I found your previous training a little too intense. I've several other crew members who are interested in physical improvement without the grueling and often dangerous hand-to-hand combat training of your previous group exercises and their vids."

"Vids?" Jesse asked.

"You had to expect that," Rae said, her smile filled with irony.

::Combat free exercises will be just as demanding,:: Jet advised. *::I've been working on it. Finding time in the training room will be difficult.::*

"Let me guess," Rae said. "Any training with Jet will be grueling, but of course, it keeps your body superbly fit. Something many envy, and conditioning is much needed onboard."

Jesse blinked, disconcerted with so many mentioning her others in open conversation. "She'll probably have a regime scheduled within days."

"Thank you, Jesse," Murray said with a friendly smile.

The two turned and headed toward their duty stations. Jesse resumed her journey to the embassy deck. The human rights rep Silmyn stood on an upper balcony watching her enter the embassy deck. Jesse wondered who kept her informed. *Unless she had access to the tracer already in her body.* She decided to visit Doctor Rae later.

::*We can remove it,*:: Angie said.

The idea shocked Jesse. "That would upset Lu."

::*Lucian knows how much it upsets you, so he would understand.*::

"Maybe, but maybe not. Right now, it would cause him concern and problems. While he is excited about the baby, he will watch us like a hawk to make sure we don't go off track. When off the *Sentinel*, it might be something to do. You know it hurts like hell?"

::*We'll let Jet handle the pain.*::

Jesse felt the humor filling Angie's comment.

::*I heard that,*:: Jet said. ::*And yeah, I could. You sissies are lucky to have me to complete the dirty work.*::

::*We are a team,*:: Angie said in utter calm. ::*Melany, like Nael, knows ship operations and how to improve them and now not only does she share May's memories with us but also keeps new ones. It lets all of us understand our past. Jet, you protect us, despite what all the interfering busybodies who believe we cannot take care of Jezlynn do. Jesse, you have always been financially astute, and handle people well. When you meld into Jezet you are a bit of both as your talents as the meeting with Corrao showed.*::

"And you are the logic of Alyss combined with the compassion and passion of Lynn. You are right. We can handle this, but what will our child think of us?" Jesse asked.

::*He will think of us only as his mother.*::

Since today was Melany's day to work in the docking bay, Jesse's time on the embassy deck would be short. In their joint embassy time, Jesse, Angie, and Nohl worked closely together to arrange the details of the negotiations. Angie often took precedence when providing advice to Nohl, except when anyone else took part who became annoyed or defiant. Angie did not like confrontation. She wondered if Ambassador Nohl noticed the change but assumed he did. He usually was pleased with everything accomplished despite whom he worked with.

She shook her head. "Unimaginable what transpires."

Jesse went to Ambassador Nohl's office. His brows rose as she entered and even smiled, inviting Sutta in. His first words showed how fast gossip moved. "Do any of you practice yoga? If not, my wife is a yoga master, and she would love to teach you and other crewmembers. It would go well with Sutta's meditation training—a class of cross-species."

"An interesting proposition." She quickly accessed her comlink and sent Lu a message. He quickly replied he would contact Nohl's wife. "The captain will contact your wife."

"If you don't know the moves, you should learn them. They improve flexibility and relieve stress."

"You practice?"

"Yes, I do. I am finding hand-combat training much easier than many of the other participants despite my age, due, I'm sure, to my yoga exercises."

"I think it is time for me to explain the mission's enemies to you. Some are my personal enemies." She explained the T'Kalz's former power status history and their loss of power to the R'Kalmona. "While both descend from the same ruling family, they disagree on many policies."

"Supreme Ruler Kalmona-Rek Kerub is from the Kalmona family, isn't he?"

"No, he is from an earlier royal Rek dynasty. The only one to escape murder by the T'Kalz. Now, many of the most powerful T'Kalz are dead, but those remaining want to regain power. The remaining T'Kalz are a ruthless and dangerous faction. Some have supposedly disappeared from Khajari. The Kalmona family has claimed Rek Kerub as family through a marriage between the families."

Nohl smiled. "But you have Khajari contacts, and might know where the T'Kalz are?"

"I know where many of them are. I know the signatures of the ships they use."

"I'm not going to ask how," Nohl said in his most ambassadorial voice.

"It's enough to have the information. The Kalmona have hunters assigned to find them, but the T'Kalz are cagey. I know they know about us. We need to be aggressively proactive and defensive."

"What are your plans?"

"I will handle the negotiations with the supreme ruler and his Khajari team while also making sure they are protected. Captains Tom Thorson and Rafe Dakota will do the same for you and your team and for the trade negotiators during all the negotiations."

"And by your personal enemies, do you mean Admiral Reed Dachs and his coterie?"

"Yes."

"I have done some exploration on my own and have had a long talk with Captain Krayne, who informed me of the situation. It is hard for me to accept the truth about this family, but I do believe the allegations. I also know they still hold power."

Jesse ignored her irritation at learning this. "It is one reason I was glad to see you in training with Henry."

"That has been an interesting experience. Hard, actually, but one I am learning to enjoy."

Leaving Nohl's, office she went to her family's quarters. Margarete, Isobel, Vanessa, and Norma, who was now a regular visitor, were having tea. Aswenna sat in a Xanthean fold position with them. Jesse paused, wondering at Aswenna's purpose. She greeted her family and spoke to Aswenna in her native language. "Do you subvert my family relations in some fashion?"

"Assuredly," the genitor said with what Jesse recognized as a Xanthean smile. "I teach them the language. They improve my Space Standard, and we talk, as they are now part of my Amber Circle."

"Willingly so," Isobel said, smiling widely at Aswenna.

Jesse knew from Sutta that the Xantheans all showed a more aggressive and animated manner than she had ever encountered, and from him already knew Aswenna, who also looked sturdier, had formed a new circle for Ezredin. Shortly after the Xantheans arrival on the *Sentinel*, she had introduced Renny Lebeau and Monica McEntire to Aswenna. With their introduction, she felt the matriarch had enough human contacts, so she could limit her visits with the Xantheans as they began treating her with what seemed like reverence. Monica had later come to her Ranger office and told her Renny and she and her husband Pir were now members of the new Xanthean Circle. The anthropologist was very excited. She told Monica not to be too excited, but Monica had only smiled and thanked her for introducing the team to the Xantheans, saying, "We study them, and they study us." To discover Aswenna had now adopted her family upset her.

"We named our new Circle...Amber," Aswenna informed her. "One derived from your name, but it also represented the color of the circling sun. I was telling your family how excited my Circle is to finally enter Sigma Sector and arrive so close to our new home. Your mother's home planet, Griff, is in this sector, too." The genitor's eyes watched her, and Jesse read Aswenna's interest in her reaction.

"Yes it is, and Griff is the headquarters of my Pilgrim Lines company. I've heard you have formed Folds within your new Circle, Genitor."

"I am the Circle Amber's Matriarch. You are their genitor, Dronai Jezlynn."

That shocked Jesse.

"Margarete has asked us to live with her," Vanessa said, changing the subject in the following silence. "However, as all of us are rather independent women, we might need a moderator. From what I've heard, Illa Jakle might work well in that capacity. We are working out the details. All of us think we can work together to improve the farm further."

Jesse blinked. *Poor Illa.* She stowed away the purpose for her current visit.

Vanessa grinned, noticing her reaction but continued unabated, "I've also been thinking it might be interesting to stay with Aswenna." Her smile widened. "I never knew such an exciting adventure would come into my life at my current age."

"Worry and dread of what your family members might be up to less consuming?"

"Jezlynn," Margarete rebuked. Jesse looked at her mother. After a few shocked seconds, Margarete snorted and put her hand over her mouth to stop her laugh.

Vanessa laughed outright while Norma hid her smile as she sipped coffee.

"Just dropped in to say hello. I have duty I must attend to."

"Melany's job in the docking bay?" Isobel asked.

Jesse froze for a second. "Just so." She rose and left in a quick exit.

"Well at least she didn't eviscerate you," Margarete said.

Isobel laughed. "If a man like Lucian Krayne can accept her as she is, she should let others do so."

"She had another purpose in her visit, but didn't ask her question," Aswenna said.

"How do you know?" Vanessa asked.

"Beneath her calm, she is anxious."

"You should be careful," Norma said.

Margarete looked at the young woman who looked worried.

Norma looked concerned. "You don't know what happened to her on Ezredin."

"You do?" Vanessa asked.

"Not everything, but I've seen a medical scan of her scars. I don't know how she lived through such torture.

"What did they do to her?" Margarete asked, looking stricken.

"She was whipped with an old-fashioned whip...the lashes cover her back, and they branded her."

~ * ~

Melany took over from Jesse as she entered the maintenance compartment next to the docking bay. While the *Crusader*'s changes were nearing completion, the *Delve* still had some details Melany wanted to change. Remembering Nael's former team, she had asked for the return of Lieutenants Lenoir Blunt and Michael Swoboda, and Ensigns Wyatt Hecht and Les Schug. Surprisingly, they seemed pleased by her request. Blunt often gave her looks that Melany interpreted as recognizing her difference from Nael, but they had all worked hard.

Mikel Swoboda stood with his hands on his hips looking at the shuttle supported in a huge sling. "She looks really good, Major. The hull integrity is far above SSC standards as is the interior. The flight deck monitors and equipment excel, and the interior remodel can only be described as sumptuous."

Melany had special lighting installed in the section of the docking bay area that exposed the black hull's complete structure. Some of its disappearing qualities seen in space also happened in docking bay and with Melany's additional innovation, often under normal light. The microscopic processors merged in the coating on each side showed the images captured on the opposite side of the ship's hull, making it look invisible.

"Glad you like it. We will have this one completed before we dock at Starbase Celeste. You will also be glad to know Vice Admiral Tuen has upgraded all of you to experienced design crew with this type of hull.

"Without your permission, I will not discuss any of the innovations you've had installed," Swoboda said.

The others all agreed before Melany said, "I have been working on some new sensors I hope will improve tracking and preserve ship concealment even further when necessary, plus we will install a new warding weapon."

"Is that legal?" Wyatt Hecht asked, looking a little dubious.

"The *Delve* is a Ranger shuttle, and I've checked with General Roberre and with embassy legal, so yes, it is. I have something else to tell you." She stared at them. They stood waiting for her to say something. Their previous promise created a desire within her for them to know who she was. "You probably have already heard that Jezlynn Chambers is more than one person. I am Melany. Jet and Jesse are the major."

"Yes, ma'am, Melany," Lenoir said. "We had heard this but thank you for trusting us enough to tell us this."

"You are a major, too. We agreed long ago that nothing said in here is spoken off-duty," Wyatt said.

~ * ~

Opening the door into the captain's quarters, Jesse found Lu already there. "Do you cover bridge duty tonight?"

"No, I just finished my watch." He came to her as he talked, kissed her cheek, and ran a hand over her stomach where he had been staring. "You are beginning to show. Henry came to me and asked to take third shift. Before the *Sentinel* left port, he requested bridge training. He passed the test and received certification this past week. You haven't noticed his absence?"

"He isn't absent in the training room."

"You are usually there after your duty hours, and since he has chosen ship's night shift, that is just before his shift starts. I have taken the day shift seven hundred hours to fifteen hundred. Ribberdan takes over at fifteen hundred hours, and Henry takes over at twenty-three hundred hours. It works, and he had some experience. He shared the twelve-hour with Ribberdan until approved for the position."

"You mean we can spend the nights together?"

"How are you feeling?"

"Jet ran after Melany's duty. Gunnerman had two Rangers following her along with Sutta." She huffed. "Jet is frustrated. Since no one will spar with her, she hits a bag, and everyone watches her as much as Henry does."

"Henry and Gunnerman, the dervish, have kept me informed." Since Gunnerman took over Lu's training, Lu had referred to her Ranger leader by that epithet. "Gunnerman tells me Jet is overly aggressive in attacking the bag but also does other weight-bearing exercises. Those in her exercise and yoga-meditation group also have told me how much they enjoy it."

Jesse sighed. "Being watched drives Jet to extreme lengths, which Gunnerman or Henry often quash. The workouts help her contain some of her energy."

"Henry told me about an episode several months ago when she attacked Gunnerman for his interference in her extreme workout."

"He didn't fight her, and Henry helped him. You at least didn't have to endure Jet afterward."

He laughed. "Yes, I did. You visited Liz Rae with no qualms about entering sickbay. She is pleased Jet keeps running."

"I wanted to know if the Individual Rights Bureau had access to the tracer you have kept inside me. Their rep is always present whenever I enter the embassy deck."

"They did, but Rae has had that access ended."

"Can she remove the tracer?"

"No. Don't sound so grumpy, and I don't want you or Jet or anyone else to remove it."

"I've had one removed before. You may think it protects me, but the last time it led my enemy right to me, and nearly got you killed."

Jesse watched stricken guilt cross her husband's face, but he ordered, "It remains in place."

~ * ~

Angie kept track of Margarete's journey as she went to meetings about the trade negotiations. *::She's leaving now,::* she told Jesse.

Jesse excused herself from a meeting and met her mother in one of the side corridors as she traveled back to her suite. Margarete smiled as Jesse approached.

"Could I talk to you privately? There is a meeting room just a few doors down."

"Of course."

Once they sat across a table from each other, Jesse spoke. "I don't know what kind of mother I can be. I'm sure you know..." She took a breath and fell silent.

"...that you are different people at separate times. Yes. Ben explained it to me, and yes, it took me some time to adjust and accept the concept, but then I realized you all together kept my daughter alive. I am glad you finally trust me enough to talk about it with me. I know you are Jesse. Ben told me there were five others. I don't care, Jesse, it makes no difference to me, except for my guilt that I did not help you then."

"When Ben told you, and up until relatively recently, my condition was considered bizarre. Changes have happened recently. Nael and May combined into Melany, and Alyss and Lynn into Angie."

"I know. It has been a reoccurring topic among ship personnel, as has been the aspect of dronai. Aswenna told us, too. She said your dronai were freely willing to move to other bodies. I guess that is unusual. As far as becoming a mother, no one knows what type of mother they will be until they are one. And you no longer have to worry about doing it alone."

Jesse breathed a soft laugh. "Not with four of us."

"And with Lucian, me, Isobel, Vanessa, and Merit, who I have not met but would like to. Your cousin Norma wants to help you before then."

"Thank you." She took a breath. "I have a problem. I'm having trouble finding a correct style of clothing to wear."

"I think Isobel has found a seamstress onboard who is making you a new Ranger uniform to fit your pregnancy, plus some more casual clothes."

Jesse looked at Margarete who smiled back at her, answering, "I haven't had the chance to be casual in months. I look forward to it."

"I have a question, too."

Jesse looked at her in inquiry.

"Can you let your family meet all of you?"

"Now?"

"If you can manage it."

Jesse closed her eyes, feeling something akin to terror. A hand touched her shoulder.

"Only if you want to. They already know about you."

She exhaled a soft breath. "All right. Let me think about it."

~ * ~

Lu had invited Jesse to the bridge as the *Sentinel* reentered normal space in Sigma Sector. It was a unique experience, her first time on the bridge while aboard a ship of this size during a transition, and an SSC ship at that. She stood behind his command chair as the ship emerged. Within ship's visual range was Starbase Celeste, still sixteen days' travel, but protecting the major trade psiroute to Alpha Sector and Alliance Headquarters. Sigma Sector was her old hunting grounds.

"Bring back fond memories?" Lu asked, looking over his shoulder at her.

Jesse smiled. "I have done a lot of finagling in this sector."

A few quickly quaffed snort-laughs came from the crew. Lu threw her a humorous glance showing his commiseration with loss of privacy before resuming his command expression.

In this sector, the Bant Shipyards orbited the planet Arlon, the place where her first Pilgrim Line ship was redesigned from space wreckage. It also contained Ezredin, now a non-inhabited mining planet soon to be a Xanthean colony, and the Planet Griff, where she grew up and where her company Pilgrim Lines headquartered. All existed here. It would be a few days before the *Sentinel* docked at Celeste and her new duty began. Henry entered the bridge to take over bridge duty, so Lu took her to their quarters where dinner waited.

~ * ~

The captain called Jezlynn to his office. Angie smiled. Comlink contacts were always to Jezlynn, but Lucian always knew who was with him when they met face-to-face. She excused herself from Nohl's meeting with legal as they finalized the embassy's topics for negotiation. She knew while Jesse would negotiate them, she already knew which portions Jesse would fight for and which she would give away. On the other hand, Lu calling her to his office was unusual.

Henry stood inside the office, standing next to Krayne when Angie entered. A container was on a table, pre-certified as clean from the delivery service.

Krayne spoke as Henry watched Angie shift to Jesse.

"I received a message from Zerka, the new owner of the *Migrant Sun*. Its previous owner, Sanker Tricome, left it to him with stipulations this be sent to you," Lu said. "Henry informs me Tricome was a confirmed pirate in this sector along with a few others."

"Yes, he was. Sanker died?" she asked.

"Yes, natural causes according to Zerka. Upon Tricome's instruction, he sent you this."

Jesse slowly opened the container. A box lay within. She lifted it out and opened it. With slow movement she pulled out what looked like a brown leather wrap. Recognition came quickly. She dropped the wrap and rushed to the hygiene facility.

Henry heard Jesse vomiting and watched Krayne rush to her. He swore vehemently, grabbed the wrap and held it up. His stomach turned when he realized he held the skinned remains of a person. The leather was made from the skin of a person, a Visekan by the look of the face spread flat. The skin was sewn together into a cape-like shape. He nearly puked himself. He stuffed it back in the box. Within a few minutes, the captain led Jesse back into his office, making her sit on one of the couches.

Shortly, Doctor Liz Rae entered the office. "What happened?"

"Jesse told me the past rose up to bite her," Krayne said.

Liz monitored Jesse and looked at Krayne.

Jesse spoke. "It happened before we found you, Henry. I had served briefly on Sanker's ship; learned a lot about pirating, but then found Tom, and my purpose changed. Sanker hated Tom, so I decided to leave with Tom and Merit. Later Sanker came to me and told me he knew where some of the people I searched for were enslaved. It was a trap manufactured by Rosche, one of my Dachs family's enemies. We managed to get out of it, but I guess Sanker never let go of his ire. The box held the skinned remains of Hazra, a Visekan slave trader. Hazra tried to do the same to me. He just didn't know about Jet or about Nael's creative weaponry." She gave a weak attempt at a laugh and removed Rae's device. "I don't need medical care, Doctor."

"Maybe not physical...how about mental?"

Henry watched Jesse who was more shaken than he had ever seen her.

"It was a shock. Now one less enemy to be concerned about. I've dealt with worse, including Hazra's dinner party. I'll survive. I wonder how Sanker accomplished this? He was non-violent, but where in hell did he find a flayer?"

"You're rambling," Lu said.

Jesse looked at him and fell quiet.

Howard entered the office. It had to be important because he seldom entered the captain's office, usually sent a notification.

"Captain, Admiral Reed Dachs requests to speak with you."

Jesse laughed weakly. "Former admiral...saw to that."

"Yes, you did, deservedly." Despite protocol, the former admiral had followed Howard into the office. Henry noticed his likeness to his son Morgan. The admiral looked at those in the office and asked, "Bad timing?"

Fourteen

Krayne looked at Jesse who nodded her head. "No, Admiral Dachs. Doctor, later," he said dismissing Rae. "What is your purpose?"

Rae left the office at Krayne's command as Reed Dachs spoke. "I have a request. One I would label an extreme favor. I have heard the Xantheans are taking over Ezredin and that an organism there helped Major Chambers recover from her disamine overdose. I would like to request they take my son with them so he might, hopefully, be cured."

"Morgan?" Jesse asked.

Krayne was surprised at her self-control and noticed Henry observed this, too.

"Yes. I understand he caused you inordinate pain and trouble, but he is my son. I love him and this all happened while he was under the drug's influence."

"He raped my wife." Krayne heard the belligerence in his voice.

He saw Henry prepare himself to intervene in the worst-case scenario he must have envisioned. Krayne realized that both he and Henry wanted to see Morgan in a box like Hazra, but Jesse did not. She placed a hand over his. He looked at her and retreated from his confrontational position. So did Henry.

Seeing this, Dachs resumed talking. "I know, which makes this exceedingly difficult for you. It is difficult for me as well." The admiral paused. "What you did, what your investigations brought to light, were true. Somehow, we, as a family, my family, had become too overconfident, self-serving, and arrogant. Now I have learned you are a Dachs relative, my sister's great-granddaughter, so I came to request your help."

"Morgan is on Celeste?" she asked.

Krayne had only seen the admiral's image in vids. He looked different here, more aged, more somber without the haughty prestige of high rank, and his appearance held none of the insanity he remembered in Morgan.

"Yes, Austin is here, too, and, willing, as I am, to face any charges. Morgan's mind has disintegrated alarmingly. If there is the slightest chance for him to recover rather than be sent to a care facility...well, that is why I am here."

"You helped him escape?" Lu asked.

"Yes. Like your wife, confinement with the Individual Rights Bureau would have worsened his condition. Later, when I learned about the dronai on Ezredin where the negotiations would take place, I decided to bring him here and seek your help. I will understand if you won't."

"Who in command told you this?" Lu's voice turned to command mode. He rose and stepped from the informal meeting side of his office to stand before his desk.

The admiral looked alarmed. "No one did...the information was all over media long before the *Sentinel* left port at Starbase Constellation."

Krayne took a breath and pause. He looked at Jesse, and she nodded. "Let me talk with Ambassador Nohl and the Xantheans before I decide what can be done in this situation, Admiral Dachs."

"Thank you, Captain." Dachs nodded to Krayne. He briefly nodded at Jesse and left the office. Howard followed him out.

As the door closed, Jesse seemed stronger. "Well, at least we will know where one set of my enemies are."

"Can you stand his presence onboard?" Krayne asked.

"Have Aswenna watch Morgan. Her Circle..."

"...Our Amber Circle, Genitor," he replied.

"You know?" Her surprise turned to resigned recognition. She sighed, "Of course you do."

He smiled at her, but it was Angie who laughed in response. "Our Circle will keep track of all of them, and time limitations prevent Reed Dachs from being brought up on any charges of malfeasance. As for Austin, I expect his treason might be chargeable, but I think we need to let legal sort that out, or else we're doing exactly what that side of my family may have done."

Krayne went to his desk tender and a few minutes later told Angie both embassy legal and the Xantheans agreed to have the Dachs onboard. It did not upset her, but she felt gratified he felt her best able to cope with the information. She informed the others. Melany said they all needed to support Jesse.

~ * ~

Two days later Jet stood next to Krayne as the three Dachs moved onboard. "Who'd believe this?" she asked. Howard took former Admiral Dachs to his quarters on the embassy deck. Two guards also escorted Dachs to his room, one Ranger and one of T-Omer's security force. Austin surrendered himself to *Sentinel's* security after the embassy's legal bureau representative charged him with treason. Jet watched as an incoherently talking but smiling Morgan was taken directly to the Xanthean deck. He didn't notice her or anyone else.

Later in her deck one office, Gunnerman, who with one look addressed her as Angie, told her the rep from the Individual Rights Bureau demanded information and access to Morgan, which the Xantheans gave. With a mirth-lined voice, he told her, "She lasted all of five minutes. Your Xantheans scared her off. They look and are far more aggressive than reputed."

::So he knows who we are too,:: Melany said. Jesse was asleep.

::Everyone does,:: Angie answered. *::And we need to investigate the Dachs and the Vaughns further.::* After the events in Lucian's office, she had worked to protect Jesse.

"I've noticed their aggressiveness, too," Angie answered Gunnerman. "Do you suppose it is human influence? Or perhaps to rediscover a purpose?"

Gunnerman laughed. "Don't know, either is possible."

"You know about Chambers, too?" Angie asked.

"Hell, yes. General Roberre told me before he assigned me here. Explains a lot from when we served war-time duty."

"It doesn't bother you?" Angie asked.

Gunnerman gave her a lopsided smile. "Why should it? Under some circumstances, I've frequently wanted to trade places with someone, anyone else."

"Don't underestimate the Xantheans. They have always been formidable, but peaceful. Their homeworlds are usually nearly uninhabitable deserts or places most humans would prefer not to live, places needing perseverance to survive. Aswenna has already told me that my dronai have refused Morgan's body. She believes the dronai on Ezredin might accept and change him. It is worth a chance, I guess. They claim they will take Austin, too."

"He at least deserves to face charges for what happened on Gasch," Gunnerman said. "For an Alliance mining operation, led by Austin Dachs, to use slave labor is a traitorous crime. Embassy legal charged him, and T-Omer's men keep watch on him in the *Sentinel*'s brig."

"That, of course, depends on whether he is guilty," Angie answered.

"You know something?" Gunnerman asked.

"Some suspicions only. We are...exploring."

Gunnerman laughed. "Doesn't exploring mean investigating?"

~ * ~

Jet's training had turned into an exercise class combined with hand-to-hand combat moves but no contact, which was more helpful for beginners, and surprisingly, Angie attended the yoga classes. Jet finished with her class and was about to take a run, but she stopped to watch Gunnerman and Henry training their groups.

::What do you see?:: Angie asked. *::Why this preoccupation?::*

"Just precautions," Jet answered. "Worried about what's coming."

"Major?" an ensign asked having overheard her.

"Nothing, talking to myself."

"We all do occasionally, ma'am."

She looked at the ensign to see if it was an identifying or inadvertent comment. At his friendly expression, she grimaced a smile and left the training room, walking to the designated track area on deck one. She heard foot treads ahead, but she was alone except for Sutta, so started her run. *::Jesse you must do something about this.::*

::If I could, Jet, I already would have. Think of it as part of the mission. Did you know Vanessa has visited her brother?::

Jet huffed as she moved. *::Nothing surprising in that. Did she go visit Austin in the brig?::*

::Yes.::

Jet just kept running. Once finished she released to Jesse, who headed toward Krayne's quarters feeling somewhat tired, almost enervated, not entirely unusual following Jet's retiring from awareness. Lu was already there, a little early for his schedule. He was reading some information on the tender in the small sitting area. She smiled, thinking about the luxuriousness of his quarters compared to the first small quarters assigned her onboard. His was not as fine as Margarete's on deck four, but elegant and spacious by crew standards.

"Good!" Lu said, looking up as the door's mechanism worked. "Is your day finished?"

"Without all the work of leading the Ranger squad and with Nohl handling most of the trade negotiations with Griff and Rissilli, and those for the Khajari already outlined, I've much less work."

Without further preamble, he said, "Admiral Dachs requested permission to talk with you."

"He felt he needed permission?"

A warning look was flung her way. "Absolutely. How are you feeling?"

"Fit, despite the fact no one will practice hand combat with Jet. She runs and shows many beginners foundation moves and exercises."

He smiled. "Good."

"Good in that you have everyone, even Gunnerman and my Rangers following your orders?"

"Precisely."

She huffed. "And everyone claims I'm manipulative. Yes, I'll talk with Dachs. I'm going to talk with Austin and visit Morgan, too."

At her defiant look, he rose and approached saying, "You will inform me when you want the interview, and I'll make sure everyone knows. I will be with you, or you do not have permission." He ran his hand over the slight protrusion of her stomach.

"I think I felt our son move today."

His son immediately moved again as if on his father's demand. Lu smiled.

"Everyone kicks according to your order?" she asked.

"One of the benefits of command."

Lu's tender signaled and after a brief kiss, he answered the summons. His expression changed to serious with a quick command, "Send them in."

In quick order, Henry Wakeman entered wearing a satisfied look with another man whose long hair and bearded face she did not recognize.

"Thought you might like some good news," Henry said. "Jesse, this is our last missing crewman, Mapping Lieutenant from the *Constant*, Mohamad Abussan."

Jesse felt doubtful as she could not recognize him, but also astonished. "We have searched for you for years but never found you."

Mohamad spoke. "Only recently from a Tarkian stationed here on the *Sentinel* have I heard of a search for those of us off the *Constant*. I escaped slavery eleven years ago with my wife. Since then we have been serving on a Tarkian station."

"How did T-Omer know where you were?"

"He met someone off the station while visiting here."

"If you need any help or want to relocate, let me know. I also have compensation funds to give you."

"Actually, Lieutenant Chambers…"

"It's Major Chambers now," Henry said.

Mohamad smiled broadly. "Major Chambers, I don't need help or payment, and right now my wife and I are content where we are. Since talking to Henry, I have learned how long and how much effort you have put into our recovery. Luckily, I didn't need it but wanted you to know I survived and escaped."

"I'm taking him to meet Tom," Henry said, and the two left.

"Looks like my search has reached an end," Jesse said.

"Certainly...an eventful day," Lu said watching Henry and Mohamad leave.

She turned to Krayne. "While I'm here, and since even with my rank I need your permission, I have a request...two actually."

"Yes?"

"As well as talking with Admiral Dachs, I would like Austin present." She noted Lu's hesitancy and heard Henry's outright negation from the door.

"That was quick," Jesse snapped.

"Tom's in the adjutant's office."

Tom appeared in the doorway behind Henry. "I think I'd like to listen to this interview, too."

"Why do you want to do this, Jesse?" Henry asked.

"Well...the situation has somewhat changed, and I've been thinking about things and investigating, as I presume you know, through T-Omer," she added with a glance at Lu. "Austin and even Morgan might provide some information I need."

"About?" Lu asked.

"I have some suspicions about who set up what and why, and certain things are not adding up." Looking at the suspicion lining Lu's face, she added, "I have not free-ranged but come to you with my request. I expected you, or Henry, or both of you would accompany me, I've never spoken with Austin, plus the most troublesome Dachs are now under your control, and I need to determine exactly who might be working with the T'Kalz."

After a moment of silence, Lu moved to his tender. Within a few minutes he looked at Henry. "Are you currently tied up in any duty?"

He shook his head.

Henry, Tom, and Mohamad were already using their comlinks.

When they looked up, Lu asked, "Schedules all cleared?"

"We will meet at once, talking with both Admiral Dachs and Austin at the same time." He glanced at Jesse. "This is not just your investigation, but concerns the entire mission, and I'll deal with your insurrection later. I've contacted T-Omer to bring Austin from the brig. We will meet in the wardroom next to my office."

He looked at the men, now including Mohamad Abussan, waiting in his office. "You may watch from here." He called Andrew. When his adjutant entered, he ordered, "Have the viewing screen for the captain's wardroom up in here and keep a recording of the upcoming meeting."

Jesse rolled her eyes and groaned, looking at the ceiling. "I suppose you've contacted Rae, too."

Lu smiled. Jesse thought it a smug and superior look. "I'm glad to know you understand how far I will go to protect you. And thank you for not going rogue on me."

"Lately it hasn't accomplished much."

Ten minutes later, Lu asked, "Are you prepared for this?"

"Yes."

"Glad to hear it." He turned to the other three crewmembers of Constant. "And you?"

Tom answered. "This works. I'll hold my temper until I hear what is confessed. You do the same." His concerned gaze targeted Jesse.

Lu stared at Tom a moment before saying to Jesse, "Let's go."

Jesse followed Lu into the small wardroom where Admiral Dachs and Austin already sat at the conference table waiting. She recognized an embassy lawyer sitting beside Austin. T-Omer stood against the far wall. Jesse guessed he had more security outside the corridor's entry door. She felt impressed Lu had arranged this meeting so thoroughly within minutes. Angie and Melany both infringed on her space, listening. Reed Dachs smiled when he saw she was accompanied. Sutta had followed them in and squatted Xanthean style next to the captain's office door.

The former admiral rose as Jesse and Lu approached, extending his hand in formal greeting. Jesse shook his hand. Austin remained sitting.

"Thank you for agreeing to meet with me and for including Austin. He needs to hear this, too."

Before she had even set down, Austin asked, "Are you always so impromptu?"

"Often, yes." Taking her seat, Lu sat down next to her with his neutral, judging mien in place.

The admiral was silent for a moment staring at Jezlynn. "I know you think of me with contempt, deservedly, I know, but I would like to tell you my version of what happened and what I have recently learned. There is information you would not have discovered in the records you must have searched."

"Information about Admiral Ries Vaughn?" Jesse asked. "I knew his Corps record had major incongruities when I began exploring, but then those records disappeared when you retired."

Reed exhaled, looking astonished. "No one should discount your talents as an investigator; however, I did not remove the files. Ries Vaughn was my mentor in the early part of my Space Corps career. He retained his office after I left in disgrace. Before that, I had looked up to him, and if he asked me to do something, I did it. I trusted him implicitly."

"He *was* the son of a former president, but I now know he purposefully shifted his own guilt to you," Jesse said.

"Yes." Dachs looked at her before lowering his gaze to the table between them. "He introduced me to my second wife, Lacey Nguyen. Hell, he practically arranged the marriage. It was shortly after our wedding that the things he requested started sounding sketchy. By that time, I had also risen to the rank of admiral. Much later he appointed Morgan for first officer on the *Constant*. It was a quick rise in rank for Morgan, and it pleased me. After the debacle with the *Constant*, I learned he also had appointed Doctor Betzen, someone I knew had been in trouble on another ship. After Morgan returned, I learned Betzen had paid Vaughn a huge payment for the position. I believe Betzen was also somehow involved in introducing Morgan to disamine and helped develop his addiction." He glanced at her. "I admit after my son's return that I did some crimes of my own for my family's interests, but by then Vaughn was blackmailing me, and at the time I didn't know about his own crimes. Since then I have learned some of them."

After a pause, Dachs continued. "My wife Larkin had had a few mental problems before the birth of Morgan and Phelan. Afterward, they became worse, leading to her confinement. I learned Ries knew the truth about her mother, Lacey Nguyen."

"Lacey was adopted by Farrland Nguyen, but, in truth, she was the illegitimate daughter of Senator Franklin Vaughn," Jesse said.

Reed Dachs looked surprised. "Yes."

Austin started and looked at his uncle, his uninterested expression sharper, but he said nothing.

The admiral didn't notice. "She married Franklin's son, former President Dickka Vaughn. Franklin had already died by then, but now I believe Ries knew about the incestuous relationship."

"It might explain a lot about your sons, and I know Vaugh and your sister Laurel's husband, Durrant Rosche, worked closely together," Jesse said.

"Yes, Durrant was my brother-in-law and another lying, cheating abuser. By then I knew Ries had also corrupted me." His gaze rose to hers in sad irony. "I always thought of myself as an honorable man. I know, hard to believe now. I believed my rise to a two-star admiral was legitimate."

"Rightfully so, you completed some important missions successfully," Jesse said.

His head rose and he sat back in his chair. "Thank you. Yet Vaughn was a four-star admiral. Throughout my career I thought the orders he gave me were legitimate. It was only after Morgan's return from the *Constant* that I became aware of some of the awful things Admiral Vaughn had secretly arranged. Things to hide his service violations, including the situation which led to the *Constant*'s destruction. He wanted both Morgan and Phelan dead."

Jesse stilled and felt Lu's hand grasp hers.

Admiral Dachs continued. "We were at war with the Khajari, but later I learned the enemy had reached out for talks. Vaughn ordered the

Constant to the mission. What he never revealed was his involvement with a major corporate interest making huge profits from the war's continuation. Vaughn also had a grudge against the *Constant*'s captain, Ed Quante. Quante had disagreed with Vaughn's orders and observed some of his illegal actions. He had filed a malfeasance report to the Secretary of the Military. After the ship's destruction, I began adding up all the evidence and realized what a diabolical conniver and cover-up expert Ries Vaughn really was, and what an unquestioning believer I had been. Before the *Constant*'s mission, through an inadvertent encounter with a Regent Lines owner, I learned of Vaughn's involvement with the company. I confronted him about it. He told me it was nonsense, and the owner lied."

Dachs wiped his forehead and straightened against the chair's back. His gaze returned to Jezlynn.

"The admiralty's plan was for the *Constant* to meet up with the Khajari just out of Alliance space to talk about an end to the ongoing war, a top-secret mission. When the Khajari ship showed up, another ship, a Regent vessel, was already there and armed."

"The ship attacked the *Constant*?" Jesse asked, amazed at her own calmness. "How do you know this?"

The admiral emitted a sour laugh. "Vaughn, who else? He gloated about it. Told a mutual acquaintance he had made a mint from the company involved in the attack. He had arranged for the weapons installation on the trader, and of course, Quante never worried about a supposedly unarmed Alliance merchant ship. Vaughn laughed about Morgan's unexpected escape, because as you know, a Visekan slaver also waited hidden behind a local asteroid."

"Command knew that a white dwarf system was a relatively short distance away and that it still had orbiting bodies. How could the Visekans have known the *Constant* would be there?" Jesse asked.

"Vaughn planned it," the admiral said. "I learned Vaughn had covert business dealings with the Visekans. The Visekans would claim the ship's remains since he knew the explosion would not destroy the entire ship. He believed it would kill the entire crew. Morgan was supposed to die. That didn't happen." His gaze never left Jesse. "He didn't foresee you and the engine crew's ability to save the *Constant*. He did not want a treaty with the Khajari, and he didn't believe anyone would survive the attack.

"One flaw in his plan was the merchant captain was inept at shooting a missile and didn't want his ship's discovery, so quickly left the area. After the merchant ship fired on the *Constant*, the Khajari ship left. I am not sure when the slaver showed up. Ries never thought Morgan would return the *Constant* to Alliance space. When he did return, Ries destroyed Morgan's reputation."

"Along with my mine."

"Yes."

"Why did he want Morgan to die?"

"Payback for my confronting him about his involvement with those outside his command structure."

"And Phelan?"

"Phelan never wanted a military career, and either Vaughn or Rosche, maybe both, had a hand in his misbehaviors, too. He lives on the family estate now with his grandmother."

"Do you have proof of these allegations?" Lu asked.

"I've told Undersecretary Corrao all I know, and I have given him what records and other documentation I could find."

Silence reigned for a moment.

"What do you want to know from me?" Austin finally asked.

Jesse searched the man's face and saw a slight resemblance to Morgan, although his hair was much darker, and his eyes brown. He looked grim.

The lawyer gave Austin a warning which he waved aside.

"I am not here for the court," Jesse said, "and didn't want this... conversation... recorded."

"You've been overruled," Austin replied with a sad quirk of his lips.

"I know. It's been happening to me a lot lately. You probably know my research led to Morgan's downfall. You've also heard your uncle's admission."

"Yes." He huffed a laugh.

"I thought your family was my nemesis."

"In some ways we are...were, but mostly my aim was just to protect Morgan. Recently I learned how severely he injured you." His face tightened and anger crossed it. "Damn Rosche and Betzen. It's a good thing they are both dead." He stared at her. "Now I've learned, surprisingly, you're a relation, a second cousin."

"Yes." She exhaled. "A most unanticipated turn of events."

"I always liked Aunt Vanessa."

"In my last conversation with Morgan..."

"After he was arrested?"

"Yes. He related some information that made me start reconsidering some things."

Austin's expression turned inquiring.

"I began thinking...speculating...that maybe the Dachs family wasn't as guilty as I thought, but perhaps exploited by a master manipulator. Admiral Dachs has affirmed this, but I'm going to tell you another perspective." Jesse paused, crossing her lower arms on the table's edge and leaning forward slightly.

"Before leaving Starbase Constellation, the *Sentinel* was the object of a subversive drone attack. Before the attack took place, both Captain Krayne and I were in the engine compartment. Other problems were affecting the engines. They had been turned off before the attack, which is why the explosion didn't destroy the ship. Shortly after we had the ship under control, I had an unusual memory.

"Unusual in that before then I didn't have memories of what happened on the *Constant*, but now I remember how some of what happened in the *Sentinel*'s engine compartment also happened in the *Constant's*. Others remember the two ships present, the two ships your uncle just described. I have reason to believe the destruction of the *Constant* was planned before she ever left port, and I believe Admiral Dachs is correct, Admiral Vaughn planned it. Further, I think Vaughn still operates within the Alliance and has developed links to an anti-government faction of the Khajari. Your answers to some questions might help me prove this."

"Vaughn's dead," Admiral Dachs said.

Jesse kept her gaze on Austin. "You know better, don't you?"

He laughed. "Sorry, Uncle Reed. The bastard is alive and a traitor to boot. Austin's cynical sneer altered, and he looked at his clasped hands on the table. After a moment's silence, he spoke.

"Uncle Reed said we needed to pay the price for our transgression to reestablish our family name. I was more concerned about Morgan. He and I have always been close. It's odd, unexpected, that your Xantheans friends have taken him into their care." He leaned back in his chair looking unmoved before continuing. "I'm at a point where I really don't care about anything that happens anymore."

A long silence persisted as Austin regarded her. He finally spoke. "I see what attracted Morgan. He has always been somewhat of a bisexual predator. Aunt Larkin spoiled him rotten and made him feel he and Phelan deserved whatever they wanted. I always thought her a bit crazy, too." He glanced at his uncle. "Glad to hear I was right. My mom was far stricter, but Morgan and I were constant companions growing up. Go ahead and ask."

"Who promoted you to mine manager at the Gasch mines?"

"Mine administrator...not manager." He sighed. "Never managed anything." He scowled at her. "Morgan's uncle, Admiral Vaughn, suggested I apply for the position, and I suspect he pulled strings to get me there. He knew I was taking care of Morgan, who was a bit crazy by then. Vaughn said I could do what I was good at, manage the finances and trade agreements. He sent me a message your ship was coming." He huffed another laugh. "Just when Morgan was in one of his belligerent spells."

"Who operated the hidden ship you escaped on?"

"Again, Morgan's uncle made the arrangement. I discovered it was a Khajari vessel, too. They left us at Fortune Station. Odd to think he always worked both sides of any arrangement." Austin once again leaned back in his chair. "I never knew they were using slave labor. Stupid, I know. Vaughn came to visit, and the next thing I knew, he took Morgan and me and left."

"I believe he entrapped you."

"I know he singled me out because of Morgan's and my shared last name. He hated us." His face tensed. "Like Phelan, I never wanted to serve in the Rangers or Space Corps, didn't want that type of career. Didn't want to be a politician or government lackey at all. Extremely un-Dachs like, I know." He sighed. "I might have liked being a trader like you, although I really hate space travel, so that was out of the question. My parents should have let me become a financial manager as I wanted. One home, on Earth, living a grounder's life."

"I think Admiral Vaughn set you and Morgan up as scapegoats for his own crimes and as vengeance against Admiral Dachs," Jesse said. "His actions during and after the Constant shattered Morgan's reputation, and you didn't count at all to Vaughn."

Austin's eyes sharpened in deliberation. She could almost see his mind add up events. "That son-of-a-bitch. You knew this even before Uncle Reed spoke, didn't you? How do you know?"

"Vanessa Dachs knew some information, so her knowledge confirms Admiral Reed's admission. I think if you freely plead to all your dealings with Admiral Vaughn, your cooperation and testimony might help your case with the justice department."

"What about Uncle Reed?"

"Time limitations prevent any actions against him, and I expect when the truth is reported, it will greatly improve his reputation. Thank you for telling me this, Austin."

"Thank you...cousin."

"That's not necessarily true, Major Chambers," Reed Dachs said, "but thank you for listening to us."

"Jezlynn...Reed."

"Is it true what I've heard the *Constant* did to you? The split personality?"

"Yes, but technically we are all just Jezlynn and you are family."

She rose and escaped the room with Lu quickly following her. The lawyer remained with Reed and Austin.

Inside his office, Lu asked, "How did you find this out?"

Jesse started laughing. He, Tom, Henry, and Mohamad all looked affronted, but she shook her head and felt the now all-too-ready tears leaking from her eyes. "The last thing Vaughn told me after discharging me from the Corps, was the Rangers didn't expect much in moral character, so I would fit in just fine."

Lu swore, and she felt his arm around her but refused to hide her wet face in his shoulder.

Aware Henry, Tom, Henry, and Mohammad were watching, Jesse pull away from Lu, wipe her face, and took a deep breath. "I suppose this means I need to do more investigation."

"No, it doesn't. It means the SSC needs to investigate, and I'm sure Corrao has already set a governmental investigation in place. You will stay out of it."

She listened but with a slight smirk. "Is that an order, Captain?"

"Yes, it's an order."

She looked away from everybody and took a deep breath. "I always assumed Vaughn was a sycophant of the Dachs. I now wonder at my short-sightedness. Things just never added up. Recently I set aside all my assumptions and just looked at what I knew from my...explorations, I explored some more and came up with another assumption. One that new facts seem to be supporting."

Sutta spoke from behind her. "Genitor, Aswenna asks that you not visit Morgan yet."

Jesse sighed in resignation. *::Talk with Aswenna,::* Angie said.

"Maybe not any time," Henry said.

"There's more," Jesse said. She looked at Lu. "Since the engine incident, Melany has explored every nook and cranny of the *Sentinel*'s engines."

"I know," he answered.

She gave a half-laugh response. "She thought she had hidden that from everyone. She removed anything she perceived as off-kilter, but someone, probably no longer onboard, made alterations to essential codes and rigged certain operations to fail. They won't. Yet I think Admiral Vaughn was behind the subterfuge. I think he is working with the T'Kalz, and we need to plan more defense strategies for this mission."

The captain's tender link sounded, and Lu moved to receive his message. When he turned back to them, he looked upset. "The Starbase Post Commander Admiral Otrika requests our presence at a social gathering."

Henry swore. Tom stood frowning with his arms crossed over his chest.

"My time to leave," Mohamad said. With a brief smiling farewell to everyone and a warning from Jesse to be careful, he left. Lu ordered guards to make sure he was safe on his trip back to the ship he had arrived on.

Jesse laughed. "Maybe Angie can play the piano and relieve us of all conversation. Maybe my formal black uniform will put off the inquisitive."

Lu's lips were pursed in contained humor. "I doubt it, but the contingent of security surrounding you will."

Fifteen

The walk from the Corps docking facilities to the commander's headquarters on the starbase was relatively short. With six Rangers, T-Omer's security group, and four unnervingly observant Xantheans surrounding them, few dared to approach the large group of officers and embassy personnel. Few had ever seen a Xanthean, and they appeared far more hazardous than when Jesse had first encountered them on one of their home planets, Çiro.

Gunnerman stayed on the *Sentinel* in charge of ship security while T-Omer protected the captain and the mission's ambassadors. Ribberdan also remained onboard at the *Sentinel*'s bridge, but other officers and embassy personnel accompanied them for the event. Jesse heard and saw the attention she had garnered.

::*Meld with me,*:: Jet demanded. Her confrontations with Jet persisted, but Jesse thought this suggestion helpful.

"I haven't seen you for a while," Krayne said.

"You recognized me in one glance? Yeah, well, it seems I've not been needed," Jezet said. She surveyed him, giving him a quick smile, but her gaze quickly scanned the balconies and their current walkways, showing Jet's part of her. "It's a deflating admission, but Jet is as wary

189

as a hunted cougar, and Jesse refused to release her control. Don't stare, Henry."

"The exposure doesn't seem to bother you," Henry replied.

"Why should it? Few know about me, so I remain essentially anonymous." She glanced at her captain again. "Don't worry. I'm sure Jesse will boot me out once we're in the headquarters department. Good thing, too. Jesse is much better at small talk with strangers. Strategic meetings are one thing, but these meet-and-greets are tedious. Is this affair a fillip for the post commander? I didn't think such events standard for visiting ships."

"For a known embassy mission of such importance, it is."

"Just dratted publicity."

"That, too," her captain added with humor.

"Just to let you know, Angie thinks some adherents of the T'Kalz are on the starbase."

"And Jesse didn't see fit to tell me?" he asked.

"Angie didn't tell her or Melany. She told Jet. You'd think internal communications would be easier, but hell, no one tells everyone everything, and Jet's been snide and snippy."

"I've noticed."

"She knows I can react just as effectively, if not as fast, as she does." She grinned at her captain. "I'm a good intermediary."

Krayne also noted that Jezet's assumption turned true when Jesse joined him at the department's conference room door.

"Are you ready for this?" he asked.

"I'm always prepared, just not always pleased, especially with Angie's revelation. I think I need a long discussion with Angie and Melany." She huffed. "Why she contacted Jet and not me..." She fell silent for a moment. "I always thought Jezlynn's condition gave us an advantage. Now I'm gaining an understanding of the drawbacks."

Many of Celeste's staff and residents filled the room, along with invitees from different docked ships, including a few from the *Sentinel*. Krayne watched Jesse smile and make affable comments to those who spoke to her; but again, Admiral Otrika stood on her other side, introducing guests as they approached him, so few lingered.

Henry stood on his other side, and Sutta stood in intimidating grandeur behind them. Sutta's presence discouraged many from even approaching.

Afterward, the admiral asked Jesse if she would entertain everyone with some music, which Angie did with a smooth and inconspicuous switch. Krayne watched her while she played, and noticed many other men did too. He did not like seeing what he considered lust-filled looks. She played for thirty minutes. After she left the piano, she rejoined him. Admiral Otrika brought her a glass of wine from the bar, which Krayne, with a smile at Jesse, took and drank himself. She gave him a disapproving look only he could recognize.

She smiled at the admiral's confusion. "Thank you Admiral Otrika, but Doctor Rae ordered me to a diet that doesn't include alcohol."

"You are on a diet? You look physically sound."

She did. Her Ranger's black formal uniform jacket hid her beginning bulge.

"Not for improving her health," Krayne said, "but for her pregnancy."

Otrika smiled. "Congratulations. I had not heard."

A few minutes later, Sal Imada approached. Jesse smiled at Krayne. "Since Tom's exhibition, Sal and I have worked out a compromise. Whenever we meet, which is usually on the embassy deck, I agreed to answer one question."

Imada smiled at Krayne. "A most unusual method to conduct an interview, but it is working, plus I am sending monthly updates to my publication on the ship and its mission. Hello, Jesse. How do you handle all the attention you gather, especially at events like this one?"

"I was more comfortable before my recent notoriety. Then, I could travel mostly unobserved. It served my disreputable purposes. Now, as you have certainly noticed, I always travel with a coterie of security. While I find this most unpleasant since it gains so much unwanted attention, few speak with me."

Imada regarded her with a slightly smirking smile. "I doubt that you ever traveled unobserved, but perhaps just unknown." He nodded and moved away. Krayne noticed he watched Jesse, which she likewise observed, while he talked with other guests.

Krayne was surprised at her honest answer about her aggravation to Imada. He placed the wine glass on a server's platter. "Admiral Otrika has provided many vegetarian selections."

"How did he know?" she asked.

"I informed him. We will act like polite guests and enjoy the fare, and afterward, swiftly leave."

As their parade of personnel and security left the governing department's confines, Krayne felt a startling, burning pain in his back. He struggled when he heard Jesse scream. Something pressed on him with agonizing pain before blackness enveloped him.

~ * ~

Jesse felt Sutta shove her aside and bat at a flashing projectile. Another Xanthean pulled Lu aside, but the projectile's changed direction hit him in the back. She screamed as he fell to the deck. She broke free of Sutta and knelt by him, seeing his uniform melt away. Rae had not attended. She looked around to see who could help him. Norma was quickly beside her, pulling a container from the bag she carried and spraying it on Lu's back.

"It's a poison nullifier and will cool the burn dramatically!" Norma shouted at Jesse as the noise around them dramatically increased.

Over the tumult, Jesse heard Henry and T-Omer shouting orders for the party's safety and for alert measures. One Xanthean vaulted against a wall, pulling down a surveillance module. Sutta picked her up, pulling her away from Lu and ordering her to silence while another of his team carried Lu. Within minutes they were within the *Sentinel*'s sickbay. This time Rae ordered her to the waiting room.

~ * ~

Krayne woke in a place he recognized—the *Sentinel*'s sickbay. Someone held his hand. "You're awake." Jesse's voice reassured him. "Rae has you lying on a treatment sheet filled with painkillers and regenerative medications. You probably don't feel much, but she said you have to remain on it."

"What happened?" His voice sounded groggy.

"A weapon hidden in one of the surveillance modules. Sutta heard it and pushed me out of the way, and even butted the projectile weapon off course, but Henry and T-Omer think it changed course to hit you, but at a far less lethal speed." Her hand squeezed tighter on his. "During the resulting chaos, the team reacted. Norma gave your back initial treatment and the Xantheans carried you and me back to the ship. The scene is playing on media throughout the starbase."

He groaned but noticed her quick grin.

"Welcome to notoriety. Rae says the weapon's charge knocked you out. You have a serious burn wound on your middle back, but you will live."

"Did they find out who did it?"

"The starbase's security contingent is investigating...but one of Sutta's group pulled the module off the wall. T-Omer has it. You would have been amazed at the increased agility and speed of the Xantheans. T-Omer told port authority his crew would inspect the module before turning it over to their security office."

"You've been here since it happened?"

"Yes."

"How long?"

"Eight hours. T-Omer is impatient to apologize. He sees it as a dereliction of his duty. Sutta wants to apologize for causing your wound. He has a sizeable injury on the arm he used to bat the charge aside."

"He saved you from being hit. No apology is necessary from anyone. Damn, another uniform ruined."

Jesse laughed. "You still have three from the ones I had delivered to *Constellation*."

"It certainly shows your foresight."

"Admiral Otrika ordered the starbase to high alert, and I've been exploring the tender here in this room, but I don't think any evidence of the culprits will be found. It was too well planned."

"But you have suspicions?"

"Not yet, just collecting information."

"You've investigated?"

"Explored."

He grimaced. "What did your exploration expose?"

"No ship left the starbase for six hours before the attack, and no Khajari are on Celeste, which means malefactors aboard instigated the attack. Allied supports for the negotiations are docked here... but most arrived after the *Sentinel,* but I've checked them out and doubt they were involved. I do have a few suspicions about a few people in residence. I think the module will show it included a trigger device. Supposedly this module was checked last week, so a time frame might be established from the module." Looking at his face, "Which I am sure T-Omer will explain when you are released from here."

"And?"

"The chief investigator on Celeste is Colin Colend."

"A Vaughn adherent."

"I've sent the name to Admiral Wakeman. Right now, I am sure of Admiral Otrika's capability and allegiance to the SSC and the Alliance, but uncertain about his staff. He doesn't have any idea of the morass Ries Vaughn has created, or even the connections between his staff and Vaughn cohorts. Since no public information has been released on retired but esteemed Admiral Vaughn, I doubt Otrika would believe any allegations against his chief investigator."

~ * ~

Several weeks later, Jesse stood once again looking out the window. This time in the wardroom next to the captain's office while he was on bridge duty. Lu had left sickbay two days after his injury and immediately returned to his captain's duties even while on pain meds. She had noted he was as cranky in sickbay as he claimed she was.

The *Sentinel* had reached its destination. The nemesis of her sleeping hours lay below. She watched the planet Ezredin as the *Sentinel* settled into orbit. Sutta stood next to her, much straighter than she had ever known him to stand, making him much taller. His four hands were clasped behind his back. He said nothing, but his eyes were wide open and attentive, not the lid-shaded version she had associated with all the Xantheans.

Ezredin looked the same as the last time she had viewed it years ago with Tom. Just the sight still disturbed her. Melany and Angie were also upset. Although Nael had been oblivious, melding with May meant Melany had access to all of May's memories of what she endured on this planet. She became aware Sutta's attention had shifted to her. "Your new home," she said, stating the obvious.

A soft croak answered her. "It needs much work."

"Change of heart?"

"What?"

"It's a snide human comment meaning the actuality of the planet might be more than even the Xantheans expected. They might change their minds."

"Ezredin has far more vegetation and arable land than any other Xanthean colony. The soil is rich with minerals. Our bodies use both the oxygen and the carbon dioxide the atmosphere holds. We know deep wells of water lie on the surface and underground. We are most excited to move to it."

"By the way, your Space Standard has greatly improved."

He croaked. "We know what lies below and look forward to founding Amber Circle on Ezredin's surface, Genitor, but my declared duty is to you."

She rolled her eyes to side-glance at her Xanthean guard, still aggravated he refused to address her by any other name. At the sound of the door opening, she turned to see who entered. Lu came in with Aswenna, who no longer seemed to need help. The Matriarch of Amber Circle stood straighter and looked stronger, as did all the Xantheans who followed her. Renny Lebeau, Monica, and Pier McEntire came with them, as did Kizz and her family. Although Margarete, Isobel, and Vanessa did not have dronai, Aswenna predicted they would and held them in her Amber Circle.

"Greetings, Genitor," Aswenna said.

"Please call me Major Chambers, Matriarch, if you want to be formal, otherwise, Jesse or Jezlynn."

"Except when it isn't you, Jesse?" Aswenna asked in her own much improved Space Standard.

"Jezlynn works for any of us, Aswenna. Your Amber Circle has increased significantly."

"Isobel and Vanessa are transporting to the surface with the Circle."

She gave the matriarch a gentle glare. More muted laughter-croaking sounded around her.

Jesse greeted Renny, Monica, and Pier, and all the Xantheans following Aswenna. Whenever she named a Xanthean by their name, their eyes glowed. She looked at her mother, grandmother, and great-grandmother, who were the last to join the crowd.

"I stay for the negotiations to finalization," Margarete said. "Otherwise, I would have enjoyed visiting the surface. Buildings and structural facilities from former colonies remain. It cannot be too barbaric."

"There are reasons those colonies failed."

"Your shared-blood family will be safe below. Amber Circle will ensure this," Aswenna said.

"Take care of my friends, too."

"They are all members of Amber Circle, so we will share information with them which will bring human understanding to Xantheans and Xanthean understanding to humans."

Lu quietly wrapped his hand around hers, but he did not look at her. He had to feel the tremors running through her, but contentment seemed to seep through their clasped hands as she looked at the view. "Are all the ships in place?" she asked.

"Yes. We just wait on the Khajari. T'Carta Kar has contacted me. They are seventy-one hours out. The *Dark Traveler* and the *Polestar* have formed an orbiting triad with the *Sentinel*, and the *Crusader* orbits within this circle. It is certainly a new maneuver for my crew. Olson's crew is preparing two shuttles to land the Amber Circle."

"Since I will take part in the talks, I will stay here," Aswenna said. Her usually tranquil gaze, like Sutta's, was locked on the planet below and seemed to exude excitement.

Looking about her, Jesse realized all fifteen Xantheans, the humans present, and Kizz stood watching the planet. All seemed enthralled with the view.

Ahjias moved next to her. "I go below to hold the Amber Circle until the Matriarch Aswenna joins us. Before we leave, we wanted to tell you...now dronai, your dronai, live in all of us. Thank you, Genitor.

Because of you, we already feel restored, feel the pull of Ezredin for a new journey, but also sorrow you won't join us."

With her gaze never leaving the planet, Aswenna spoke. "Your mother has asked me to stay with her during the time of the negotiations. Sutta stays with his Rangers unit with a few others from Amber Circle. They will share a room in the Rangers' area. All of the Dachs onboard move with the Circle to below."

"They are going aground?" Jesse said in surprise.

"Yes," Ahjias answered. "When their talks with security end. Morgan goes with us now."

Jesse took one of Ahjias' hands, pulling it close to her mouth. She kissed the back of the hand. "A merging of more than dronai, my sister Ahjias." She swore Ahjias cried although no tears emerged, but her eyes glowed with emotion.

Aswenna smiled. "New beginnings."

Lu's hand tightened on hers as he told Ahjias, "Your shuttle to the surface is ready, whenever you wish to leave. Jesse and I have some business to complete."

In short order he had her out of the wardroom and in his quarters.

"How are you holding up?" she asked him.

"Fine. How are you dealing with Ezredin?"

"Since I don't have to go aground, fine."

She saw suspicion enter Lu's expression at her admission. "Like you accede to my orders?"

She smiled and wrapped her arms around him. "I've never liked having anyone order me about. Well, not at least since the *Constant*. While obeying your orders, letting you place protection on me, managing my decisions and my actions often provokes me, it is also oddly comforting. It reassures me of just how much you care for me."

His expression softened. "Far more than you can imagine."

"Only if it encompasses the universe, which is what you are to me."

He laughed. "Not if you consider Jet's frequent outbursts."

"Well, before my universe explodes, I need to tell you something."

"That you've already been in negotiations with Kalmona-Rek Kerub and T-Carta Kar? Glad to hear you admit it, but as an ambassador with a standing relationship with both, not unexpected."

She punched his arm; he grunted but smiled. "T-Omer's study of my communications informed you?"

His smile grew broader, but he only kissed her.

An hour later they went to the docking bay to say good journey to those entering the shuttles. Jesse watched them leave the ship through a view portal. *::They begin a new journey,::* Angie said, *::we do, too.::*

Sixteen

Ambassador Nohl, his assistant, three Ranger security, and three Corps security, waited on the *Crusader* with Jesse for the Khajari delegation to board. Tom Thorson, Rafe Dakota, and Henry Wakeman stood with Jesse, and T'Carta Kizz stood next to her as the Khajari delegations' shuttle joined with the *Crusader*. Sutta stood behind her. Lu remained on the *Sentinel*. As T'Carta had informed her, five Khajari ships orbited Ezredin, including the *Azreal*, now independent of Pilgrim Lines Shipping.

Today Jesse did not wear a service uniform but an elegant royal blue professional suit with her long black hair carefully braided and gathered to hang down her back. Ambassador Nohl had looked approving upon seeing her in the docking bay before boarding the *Delve*.

Melany's docking bay team piloted the *Crusader*. She appointed Mikel Swoboda as pilot with Lenoir Blunt as copilot and permanent residents. The shuttle remained in place with different support teams switching daily. Jet piloted the *Delve*. Having an ambassador as pilot surprised many, but Nohl had reassured them.

One of Jet's Ranger security stood as guard at the hatch as it opened, coming to alert as the mechanism sounded.

Three Khajari security officers entered first and moved to a side bulwark to stand at duty, followed by a few Khajari Jesse guessed to be officials. One stood out as much taller than the others and overweight, an unusual condition for a Khajarian. He introduced himself as the trade negotiator, D'Kelv Uve. Despite his imposing size, his voice was pleasant, and he spoke Space Standard. The others followed his lead and introduced themselves.

A few Khajari dignitaries and T'Carta Kar, along with a Khajari woman who caused Kizz to start slightly, entered next. She had to be Kar's wife. The woman immediately moved to Kizz and touched her cheek against her son's in Khajari family greeting, confirming Jesse's guess. Tuning from Kizz, the woman gave Jesse a brief contemptuous look.

Last came the Supreme Ruler Kalmona-Rek Kerub, who had recently come to power. Although he was once far from the inheritance of power, war between Khajari factions had decimated those eligible to rule. Now Kerub was the best and safest candidate to govern and had the powerful Kalmona family supporting him. Jesse knew the Kalmona family was an offshoot of the previous royal Rek family before the T'Kalz takeover, and Kerub was the last Rek family member. He had placed their name before his family name for the support they gave him. His gaze immediately found her. He smiled. His demeanor was always resolved, but now his dress was far more formal and elegant. He came directly to her, and rather than give her a formal greeting, he touched her cheek to cheek, except in an instant his hand brushed aside the edge of her dress jacket and ran over her belly.

"My cherished Jezlynn, I had heard about your increase." He smiled with a slide glance at T'Carta Kar. Jesse recognized the Khajari baiting tactic, but Kar was unperturbed at his leader's goad. As Kar provided his supreme ruler no reaction, Kizz immediately moved to stand behind his father's left shoulder. Jesse noted his mother's startled reaction at her son's move, a declaration of sworn support for his father.

"I see we've become far less formal since I'm no longer your boss," Jesse said.

Kerub laughed. "You will always be my friend and my liberator. After all, you saved me from slavery."

"As Kar saved me from the same."

"Ah, feisty Jezlynn, I wanted to prevent you from giving me any formal dignitary greeting, and I knew Kar would insist on protocols. Yes, as you've said, once you were my boss, but never doubt my mission—I will do what is best for Khajari."

Jesse saw his stratagem for the Khajari: admit his acquaintance with the Alliance's ambassador while proclaiming his loyalty to his home world.

"Jezlynn," Kar stepped forward to also greet her cheek-to-cheek with a sly look at Kerub. "It has been a long time, and now you return my son to his family."

"She has also saved your shuttle, Father, and even enhanced it," Kizz said. He smiled as he looked at her.

Kar's wife looked irritated.

Jesse bowed her head to Kizz in Khajari manner, as he did to her, and turned to Kar. "If one of your pilots can return to the *Sentinel* on the *Delve* with me, they can reclaim your shuttle and the remaining members of Kizz's team who came with the Xantheans from Asedin."

"I can pilot it," Kerub said, earning an almost imperceptible glare from T'Carta Kar. "And I would like to visit the *Sentinel* as a guest rather than an enemy."

Jesse politely smiled. "We are all representing our relative nations, so perhaps it is appropriate now to establish a little more formality."

She turned to those in her group and introduced Ambassador Ang Nohl, who looked more amused than diplomatic. Kerub nodded, but T'Carta Kar stepped forward and offered his hand to the ambassador in Alliance fashion. Jesse kept introducing her team. When finished, Kar introduced the dignitaries who had entered with T'Carta, which included T'Kalz Zef, one of the previous ruler's family.

Jesse showed no reaction, and the security men who stood in formal stance behind their supreme ruler relaxed slightly. With all formal negotiation delegates introduce, Kar grasped his wife's arm. She stepped forward to stand next to him. "Let me introduce my wife, Gana."

Jesse extended her hand. Gana's fingers merely touched hers and quickly withdrew while she remained looking somewhat aloof. "It is a pleasure to meet you at long last, Gana."

Gana nodded her head but made no reply. Kar's equanimity faltered briefly as he gave his wife an annoyed glance.

"Tom, Henry, and Rafe, I am glad to see you, too." The supreme ruler put aside his regal bearing and Jesse's request for formality and gave them family greeting of hand on shoulder, which made all three men smile. All three placed a hand on Kalmona-Rek Kerub's shoulder in return.

Jesse noticed her delegation watched with great interest, so she resumed formality with her opening speech. Kalmona-Rek Kerub also became far more formal and proper in address. She noted T'Carta Kar looking around the *Crusader*. He spoke when she finished her formal speech for the beginning of the negotiations.

"Your Melany reconfigured this shuttle for the negotiations? She did an excellent job," Kar said. "The *Azreal* is hard enough to find in open space, but this shuttle was not at all recognizable by either vision or instrumentation until our ships arrived and the signal lights and insignia appeared."

Jesse paused at his knowledge and noticed Supreme Leader Kalmona-Rek Kerub wore a suspiciously innocent-smug expression. They all knew. It meant Kerub had kept a discreet communication link with Pilgrim Lines.

"We needed a large, but safe and neutral conference room. The *Crusader* can hold sixty comfortably, if needed. The table and seating remain compliant with Alliance and Space Service Corps' safety requirements." She took a breath. "We should start, so everyone please take a seat."

Kerub spoke before moving. "I know of your suspicions of the former rulers of Khajari, the T'Kalz family, but all here have helped to develop what our government wants from these negotiations. Those T'Kalz present want to reintegrate with the Kalmona and my government." Kerub stared at Jesse and his lips cracked a brief smile when she showed no reaction.

"Thank you, Supreme Ruler Kalmona-Rek Kerub. As I have already been introduced to T'Kalz Zef, I speculated this might be the case. It seems your leadership has made many advances toward both inner and outer peace." She smiled. "I'm sure you've vetted all of your delegation for their peaceful intentions, as I have with mine."

T'Kalz Zef stepped forward. "He has, Ambassador Chambers. Many T'Kalz knew and understood the enormous problems of our family's leaders, including the capture and imprisonment of good but challenging Khajari family members, including T'Carta Kar and now Supreme Leader Kalmona-Rek Kerub. It seems all Khajari owe you a debt of honor."

Jesse hesitated a moment. "Thank you, T'Kalz Zef. It pleases me to see your support for your new leader, but neither he nor any other Khajari owes me anything." She extended her hand to him and he took it. "It will be a pleasure, though, to work with more Khajari toward peace."

He smiled and bowed his head as he stepped back.

"Despite T'Kalz Zef's presence, there are still T'Kalz who want to reclaim leadership," T'Carta Kar said. "However, many more Khajari want peace and safe international trade agreements. You, Ambassador Jezlynn Chambers, have already worked with many of the Khajari traders who have joined us. And you arrange a neutral Xanthean planet where we can meet in peace." While Kar talked, she noted Gana looking at one of the Khajari traders and saw the trader, who introduced himself as D'Kelv Uve, give Gana the briefest of nods.

She smiled at the group saying, "As to our trade negotiations, Lieutenant Commander Henry Wakeman and I will negotiate the space-protocols agreement between our two nations here on the *Crusader*. Captain Rafe Dakota of the *Dark Traveler* will handle trade negotiations with the Khajari among the Rissilli, Griff, Ezredin, and Tarkia representatives, and those from the newly formed Xanthean colony. Many of whose delegates have only recently joined the negotiations. Ambassador Nohl, from the *Sentinel's* embassy, and Captain Tom Thorson will be handling trade negotiations with your team and the Alliance aboard the *Polestar*. As the Alliance ambassador, I listen, advise my team, and translate when needed."

When the initial talks ended, most of the Khajari delegation wanted to go to the *Sentinel*. The *Delve* was too small to take them, so Tom had many of the negotiation team go with him on the *Polestar's* shuttle. Jet took the *Delve's* pilot seat. She knew Henry was contacting the *Sentinel's* captain before the *Delve* left the *Crusader*.

The *Sentinel* was the largest ship orbiting Ezredin and entering just the docking bay impressed her guests. All major officers waited with Krayne in the docking bay with appropriate security contingents in view. Henry disembarked first, guiding the Khajari negotiators to Captain Krayne and First Officer Ribberdan and performing introductions. Kizz remained in the *Delve* after the rest of the Khajari disembarked.

"What should I call you?" he asked.

"Jezlynn always works," she told him smiling.

He took a breath before speaking. "I owe you an apology for my actions on Asedin and I am overlong in saying them."

"Did Kar ask you to do this?"

"No, although he was disappointed at my previous actions. He told me what you two had shared, and what you had accomplished. While you might have goaded me about my actions, you never took retribution."

"Only in escaping with the embassy team."

"Yes." He gave a reluctant grin. "Which taught me the valuable lesson to never underestimate anyone. I must also tell you I've learned things since then that have cemented my allegiance to my father."

"Kizz, I was never your enemy."

"Which you proved, and the Xantheans have informed me."

"Have they added you to their Amber Circle?"

"Yes, along with my father and the supreme leader. We all carry dronai. A somewhat surprising discovery."

She indicated the open hatch...he nodded and stepped through it. Following him, she noticed Chief of Transport officer John Olson's crew waited to secure the *Delve*. She nodded to him as she left the shuttle's gangway. "The rest of the piloting and security team remains on the *Crusader*, Chief of Transport Olson, to ensure security, but all the delegates wanted to visit the *Sentinel*."

He smiled. "As expected, Ambassador Chambers. When things are done here, the *Delve* will make a return trip to the *Crusader* and we'll get the crew back."

· Tom's shuttle was berthing, and she watched the process repeat as more delegates emerged into the docking bay.

"Please have the Khajari shuttle cleared and ready for launch, as they will be returning on it."

"Already prepared." He winked at her in an unprofessional manner, and Jesse nearly burst into laughter.

Walking to the main deck, she saw that Lu stood alone except for a few security guards. She guessed Ribberdan was performing the tour duty.

Lu smiled at her. "We'll wait here for the short tour to finish. How did it go?"

She noted T'Carta Kar's private shuttle already prepared for departure as she explained events on the *Crusader*. Finished with the important information, she added, "Kar's wife Gala hates me. What I have recently discovered is she is also related to the T'Kalz family. However, Kerub is working with some success to persuade the T'Kalz to join his government."

"When you addressed both by their given names rather than formal family name probably upset her," Henry said approaching.

"You met Kar and Kerub. What did you think?" she asked Lu.

"Both are astute and enamored with you."

She sputtered a laugh. "Kerub still feels he owes me for freeing him from slavery but sees me more like a sister than a potential lover. Kar and I are friends with a precise line of limits between us."

"He gave me this." He held a small, secured data clip. The screen showed her slave deed. He handed it to her.

"Free at last."

"Hopefully, you will not want to discard me."

Her smile widened. "Never."

Norma Hughes entered the area carrying one of the drinks Rae prescribed for Jezlynn's pregnancy. Jesse groaned, but Lu took the container and thanked Norma, who smiled at Jesse and immediately left. Lu watched her sip the container's contents. When she finished, he took the container and left to talk with John Olson on the other side of the bay. Gana returned. She walked to Jesse.

"You will address my husband by his full name and title during negotiations for our supreme ruler's mission, and you will not talk to him or to my son at any other time, or touch either of them."

"Did you decide to come on this mission to protect Kar and Kizz from me, or were you afraid of what they might learn?"

Gana slapped Jesse's face with a loud cracking sound. Jesse felt Sutta move, but she held up a hand to stop him. At the same time, a fast-moving Kizz appeared. Jesse had not seen him approach as she had watched Gana. His hand grabbed his mother's arm and pulled her away from close contact. Lu quickly returned to Jesse's side, looking furious.

"You will tell Kar nothing!" Gana shouted at Jesse.

"She doesn't need to," Kar said from behind Gana. Kerub stood next to him. "I already know who was responsible for my capture and slavery."

Gana looked shocked and stuttered. "How could you? Did she tell you? And you stayed?"

"I've always known. The T'Kalz who captured me talked freely, often informing me of my enemies' actions. They laughed about my gullibility. And why stay? To try and reestablish our relationship, and later for my son."

"It was fortuitous you knew where your wife might go when she disappeared from our tour," Kerub said in a calm and unemotional voice, which contrasted with the ferocious gaze he aimed at Gana. "When you have served Khajari as Jezlynn has, you may disapprove of her. However, always remember, I owe her my life and my freedom," he said the last in slow, stressed wording, "and Prince T-Carta stood by me when many Khajari threw me away, including members of your family. They will pay. Make sure you don't have to." As the remaining group returned to the docking bay, he bowed to the *Sentinel*'s captain. "Thank you for allowing us to view your magnificent ship."

Kar was less formal. "Thank you, Captain Krayne. We will leave now." He nodded at Jesse.

Within minutes, T'Carta's shuttle left the *Sentinel*'s docking berth. Shortly the *Delve* and Tom's shuttle left.

"Well, that was unexpected," Jesse said, aware the entire docking crew stood nearby looking livid.

Lu's hand gently encircled her arm, and he began leading her away.

"Where are we going?" she asked.

"Sickbay to have the bruise on your face treated."

As Rae finished treating Jesse's face, Lu was called to the bridge.

Jesse left sickbay and started for Lu's quarters but hesitated in the corridor. She just wanted to be entirely alone for a while.

::I can hide the tracer,:: Melany said.

::You can? Since when?::

::Since I was bored and looking for something to do after finishing the shuttles. I even know a place you can go.::

"Lu's busy so probably won't notice. I can leave through his office's back exit so no one will notice I've left. Lead on."

::There is a little-used viewing room in the embassy.::

::Why isn't it used?::

::The space view diverts many new visitors for a brief time, then they ignore it or become afraid of the view when in psiroute passage. With fewer embassy staff on the ship, and those busy on other issues, it has usually remained empty. Before you go, get the de-tracer from the bottom of our clothing drawer in the captain's quarters.::

A few minutes later, Jesse entered the lounge. Melany was right. The small viewing room held only two sofas and what had to be one of the largest windows on the *Sentinel*.

"How did I not know about this room?" She spoke aloud, asking in a more rhetorical than question way. Melany answered anyway.

::On the embassy deck, you have traveled the corridors to talk with your on-duty Rangers, or to meet with Ambassador Nohl in a meeting room, or you have gone to Margarete's apartment. You've always gone to your office to escape. I searched the entire ship.::

Jesse sat on a sofa and looked out on Ezredin. Except for the window's planet view, the room was dark and silent. Perhaps for the first time in two years, no one knew where she was. She briefly closed her eyes and felt an unusual comfort. The dim light from space diminished the darkness within the compartment, so it lacked the total blackout in after-work time in the mines, the hours when the supervisors withdrew all lights from the mineshaft where she and Kar had been kept. A place where one could only use touch or sound to move around. Gana's slap had brought back unpleasant memories. And she, for an ambassador, had acted in an unprofessional manner, reacting in anger rather than logic.

::*Kar used to talk to Maizka,*:: Melany said, ::*she could not hear or speak, so didn't know what he said until Lynn emerged. Experiencing only bad memories, May was always afraid, but Kar tried to protect her and offered comfort when the mine supervisors abused her.*::

"We've had an unusual life." She felt tears running down her face; she had never cried before and now she found she cried frequently.

::*We are all changing,*:: Angie said. ::*Becoming more like the original Jezlynn.*::

"Will we all merge?"

::*Maybe, but I doubt it. Jet and you are both too independent, and now that Angie and Melany are part of Chambers, neither of us wants to lose ourselves.*::

"What about our son, what will he think?"

::*As Margarete said, and Isobel told you, he will know it is his mother's normal existence.*::

She gasped as a hand touched hers. Twisting her head to see who it was, she relaxed as she recognized Lu's shadowed face. She hadn't heard him enter. He picked up the de-tracer device on the table before settling back on the couch. After glancing at her, he looked at the view, and Jesse judged he did so to relieve his distress...or anger.

"I needed to get away from everyone and everything for a few minutes. Melany devised the de-tracer device in her free time. How did you find me?"

"Rae alerted me when your monitor ceased working. When you weren't in our quarters and the system couldn't find your monitor's presence, I knew you had to be onboard. I had a surveillance check done to look for any solitary lifeforms." He looked at the device in his hand. "This hides the signal from your monitor..."

"Tracer."

"... but not life signs."

"I acted unprofessionally on the docking bay. I goaded Gana."

"She did most of that herself. This room holds a spectacular view while being both wonderfully quiet and peaceful. Are you facing your demons here?"

"Gana brought back some unpleasant memories. Have I upset you? I expected you to be tied up in duty a little longer. It is rather disquieting to remember things I never knew."

"I can only imagine. Are you all right?"

"Somewhat calmed, so yes. Let's go."

"Let me talk with Melany first, please."

Jesse relinquished control.

"My apologies. I didn't think about anything but what Jesse wanted...needed."

"I can understand Jesse wanting privacy, but do you know how important her mission is and what danger constantly faces her?"

"Well no, I don't. Nael and May were never much involved with either Jesse's or Jet's activities when they held control. And while May had many memories, there are few of when Jet or Jesse was in control. I would not want to endanger either." She nodded to the device. "It is a small prototype for something else Jesse asked me to try to make some time ago. I don't think she remembers even asking me to do it."

"Would you confide in me anything you design and its use?"

She regarded him briefly. "Your suggestion might be a good practice until I become more aware of what is going on, maybe even after. Perhaps we could set aside time where you can tell me more about Jesse's goals and problems?"

He smiled. "Good idea."

She looked out the window. "You should bring Jesse here more often."

"Maybe until it is discovered we come here. Then it will be used frequently."

"There are other places to escape on this ship; you just need to be inventive."

Within seconds Jesse was back. At her inquisitive look, he smiled. After a few minutes he pulled her to her feet. Jesse sighed, learning Sutta stood outside the door.

~ * ~

"Don't tell me you've already learned about the docking bay incident?" Jesse asked Tom, looking at him in their communication link.

"Gossip travels fast. You didn't tell me."

"There was no need. She thinks Kar's in love with me."

"Not about Gana but my father. You reimbursed his losses from our raid."

"He was your father. Even if he disowned you to survive, and even if we robbed him. However, in doing it, we did find Rafe, so we kind of owed him. I'm sure he wasn't aware one of his ships was carrying slaves."

"He thought I paid back his losses. The money just magically appeared in his business account. He explained everything, even his shame at disavowing me as his son, and knowing nothing about how his shipping lines were being misused." He looked away from the screen for a moment.

"It was a long time ago, Tom. You've finally talked to him?"

"Yes—at Starbase Constellation. Merit goaded me constantly. He was at Celeste, too, and now he is here. He is involved in the trade negotiations. Merit invited him to stay onboard. He seems remorseful."

"And you've worked hard to avoid any personal meetings with him. Are you going to try to restore a relationship?"

His lips formed a quickly-ended smile. "We have, sort of."

"Merit?"

"Yes. She never had family and now wants as many members as she can find...or invent."

"I hope you don't mean me?"

"Hell no. You've been family since you rescued me."

Seventeen

During the negotiations, Jesse, with Angie's help, and Jet's and Melany's advice, had argued and compromised on the travel protocols and routes. Surprisingly, T'Kalz Zef on the Khajari team had suggested the Xantheans should act as the neutral regulators and as arbitrators of any conflicts since it appeared they would be traveling space again. Alliance and Khajari approval of the proposal gave Aswenna a powerful place within the negotiations. While impartial on issues between the two negotiating factions, she was obdurate that Xanthean protocols would be observed.

In some ways, it did not surprise Jesse that the day before being asked, Aswenna had already agreed to join the regulatory negotiations—even before it was mentioned by T'Kalz Zef to Jesse. Aswenna explained what her part in the treaty would be to the genitor, finishing by giving Jesse an order. "You will go to Griff and design us three ships to Xanthean specifications with a mix of current technology. We have remembered the requirements for the Xanthean ships," she commanded, with what Jesse thought a lofty-looking Xanthean grin, but the demand pleased Melany.

The title genitor still annoyed Jesse, but during the following days of negotiation, Aswenna pointed out both the benefits and the problems regulating space might cause the Xanthean colony, telling the committee the Xanthians would decide on whether to agree or not, and almost instantly saying, "The colony knows the current agreements of the committee and so far agrees with them. We have a strong wish to reenter the universe as peacekeepers after our long retirement." Turning to Jesse she added, "You will be at Griff at least once a year to continue your trade business and to produce their ships. Five Xantheans have agreed to go with you to advise you on our requirements and help with the design."

"How do you know all this?" Jesse asked.

The committee members watched the interchange, unsuccessfully hiding their interest and mirth.

"Your Amber Circle informs me."

"Please, Aswenna, your Circle not mine." Jesse wasn't sure but swore the Xanthean's bony face wore a complacent expression.

After each day's meetings, and once all the delegate shuttles left the *Crusader*, Jet piloted the *Delve* back to the *Sentinel*. Lenoir Blunt kept in touch with the *Sentinel* for all the *Crusader*'s needs, so the *Delve* was often carrying cargo for the next meeting.

Although Angie helped in the negotiations, the work left Jesse feeling both mentally and physically exhausted. Stepping off the shuttle, Jet stopped and paused for a few seconds before moving on and switching to Jesse.

::Lucian may not be on the Crusader, but he watches and notices wherever you are on the Sentinel.:: Angie's thoughts prickled both Jet and Jesse as they thought he had stopped monitoring her.*::You need to call Tom. I've been thinking about and replaying some of the details and events leading to this soon to be finished treaty, and I have some misgivings.::*

"What is bothering you?" Jesse asked.

::Not with the negotiations on the Crusader, but other incidents. I'll tell you when I have more information,:: Angie replied.

Angie's tone of mind alarmed Jesse. In her daily talks with Tom and Rafe during the last five weeks, she knew they had mediated some intense talks and arguments. Ambassador Nohl, with Tom's and Rafe's help, had worked through their negotiations and already finished the trade agreements among the Alliance, Griff, Rissilli, and Tarkian representatives, which now also included other colonies like the traders from Çiro colony and even some Xantheans from Asedin City, who had shown up to participate.

After meeting with Aswenna and other Xantheans from Ezredin, she suspected those Xantheans might never return to Asedin.

Leaving the docking bay, she went to the lowest deck and her Ranger office. Jesse sat at her tender and opened a link to Tom. He looked pensive while he inspected her face. "How have your negotiations progressed?" she asked.

"I think everything on this side is completed. Nohl has approved the results and sent all the sign-off documents to Constellation. As soon as Nohl hears from President Uebel, and he returns the officially signed agreements, we're done...a few more weeks or so at most."

"We have a few more issues to wrap up to complete the travel treaty, but we are all in accord. Nohl should be sending those documents to Constellation soon. Angie has some misgivings, not about the negotiations, but about some of the players."

After a long hesitation, Tom spoke again. "Rafe and I have been talking," he said at last.

"And?"

"With all the ships from various companies arriving, and their requests to give information and receive permission from the Xantheans for commerce, we have both detected what we suspect are some dodgy applicants. With Aswenna helping you finish the travel regulations, we've missed her acumen on our attendees."

"Her accuracy tends to be scary, doesn't it? Will they shuttle to the new colony for the final festivity at the end of the negotiations and their signing? If so, the Circle will decide their reliability."

"Many have already indicated they would, but as I said, we still have doubts. Plus, Rafe's had a message from Adessa. She thought contacting you aboard the *Sentinel* too dangerous, so chose Rafe to relay her information. She had some knowledge about Ries Vaughn's alternate identity. Rafe now thinks he is someone who came aboard the *Dark Traveler* as a Çiro colony representative. He said they took a private shuttle groundside several times. If Vaughn, he probably has maps of the entire mine system. The mine still holds a tremendous fortune in minerals. Furthermore, we think news of Ezredin's Xanthean colony spread, which presents a possibility of others hiding on the planet. Some who might have arrived before the *Sentinel* came."

"It might be possible."

"It's possible the mines might have had other valuables stored in it."

"Like T'Kalz Smalik? Vaughn's partner in crime?"

"Yes, among other things. I've already forwarded Adessa's info to you."

Jesse swore. "I'll get back to you." Ending the call, she used her private link to T'Carta Kar. Finishing a brief conversation, she rose to her feet. Her hand slid over the ever-enlarging bump below her now nonexistent waist. It still surprised her but also filled her with a strange feeling of pleasure-dread and fear-lined hope. She checked where Lu was. His position appeared in one of the ship's more remote areas. She let him know she needed to talk with him in his office. Sutta had already risen from where he squatted near the door. "Ready to move, partner?"

When she had first called him such, he had looked puzzled. Within an hour he had looked pleased. She suspected he had contacted someone to discover the meaning.

He answered her in the deep-throated Xanthean word advance, which emerged like a growl and meant he would follow. She had at least managed to stop him from calling her genitor.

Arriving at the captain's office, she knocked and entered. Sutta followed her inside. She saw Lu was already seated at the less formal couches surrounding a low table with three late lunches laid out. She guessed for herself and Sutta and wondered who reported to him about her eating activities.

He smiled as she moved toward him and nodded for Sutta to join them, saying, "As you now report to Aswenna on these matters, join us." Sutta squatted Xanthean style at the table's end where the third plate waited.

She shot a glance at Sutta before sitting. Lu placed a plate in front of her, indicating with his hand that she should eat. Picking up a fork she took a bite while he leaned back and stared at her.

"I know you have information, but we'll eat first."

She found she was hungry. Once finished, but still chewing, she spoke. "Tom passed on some information from Rafe, along with some observations. A former associate of mine, and Rosche's, also passed on some compelling confirmation.

"Adessa?" Lu asked.

She huffed. "Tom and Rafe have reason to believe Ries Vaughn has been on one of the ships participating in negotiations, and T'Kalz Smalik might have landed groundside before the *Sentinel* ever arrived. I think the two are planning something."

"T'Kalz Smalik, cousin to the former Khajari ruler?" Lu asked. She read his initial reaction before he sat back in thought. Then his inscrutable look followed.

She looked at Sutta. "I know Xantheans always know about what topics interest them, but they often ignore dangerous situations. Do you know if they have searched the mines?"

Brief surprise and anger flashed on his bony face before he became self-absorbed, almost freezing in place.

"Tell me what you know," Lu ordered in captain's mode.

When she finished repeating Tom's information, she added, "All foreign ships are considered territorial ground and unassailable, so unless you have verifiable proof of a crime, which we do not have on Vaughn or T'Kalz Smalik, they cannot be arrested on any ship they are aboard. As you know, the human Çiroean colony has reason to dislike me. I have already notified T'Carta Kar."

He nodded. "Neither Tom nor Rafe identified Vaughn? Either amazing medical transformations or a unique disguise. They also might have been on Celeste when we were there."

"Yes. They probably waited for the *Sentinel*'s arrival. Several of the ships participating in the negotiations did. They might be behind the attack on you."

"It was aimed at you and only caught me by deflection. Perhaps, though, they still lay in wait for an opportunity to arrange another covert attack. Does Tom have images of them?"

She handed him her comlink. "These were from Adessa." The images showed a younger-looking admiral with different colored hair and facial structure, but the eyes were those of Ries Vaughn.

Lu looked at the images and handed her link back to her.

"Send copies to my tender." He looked at Sutta. "Does the colony know?"

"Informed already, but so far, no one identified," Sutta said. "Those on Ezredin have not been to the mines."

Jesse flashed a grin at Sutta. "That was quick."

Sutta's expression quirked in a Xanthean manner. Jesse turned her gaze back to Lu. "I have a suggestion."

Sudden alarm lined Lu's expression, and Sutta's position became more rigid. "What?" Lu asked.

"I suggest a trap." She waved a hand when she saw his objections form, and before he even spoke, she began laying out a strategy.

"No," Lu said emphatically, interrupting her. "You carry our child, and I will not allow either you or him to be endangered." He stared at her for a moment while Sutta uttered a Xanthan word of agreement.

"My mission is nearly complete, even if anything happened to me, the plan would not change. I really no longer need so much security."

"You will promise me right now that you will not do one thing toward carrying out any such plan or any other one you dream up."

"Or you'll put me in the brig?" At his enraged and adamant but concerned expression, she slowly exhaled, realizing she been holding her breath. Some things were far more valuable than others. "All of me promises that. We will be in your room every night and only carry out our assigned last duties of the negotiation completion on the *Crusader* and the resulting final celebration. What happens to those two scoundrels is no longer my concern."

"Jet promises, too?"

"Yes."

His look measured her truthfulness, knowing many of her previous actions gave him reason to doubt her, but she hoped he read her commitment.

"Good. Thank you."

When Sutta shared a look with Lu, she knew her promise backed with another. Since Lu never mentioned what he was doing in the *Sentinel*'s outlying areas, she also knew Lu wasn't telling her something. His tender chimed and he went to check it. He flipped the reception screen to the wall.

T'Carta Kar and Kalmona-Rek Kerub appeared on the screen. They asked for Jesse, too.

"You have security on?" T-Carta asked. Once assured, he asked, "You are sure of your information?"

"Yes," Jesse answered.

They discussed the various aspects of where to find the two malefactors. Kar added, "They may have more supporters than we think."

"You will stay out of all searches." Kerub's statement was clearly an order.

"I've already ordered her out of the mission, and she has promised me," Lu said.

"We seem to have switched positions," Jesse said, and at their reaction felt her lips firm. She added, "Besides, I am not sure what their reasoning is for this subterfuge. They can gain nothing at this point in the negotiations."

"This is about revenge," Kerub replied. He turned to Sutta. "Keep a close watch on her."

"They will be after both of you, so you also better keep a tight watch," Jesse said.

Lu and the two Khajari discussed security measures and possible capture before problems developed. Once they were in accord, the link ended.

Jesse left Lu to see her mother. Margarete was thrilled with how her participation worked out for Griff in the trade agreement. Isobel and Vanessa had returned from Ezredin to finish their plans with

Margarete. "Captain Dakota was so hospitable and added wonderful knowledge and insight to the negotiations. I am glad Griff will be his and eventually Captain Thorson's home base, too. Although I know you will spend much time here. Sit down, you look tired."

Jesse stopped rubbing her back and sank into one of the comfortable chairs.

"Have you picked out a name yet?" Isobel asked.

"No, although Punter sounds good."

"Kicking, is he?" Vanessa asked. "Norma told us everything is going fine."

Jesse closed her eyes and smiled while clenching her teeth. She took a breath. "Yes, and he kicks at the most inappropriate moments."

"Well, dear," Isobel said. "We know you are not used to interference from family, but with all the bossy women in your family, you have to expect help with Punter. And Norma, too, is very glad you recognize her as family. We will help in any way we can."

"I now think of her as both family and friend," Jesse said.

"She will be glad to hear it. Now that most of your mission is complete, you can begin to relax more," Margarete add.

She looked at her mother. "I'm worried..."

"About your mission? Rafe told me you have done an excellent job that is nearly completed," Margarete

"No, not about the treaty, but about my child and what he will think about such a...

strange... mother."

Isobel clasped her hand. "He will grow up knowing all of you and never doubt your devotion to both him and his father. And we will support you, and you will come to learn my devotion to you as my granddaughter."

Jesse felt unexpected tears on her face. "I've already learned that."

Isobel handed her a wipe. "Not entirely, not yet, but it will continue as long as I live." She sat back. "Well, at least you have four babysitters all lined up."

Margarete patted her shoulder. "It is amazing what is available on this ship. Did you know they have furniture and supplies for babies in the medical department? Norma showed us some. We asked Lu if we could outfit a room in your quarters. He's having ship maintenance form a room."

"What are you wearing to the final celebration of the treaty the Xantheans are planning?" Vanessa asked. "Margarete must, of course, attend."

"My mind is still reeling from the completion of negotiations. I haven't thought about what to wear, or even where the festivities will be held. One of the suit ensembles I've been using will be good enough, I'm sure. The *Crusader* will hold an end of negotiations gathering, but it is too small for a large affair. I haven't thought about Aswenna's plans to invite everyone to Ezredin's new colony for a celebration."

"Aswenna has already invited us to visit," Margarete said. "She is moving down immediately after your last meeting and asked us to stay."

Jesse gave a weak laugh but felt her chest freeze. "You want to stay aground for a while?" she asked Isobel. "A relief from ship life?"

Margarete sat down next to her. "We already know why you do not want to go groundside. We have talked to Aswenna and promise we will be with you."

Isobel added, "We've asked Lu if we might travel with you then, and he agreed. Believe me, it was hard to persuade him, but he said only if you agree."

"What? Have I been asleep through all these...negotiations?"

"No," Isobel said. "You've just been caught up in your own assignment, so we've sort of helped out. Even if all of us haven't been involved to formal government events before, Lu described a dress he thought would be suitable. We are working on that too."

"Let me think on this, please?"

Her family sat back and looked at her with worried expressions.

::Not worried, but commiserating,:: Angie said.

~ * ~

Days later, after the final discussions on the *Crusader*, legal representatives from both sides recorded the signing protocols and securities. Kalmona-Rek Kerub and other representatives signed the accord first. The record of Kerub's signing process included his negotiating team, and many from the Alliance's team, watching him to prove it was a unified negotiation decree. Jesse felt relieved. With Kalmona-Rek Kerub's signature duly recorded, Ambassador Nohl went through the same signing procedure. The copy was sent to Alliance President Uebel for legislative approval and signing. When it returned with the Alliance president's signature, the treaty would be completed.

With the document sent, a somewhat prolonged celebratory gathering of conversation, drinks, and hors d'oeuvres followed the signing. This time Lu was with her on the *Crusader*. Both Kar and Kerub spent a long time talking with him. While she spent time talking to the other delegates, she noticed how many Khajari conversed with Aswenna.

T'Carta approached her. A glance showed Gana stood by Kizz, nearly glowing with anger. T'Carta noticed, too, but ignored his wife. He told her how many of the Khajari delegates noticed the Xanthean's ability to reply to their thoughts before they spoke them. "It seems precognition is one of their abilities, but it comes with a total disregard for some salient information or activities."

"I've noticed that, too. They often overlook what appears obvious."

He smiled, nodded, and walked away to talk with Kerub.

Tired and noting many prepared to board their shuttles, Jesse let Angie take over. Angie inspected the crowd with interest, and a few delegates she knew approached with some inconsequential discussion. Feeling the urgent need for the hygiene facilities her pregnancy caused, she excused herself. Gana was just emerging from the lavatory. Jesse nodded and entered. Finished, she exited and felt a mask cover her mouth and nose. She jerked in reaction, but strong arms held her. In seconds, consciousness ended.

~ * ~

Krayne had watched Angie leave and guessed where she went. Sutta followed her. Minutes passed. Too many for her to be absent. Aswenna moved toward him with some urgency, grabbed his arm and pulled. "They took her."

She followed him into the hall outside the hygiene facility. Sutta lay unconscious and bleeding. Aswenna stooped next to Sutta and put the hands of one arm on his head. Krayne called Tom, who quickly appeared. Nohl, T'Carta Kar, Kizz, and Kalmona-Rek Kerub were behind him.

"Find your mother," Kar told Kizz, who quickly left.

Krayne contacted the *Crusader*'s flight captain. "Captain Swoboda, I need a list of all shuttles that have left or are leaving the *Crusader* and any shuttle that heads toward Ezredin from any ship within the last twenty minutes."

He turned to those surrounding him. "How the hell was she abducted?"

Tom was already checking the *Crusader*. He found a local interrupter canceling all cameras and audio in the short facility access area.

Lu contacted the shuttle's bridge. "Captain Swoboda, also get Major Chamber's tracking code from Commander Ribberdan. Send all information to the *Delve*, I'm taking the shuttle groundside." He heard T'Carta refusing Kerub's demand to help find Jezlynn, saying he would help find her, and heard Tom Thorson speaking further down the corridor but could not hear what urgent message he sent.

"Mother is not onboard," Kizz said. "If you go, I'm coming with you."

"If they took Jesse groundside," Rafe said, "you won't catch any monitor signal. They will undoubtedly take her into the mines."

Krayne turned to the ambassador. "Nohl, return to the meeting room and try to keep those remaining unaware of what has happened. Tell them we' have a problem on the *Sentinel*. Kalmona-Rek Kerub, please take your shuttle back to the *Azreal*, but first, go to the *Sentinel* and drop off Aswenna and Sutta. I will keep you informed of everything that takes place. Rafe, be on alert for any shuttles coming from Ezredin."

"No, Captain Krayne," Aswenna said. "You will take us to Ezredin where our healers already wait for Sutta. The Genitor's Circle will help you find her."

Lenoir Blunt spoke through Krayne's comlink from the *Crusader's* flight deck. "Found images, sir." He watched one of the tall Khajari traders drug Jezlynn. He opened his long robe and strapped her body to his and resealed his robe. He looked exactly as he did before hiding Jezlynn inside his garments. Gana was with him.

"That's D'Kelv Uve, a member of Gana's trading family. Gana took part," T'Carta said. "Kizz and I go with you."

Swoboda spoke. "Four shuttles have traveled groundside, Captain, but one's direction seems erratic. Sending info to *Delve's* com."

Heading for the *Delve*, Krayne expected to take the fight deck, but Tom forestalled him, having already slipped into the pilot's seat.

Eighteen

Jesse woke in total darkness. She lay on her back and groaned when she tried to sit up. Her bound ankles made it difficult to roll to her side. Manacles locked her hands behind her back. A massive headache made thought difficult. She ached everywhere. A strange undulating sensation crawled over her skin. She shivered. Squeezing her eyes shut, she shook her head. The pain blazed then reduced slightly. An acrid scent filled her with dread. She lay on a gravel surface. It induced panic.

Fear trembled inside as persistently as whatever quivered on her skin. "Got to get out of here." In the utter silence surrounding her, the fright in her voice hit her. She turned and twisted, trying to roll onto her knees. Terror threatened to overpower her. Her pregnancy bulge made moving more difficult. A thought halted her futile motions for a second. *I must succeed for Jedrick's sake.*

A snorted laugh greeted her. *::Already naming him?::* Jet said as Jesse fell onto her back, landing on her arms and manacled wrists.

::I guess I did. Jedrick Lucian Krayne.:: Her arms and shoulders hurt. She swore.

::Let me,:: Jet said, pushing her aside, *::and if Krayne agrees to it.::*

::*Check the shoe heels,*:: Melany spoke, sounding very shaken.

Taking control, Jet found the clothes hindered movement. "Damn skirt." She skootched downward until the skirt's hem reached her hips and swore between her grunts of exertion, using her fingers to pull upward on the fabric. Twisting to her left side, she braced herself on her elbow and push-pulled herself into a kneeling position.

::*At least I'm not alone,*:: Jet ejected a laugh. Jesse had worn the long-heeled shoes Jet hated as much as the other fashionable feminine-wear her other enjoyed. ::*At least you wore tights underneath.*:: She stretched backward, arching until her hands could reach her feet.

::*It runs the length of the right shoe's heel,*:: Melany said. ::*The base should pull off fairly easily.*::

::*When did ya do this?*:: Jet asked.

::*Not me, Nael, but he's now part of me, so I guess I did. This is so messed up; so were May's fears. He liked messing with Jesse's fashions. For security; for you.*::

::*Of course, being here altogether is a bit different,*:: Angie said.

::*We are all here with you,*:: Jesse said, more sensitive to Melany's angst. ::*This is not like before.*::

::*I know. Jet will protect us. It's just the memories are powerful.*::

A nail broke as Jet wedged the heel's covering off, but in the process of removing the heel's sole, the edge of the tool emerged. She pulled it free and cut the cord binding her ankles.

A voice spoke in the dark. "They left me here, too."

The voice spoke in Khajari.

::*Gana,*:: Jesse informed Jet.

::*She was outside the lavatory when I opened the door,*:: Angie added. ::*It was a trap. Hers. I'm sorry for my part. This is my fault.*::

::*Bullshit,*:: Jet answered. ::*They played her; she's not the planner and you're not a conniver or a fighter.*::

"Where are we?" Jet asked Gana in her language while she still struggled, tugging her hands to test the strong linkage.

::*It will cut through anything, so be careful,*:: Melany said. ::*This smells like the mine.*::

Jet cut through the cording at her wrists, slicing her left palm and fingers along with the cord, but pulled her arms forward while rotating her shoulders in a strain-relieving stretch.

"I'm not sure; a cave somewhere on the planet." Gana's voice sobbed. "I'm sorry, this is my fault. I didn't think my coconspirators would betray me and abduct me, too. We will both die here."

"Nonsense." Jet remained on her knees but quickly rose to her feet. "You didn't make the plans. Damn, I gotta go."

"Please do not leave me! Please!"

"Didn't mean go to leave." She backed several steps and bent to relieve herself during which Gana never stopped talking. The continual sliding motion over her skin made her shiver and increased to almost unbearable.

"No, I only helped the perpetrators escape the *Crusader* unobserved."

"T'Kalz Samlik and Ries Vaughn?"

"No. A third T'Kalz cousin of mine did the dirty work for Samlik. I don't know who else is involved. Samlik offered me power over Kar, power to take over his rule and gain Khajari recognition."

"D'Kelv Uve?" Jet asked as Jesse supplied the name. She rose. "Keep talking so I can locate you." Holding the sharp tool, she sliced the cumbersome skirt front and back and kicked off the shoes before she walked toward the voice that babbled excuses and apologies. Partway there, she stumbled over a body and fell. "Whose body?"

Gana choked on her sobs but finally answered "Uve. They murdered him for his help. He didn't know they planned to leave me here."

Running her hands over the body, Jet investigated the cage-clothing the Khajari wore. He had no weapons on him, or they had been removed. Jet pushed herself back to standing. "Have you learned nothing living with Kar?"

"He loved you." Gana sounded like she spat out the words, but anguish still filled her voice.

She touched Gana and the woman started and shrieked.

"Quiet!" Jet demanded. "Are your hands tied?"

"Yes," Gana said between sobs. "I've continually punished him when it should have been me receiving punishment."

Jet let her hands drift down Gana's back until she found the cord and carefully cut it. Gana pulled her hands away, and Jet heard her rubbing them together. Her hand followed down the woman's legs and cut the ankle bindings.

Gana's admission persisted. "It seems I've been extraordinarily shortsighted. I wanted you gone, wanted Kar to stop thinking about you. Now my family has betrayed me, probably planned it this way from when…"

"Did you hire them?" Jet interrupted her.

"No. They approached me. Uve, who is a first cousin to T'Kalz Smalik, contacted me. They both knew I hated you. They told me about someone who they assured me could rid the universe of your perverse presence."

"Ries Vaughn, do doubt. Did you help work out the plan?"

"No, it was Smalik's plan. My only part was getting you away from the group. I told them you wouldn't go anywhere with me, but to watch the facilities. You were pregnant and would have to go. The mask held a sleeping drug."

"They played you. Took you to punish Kar and Kizz. How long?"

"I don't know; hours, but not a day, I don't think. I have been awake the whole time. Smalik didn't care what happened to me. He blames Kar for his loss of power, so took his revenge out on me."

Jet heard the woman's gulps between gasping sobs. "Your disappearance is a bonus to their persecution of Kar. Vaughn wants me gone for the trouble I've caused him."

"Kar loves you." Gana sighed. "More than me."

Sudden memories of this place filled Jet's mind as Melany seemed to envelop her. She shook her head, which made the subdued ache increase but warned Melany to back off. "Nonsense. You are all he talked about when I was here with him." It was strange to recall those memories.

Melany gave Jet another memory of the cave. She felt May's fear and pain. It made Jet dizzy.

Gana didn't seem to be listening. "How could he love me? I caused him to be here." She choked. "We can't escape. We can't see anything."

"Don't need to see. Stand up, kick off your shoes, and put a hand on my back. Follow me when I move." Jet rose, picked up some rubble from the mine's floor, and threw it, listening for where it fell. Soon she knew the direction of a wall and started taking steps toward it. She heard Gana behind her. Once at the wall, she braced her hands against its rocky surface. She ordered Gana to remain where she was while she traveled down the roughhewn wall. When she finally came to the corner, she felt up and down the corner's edges, and her swiping fingers found the carved symbols Melany described, designating the site within the cave. She barked a laugh. Even slaves could be crafty. She tried to shake off whatever crept across her skin.

A sudden bolt of light seemed to flash through her body. She fell to her knees and felt arms encircle her.

~ * ~

Before Tom even landed the shuttle, Krayne saw Xantheans already gathered near the landing site. He helped Aswenna get a now conscious Sutta to his feet and out of the shuttle. Her people already waited and helped move their injured member to safety. Krayne immediately pulled his comlink and searched for Jezlynn's location. Tom was right...it found no signal.

T'Carta followed him out of the shuttle. He stood looking at the landscape, turning to get different views, and pointed toward some hills. "It has changed greatly, but the mines, they are ten kilometers in that direction." He turned to a nearby Xanthean, speaking their language. "Have any of your settlers investigated there?"

The Xanthean replied in a guttural, "No."

Aswenna, now that Sutta was in the care of other Xantheans, came to them. "They have been busy rebuilding and restoring the community's dwellings. No one has explored much." She sighed. "Nor do they feel any dronai here."

"Captain Krayne," Ribberdan's voice emerged from his comlink.

"Yes, Commander Ribberdan."

"A small shuttle just took off from near your location. Its direction indicates it is heading to a Çiro ship. Sending your comlink the takeoff site."

"Make sure the ship is detained. Send both of Major Chamber's Rangers squads to the ship with SSC security as backup. They have my authority to board and investigate. Send them in one of our armed shuttles."

"On it, sir. Gunnerman was already preparing."

Krayne turned to Aswenna and asked, "Do you have any ground transport?" just as one settled nearby.

"From your ship," she answered. "Since our first landing."

He nodded. "Thank you."

Tom had already moved to take the driver's seat, but the Xanthean, already in place, remained unfazed by Tom's ferocious look. He waved Tom to a seat behind him. T'Carta Kar and Kizz both took seats as he slid into the one next to Tom. He noted three other Xantheans held the back seats. He had barely strapped in when the craft moved forward at a fast speed.

As the craft approached the cliffs rising before them, T'Carta Kar spoke, giving the driver directions to the mine's entrance. They all ran to the entrance, but once there, Kar slowed. Kizz put a hand on his father's arm. Kar looked at Kizz and moved into the mine's entrance.

The Xantheans with some forethought had brought elume lamps, but Krayne noticed the nostrils of their bony faces expanding and contracting in quick motions. One said, "Dronai."

His gaze returned to his comlink. "I have a faint detection of Jezlynn's medical monitor. They're down there."

"Let's go," Tom said. They hadn't traveled twenty meters before they heard an explosion. The floor of the mine shook, and further ahead the walls along the tunnel began to collapse.

~ * ~

Noise roused her. She heard someone crying and screaming for her to wake up. She felt both awful and revitalized. Realizing arms clung to her, she remembered where she was.

"Please, please, wake up. We have to get out of here."

Memory returned like a swift kick. The all-enveloping darkness brought back horrible memories and fear.

"We will, Gana, just give me a minute." She shoved herself to her feet with one arm braced against the rock wall. Gana's hands clutched her but it felt like she pulled the woman to her feet, not vice versa. Then Jezlynn heard and felt the rumbling within the mine's shaft. She pulled Gana close and backed up against the wall she had been following which at least felt stable. Some rocks broke loose from wherever the ceiling was and fell around them. Gana screamed again. "Upper level cave-in," she murmured.

"Must have been a planned explosion," she spoke to herself. "They wanted us to live through it...prolong our agony of being trapped down here. Stop that!" she yelled at Gana.

"We're never going to get out," the woman said, continuing her crying jag.

"Yes, we will. Lucian and Kar will look for us. It isn't hard to figure out where they might have taken us. Vaughn wanted revenge. They planned well to circumvent all security. Of course, Vaughn's an expert at that." The mine had settled into stillness, but the acrid dust from the explosion filled her nostrils. "We're okay now, and I doubt they planned multiple explosions. Let's go." Wrapping her left arm around Gana, she used her other hand's fingers to roam over the wall while she walked along its edges. She finally found a message carved on its sides and read the symbols. She knew her location. Although memories of her surroundings filled her mind, she followed in the direction she needed to go while repeating a mantra: *That was past, this is now.* She knew they were four levels down, but whoever left them had not strayed far from the main tunnel's path through the mine.

"They never considered I knew another way out."

"What?" Gana asked.

"Nothing, just remembering."

Gana clung to her, so she released her tight grip on the woman's shoulders but still helped her to move through the dark abyss. Her fingers trailed along the tunnel's wall. Gana stumbled often in rocky rubble lining the mine's floor. The rocks and uneven footing battered her feet, too.

"I am sorry," Gana persistently said, breaking the silence. At least her sobbing had stopped. *She's reached hopelessness. I did once, too.* She felt a tinge of sympathy for Gana.

Keeping her fingers feeling for the wall's markings, she and Gana followed the path upward until reaching another directional marker. She started down one of the ancillary tunnels.

"Where are you going?" Gana asked in a terrified tone.

"To another exit. I hope you can climb."

After walking for what seemed like hours, she saw the reflection of water. Gana had finally fallen quiet. The sheen of strong light showed through the upward tunnel.

She stopped. "Quiet. Did you hear that?"

"What?"

"Listen." The sounds of movement filtered to her.

Gana screamed. "Kar!"

Jezlynn kept walking to the light, pulling Gana along. She noticed movement ahead. "Kar remembered, too."

Shortly elumes appeared ahead of them, the light from one landing on her clothing. Commotion broke out as shadowed figures rushed toward them.

She felt arms wrap around her, but her mind was numb. She knew someone carried her and all thought ended. Awareness returned once she emerged into daylight. They were at the top of a ridge with their rescuers walking about. Her captain sat next to her, dirt covered and distraught. "You found us." She cringed; no 'us' remained. She looked down at her ruined and dust-covered clothing, her hands and feet were covered in dried blood and bruises. The crawling sensation on her skin remained.

A Xanthean voice spoke next to her in their language. "Dronai. You attracted them." She looked at him, unable to respond. His bony face looked exultant. "They came to all of us."

A blanket was wrapped around her and within minutes she was helped into a ground transport. She turned her head to stare out the vehicle's side window.

She heard Krayne answer his comlink but didn't hear the message. He told someone, "We have them."

His hand gently held her injured one. He uttered a "Damn," probably from feeling the dronai feeding on her injuries. Her skin and places inside her body still felt a slithering-like sensation. She glanced at him, but her own changes overwhelmed her, so she said nothing. Once at the Xanthean colony, Krayne helped her out of the transport. Aswenna and Ahjias waited.

"Sutta?" she asked.

"Recovering," Aswenna said. "He apologies for his failure."

"He did his duty and was injured in carrying it out; he should earn only praise."

"I will tell him, Genitor," Ahjias said.

Jezlynn flinched at the title. They removed her clothing. Bathing removed the crawling feeling afflicting her skin. When done, a Xanthean carried the water outside and poured it into the ground.

Ahjias gave her fresh clothing.

Aswenna stood nearby. "The effect will slowly rescind. The mine's dronai recognized those in you. They have melded and journeyed with you here to our city. They will slowly spread across the planet." They led her back to Krayne, who took her arm and guided her to the shuttle. She noticed all onboard staring at her. Gana was next to T'Carta, also clean and wearing different clothing. Everyone was clean.

"You okay?" Tom asked.

"Define okay."

Tom looked shaken and glanced at Krayne. She started shaking again and was quickly guided to a seat.

"What has happened?" Krayne asked.

She looked at his worried-looking face. "They are gone."

"The dronai?"

"Did you feel them?"

"Yes. We all did. Everyone found it a little disconcerting.

"That's not what I meant."

"Your other selves are gone?"

"Yes." The thought filled her with remorse and grief.

"No, they aren't, they are all a part of you...Jezlynn?"

"I think so. It is hard to tell. On the *Constant* everyone used to call me Jay for my initials JA, but I suspect I've had so many aliases, only my given name will work now."

"You remember?"

She looked out the window. "Everything...I remember everything."

"How do you feel?"

"Abandoned."

His hand grasped hers in warm comfort. She squeezed it back wondering...*how can he love a freak like me?*

She smiled in frustration leaving the shuttle. Doctor Rae already waited on deck. "Did I doze off?" she asked Krayne. "I don't remember hearing you contact her."

Krayne's answering smile changed as she cramped over in sudden pain.

Nineteen

After leaving sickbay, Krayne went to his office, hearing many congratulations on the birth of his son as he walked the corridors. He had stayed next to Jezlynn through the whole delivery.

Once holding their son, Jezlynn told him Jesse picked the name Jedrick Lucian, but if he wanted to choose something else, she understood. He told her Jedrick Lucian sounded perfect. Jedrick was a bit early, but Doctor Rae said with all that had been going on, not unusual, and Jedrick was of a good weight and seemed very healthy. Both mother and son slept.

He had stopped to talk with Margarete, Isobel, and Vanessa who sat in the waiting room. Rae came out to show the excited women to Jedrick's bassinet.

Rae told him Jedrick's body already held dronai.

"How will it affect him?" he asked, a thread of worry worming through him.

"I don't know. Outside of Jezlynn's changes, it hasn't affected you or anyone sharing the organisms other than giving a more youthful appearance, increasing injury healing, and some cognitive function increases. The Xantheans might have more information. We'll watch him as he develops and look for possible changes."

Lu needed sleep, too, but in traveling to their quarters, the crews' congratulations pleased him. He felt pleasure not only in the greetings but also in knowing both Jezlynn and Jedrick were safe, although Jezlynn's mental condition still caused concern. She mourned her others. He did, too, but knew they were all integrated into her.

Ribberdan and Gunnerman had both come to him in sickbay with reports about the capture of those onboard the escaping shuttle. Her abductors were in separate brigs. Kerub had demanded custody of T'Kalz Smalik. Ries Vaughn sat in the *Sentinel*'s brig. The flight crew remained on the Çiroean shuttle, claiming they had no idea about the illegal plans of their passengers. The ship would stay in Ezredin space until cleared of all malfeasance. He smile-grimaced. That became a Xanthean problem and perhaps a surprise for the ship's crew.

Others who acted as staff for the trade negotiations were arrested. They would be transported to Ezredin for the Amber Circle's justice. He doubted the verdict would be too onerous. T-Omer's staff executed extensive identity searches proving previous criminal actions by many. So, after Xanthean justice, they faced more retribution from their colonies or the Alliance. The *Sentinel*'s brig was now at near capacity. He suspected the Çiroean Xantheans would know one way or another about the ship's flight crew, so they wouldn't escape either.

Inside his office, he checked his tender and found messages from President Uebel and Admiral Wakeman. His first reaction was to wait until morning, but he sat down to read them and smiled at the content. Uebel's message was full of congratulations on the completion of their important mission, saying the treaty documents were signed and would be returned within days.

Wakeman's message changed both his and Jezlynn's duties. Throughout his career he had wanted to explore the vast edges of the Galaxy. Now his orders placed his ship in the one place he wanted to remain. At the Alliance president's and legislature's request, Wakeman issued the orders that the *Sentinel* would remain an embassy ship covering a starbase's duty and business. As Jezlynn's mission was successfully completed, Uebel had ended her service in the military. Krayne briefly wondered how she would feel about her release from duty. His report on the remote sections of the ship had been handed to the embassy for further ideas on development.

He had showered and redressed in sickbay immediately on returning to the *Sentinel* even after cleaning up in the Amber Circle's colony. The creepy feeling slithering on his skin finally ended. His relief at Jezlynn's safe recovery and the long hours of his son's delivery had left him exhausted. He found his bed and closed his eyes, thinking how much he missed his wife's presence next to him.

Ten hours later Krayne was in his office and back on duty. Howard alerted him T'Carta Kar and Supreme Ruler Kalmona-Rek Kerub wished to speak with him and waited in the adjutant's office. Krayne told him to let them enter.

T'Carta had been onboard since the *Delve* left Ezredin's surface, waiting for a shuttle to the *Azreal*, and Krayne suspected, news on Jezlynn. He noted during the trip the man had kept a careful eye on both Jezlynn and Gana. Of the too, Gana had looked the most shaken and unsure.

A message arrived that Supreme Leader Kalmona-Rek Kerub's shuttle had docked in the *Sentinel*'s bay, and the supreme leader was asking to talk with the *Sentinel*'s captain. Upon entering, Kerub spoke first. "Thank you, Captain, for allowing me to join your policing operation to capture the perpetrators. I owe Jezlynn more than anyone, except perhaps Kar. Jezlynn changed me. Besides rescuing me from slavery, she made sure I learned how to survive and gave me the means to do more than to cower in fear and anger while hiding my existence. I owe her."

Krayne smiled. "She won't think so, and I know she admires your courage and determination."

"And I am glad Jezlynn has you and congratulate you on the birth of your son, Jedrick," T'Carta told him, smiling. "Unfortunately for Gana, she has a long way to go to regain my regard but is taking steps to do so." He hesitated, looking at Krayne.

"You do not need to tell me." He took a breath. "And I understand some about Gana. I know the effects jealousy can have."

"We will eventually come together. She is very remorseful and not even Kizz has yet forgiven her. You, however, do deserve to know Jezlynn's history with me. Usually I worked alone in the mine, knowing full well how I was targeted, captured, and why. The T'Kalz informed me. They felt I was not worthy of death like so many others from my family. My actions on Khajari injured their family's reputation, and I needed physical repayment for my treachery. It was a dark and dry mine and as good as a cage. I was kept separate from the other slave miners. They brought lights so I could crack rocks and load them in a conveyor. They took the lights when they left, leaving me where I could feel the walls and floor, hear sounds, smell the mine, but see nothing."

"They mined pyrite for space power collectors."

"Yes. An unpleasant smell one eventually grows used to. They abandoned me to the total darkness with some water to drink and little food. Occasionally they brought me used garments when what I wore fell apart. I never knew how many hours I worked, or how long I stayed in the dark, but I did explore it. Discovered the other slave miners did, too. Learned to communicate with them. Later, I learned I'd been down there seven years."

"When they first brought her to me, her face and body bore black bruising. My two Khajari supervisors branded her, telling me even an insignificant Khajari noble such as I deserved at least one servant. Later, they whipped her instead of me for my supposed crimes. She writhed in pain but when she screamed, no sound emerged. They left her bleeding. They laughed, too, about her probably not surviving, but then, a leader like me probably only deserved a dead servant. I did not think she would survive long either. She lay in the mine's dust and rubble. Even in the total darkness, I knew her blood covered me and soon felt a tingling sensation like something crawled on me. I constantly brushed it away but there was nothing there."

He rose and went to the window. Krayne thought so that neither he nor Kerub could see his face.

"She was unconscious for a long time, lying still on the mine's floor next to where I slept. They didn't even check her when they brought back the lights and ordered me to resume my royal duty of hacking rocks. When they left again, I touched her neck. A pulse remained. Whenever I finished work, I'd touch her hand or neck to check if she still lived. When she did, I poured water into her mouth, and she would swallow. She remained alive. Her pulse even grew stronger. I don't know how long it was before she touched my hand when I touched hers. Time was...uncertain.

"When she recovered enough to stand, they made her work with me. She could not do much at first, but they still put ankle chains on her and chained us together before they left. She never spoke, not for the longest time. Only when they had the lights on for us to work did I see what she looked like and how she healed. We both occasionally bathed using the drinking water. The supervisors liked to use her, especially in front of me. They called her Maizka, my whore. Afterward, I would hold her as she cried. I could not help myself and used her too but did not take her savagely. Then one time after the supervisors left, in the total dark, she began singing. Much later I learned what had happened to her mind. It changed nothing. She gave me a purpose to survive."

"How did you escape?" Kerub asked.

"Once a supervisor was called away from watching me to where a gang of miners worked. What they never realized was the miners often had interesting perspectives on their underground spaces. Once, while wandering in the dark, I saw the sky reflected in a small pool of water. At first, I thought it was my imagination, but it reappeared whenever I went that way. I took her there so we could bathe in the pool. I also knew of a hiding place as the supervisors seldom explored the surroundings. The same supervisor was called away again. While he was gone, I sent her into hiding. When he returned, I was ready.

"He approached too close, sneering, asking where my whore was. She surprised me. She stood behind him and smashed a rock against his head. I finished killing him with my miner's tool. Knowing we had little time, I grabbed the bits of dry rations I had been storing and forced Maizka to climb ahead of me up the small crevice above the water. Once outside, I discovered it was night. Even starlight was an amazing thing to behold. It took days to become accustomed to the brightness of daylight."

T'Carta kept silent for a few brief seconds. His anger was palpable to Krayne and he saw the same in Kerub's expression.

"After the total darkness of the caves, the night held enough light to see. I found a small stream emerging from the rock. Inside was another small cave where we stayed until I was sure no one searched for us. After several nights of crawling out of the cave at night, I noticed lights in the distance and knew a community existed. I knew about the small colony from the talk between the two supervisors and from talking with the other slaves. We walked to the community during the night. It was a human colony, and while some of them worked in the mines, they had never encountered a Khajari before. I told them I had crashed my shuttle and gave them the name of a Khajari to contact; one who I knew would help me. We were both lucky to escape."

"Your remaining supervisor didn't hunt you?" Krayne asked.

"I knew both of my keepers, both cowards." Venom filled his voice. "Neither was high on any T'Kalz hierarchy." He huffed a dry laugh. "Neither was Gana. When I escaped, I knew his first response would be to run before any T'Kalz with any power came to punish him. Later I found out who operated the mine."

"Admiral Ries Vaughn?"

"No, but close. One of his business friends from Regent Lines. The minerals we mined were exported through the company's shipping lines. He may have given permission for my imprisonment, but I doubt he knew who I was. Once at the colony, Jesse, as she called herself then, told me she needed to report back to the Space Corps. I needed to reestablish myself so let her go. Later I hunted down the remaining supervisor. Jezlynn will never need to fear him again."

"Thank you for helping save her once more," Krayne said. "You leading us to that vertical shaft into that cave saved time."

"I'm surprised she remembered it was there, certainly fortuitous." T'Carta looked at him. "I am glad she found you, and the saving worked both ways. She let me keep my sanity. If she has totally reintegrated mentally, you might face some difficulties."

"I know. She faces some hurdles, but I think Jedrick will help."

"And you. Don't let her obsession with you become overwhelming," Kerub said.

Krayne smiled. "It is a mutual obsession."

"We need to return to the *Azreal*, but we both wished to speak with you first," Kerub said. "I have heard from the T'Kalz remaining on Khajari, and from those who served on this mission. They all want T'Kalz Smalik brought to justice. He has brought shame to their name, so letting them give judgment on his crimes will serve many purposes. The *Azreal* is under preparations to leave, so we came to wish both you and Jezlynn goodwill."

Shortly after they had left, Lu returned to duty. His mind reeled with everything that had happened and with his worry for Jezlynn. His exultation for Jedrick's birth also interrupted his thoughts. Gratefully, Henry and Ribberdan told him they would share bridge duty until things settled down. He checked in with his adjutant Howard for any problems. Howard reported most ships orbiting Ezredin had departed. Krayne checked his tender for messages and finished a few reports before heading to the sickbay.

Jesse was in one of the few private rooms, showing Doctor Rae still worried about her reaction to sickbay. In the anteroom to the private area, Isobel sat holding Jedrick. Vanessa sat next to her daughter. It seemed his son's grandmothers were already there helping with their grandson's care. Vanessa sang lullabies to Jedrick.

Krayne stood watching them, knowing he knew no songs of comfort to sing to his son, and knew little about childcare. Upon noticing his presence, Margarete turned to him with a worried look. He smiled at Margarete, saying, "She will come around." He moved to briefly take Jedrick from Isobel's arms, awkwardly holding his son. Isobel smiled at him as Jedrick made a few newborn noises, but his son's eyes stayed closed. He gazed at his son for a few minutes before returning him to Isobel's arms.

He became aware Rae stood next to him. "You will learn."

"That obvious?"

"It's rare to see alarm in a captain's eyes. Those women will be very happy to show you. Jezlynn remains very quiet."

"That's very true, Lucian," Isobel said. "It's not that hard."

He walked into her private room. He had informed Rae of his wife's change when he first brought her to sickbay from the shuttle. She later informed him that while the level of dronai in her body seemed elevated, her mind showed reintegration.

Jezlynn sat in a chair near the bed, expressionless, or maybe warily watching him enter. He pulled a chair up, sat, and returned her regard. "Our son is a treasure beyond belief."

She smiled but kept silent.

"Can you tell me what happened?"

She explained the events in the mine, finishing, "When Jet touched the cave wall and felt the wall codes, that same crawly feeling crossing her skin, but…I don't know, it somehow increased and extended right through her with a shock. Everything went black until I felt Gana help me get off my knees. I knew what I had to do so followed the wall's symbols. I could read the wall codes and knew the direction to go.

"I understood I was me but different. It has been very strange. Aswenna said dronai in the mine caused my reintegration. Those in the mine recognized those in me. It seems we all carried dronai back to the settlement. The Amber Circle has declared the mine a sacred spot. She said my presence reinvigorated the mine's dronai, and the few Xantheans who entered the mines said they felt welcomed and shared bonding. The dronai from our bathing waters have reestablished within the colony's grounds. They are very pleased. "

"And?"

Her lips quivered in a manner reminiscent of May, but her gaze held the introspection of Angie. "Doctor Rae said my invasive symbiote level has increased but is lowering." She looked desolate. "And both you and Jedrick are infected. How can you want me?"

"First off, it is not an infection, but as Aswenna said a symbiotic relationship. All humans share their bodies with other life forms. These seem to be helpful ones. And why wouldn't I want you? You wanted me, gave me your love and the greatest gift I've ever received is our son."

"Can you get me out of here? Please?"

"Problems?"

"Bad memories and trouble sleeping."

"Let me go talk to Doctor Rae."

~ * ~

"Where are you going?" Margarete asked Jezlynn as she emerged fully dressed from her room.

"To an interview," she answered as she moved toward the door. "Since Jedrick has babysitters here, it is a good time."

"Does Lucian know?"

She closed her eyes, then glanced at her mother and grandmothers who had invaded Lucian's quarters after he had left for duty. "I'm a grown and independent woman, Mother, and can make my own decisions. I'll be back in thirty minutes or so." She escaped. It seemed like a replay as she guessed her mother would contact Lucian. Margarete liked Lucian. Sutta waited in the corridor and rose to follow her. It was a relatively short walk to the first deck and the brig. Before she arrived, a smug-looking Lu walked next to her.

Once inside the brig, he led her to where former Admiral Vaughn was imprisoned.

Ries Vaughn didn't move from where he sat on the bunk in his cell. His masculine attractiveness remained. His dyed hair was growing out showing the natural gray. He did look at those standing outside his enclosure. "Too bad you escaped."

"Why the vendetta against me? Why against the Dachs?"

"Like you, to prove I could. And I did." He rose. "You look nothing like Vanessa."

She didn't respond.

"You also caused me a great deal of trouble on the *Constant*. Without that crew you worked with, the ship never would have returned, and I would not have had to make so many defensive moves to protect my actions. Simple. Then you returned. I had to prevent more problems, and you needed to pay for your audacity. None of your Dachs family ever had your resolve...or cunning. The Dachs were simple. I wanted their power." He rose and walked to stand in front of her. "You are far more beautiful than when you first returned from this planet and I sent you to the Rangers."

"I hadn't fully recovered from slavery."

"A mistake on my part. Who could have guessed? What do you want to know? I think you probably know of all my misdeeds."

"I don't want to know anything, just get a little payback by seeing you where you belong. I think you are a master manipulator, so I couldn't trust anything you said anyway. And you are right, I know a lot of the crimes you have committed, and I've handed over the validated proof to the proper authorities. Goodbye, Vaughn." She turned and left.

Twenty

"Are you sure you can go to Aswenna's gathering?" Krayne asked, circling the training mat following Jezlynn's movements. He knew her gratified that her mother and grandmothers took so much care of Jedrick, freeing her to other duties. She often complained they had to believe her incompetent as a mother since they took over so much of Jedrick's mothering.

"I promised Isobel I would go, and since being in the caves again, they don't hold the same terror for me as they did for Maizka. And although I dislike being treated like some exalted being, I don't mind going down with you. Aswenna asked that we bring Jedrick with us."

She lashed out with a kick which he evaded while moving closer and grabbing her. With her response, they both hit the mat.

"I know," he said. "Our revered elder has invited many people. You have Jet's physical talent."

"Maybe, maybe not. She and Gunnerman trained you too well; you win too often."

He rolled to a sitting position while catching his breath, noting Jezlynn was breathing hard, too. "You are grumpy. The dervish still insists I participate in training. He said you will participate, too. His objectives have coalesced into determination since his promotion. Did you know your insistence on Ranger training proved very helpful in capturing those involved in your abduction?"

"I thought you released the Çiroean ship?"

"After extensive interrogations, which T-Omer and Gunnerman performed to clear the basic flight crew of any involvement. Kalmona-Rek and I both gave permission for it to leave. Most of the tradesmen were under Ries Vaughn's influence. They used weapons against the squad entering their ship but were unprepared for what the Rangers dished out. They had a few trained guardsmen onboard, too, but again, not as good as your Ranger squads."

"Anyone..."

"A few injured, all survived and took down all the offenders. Gunnerman claims their success was due to the increase in physical and combat training you demanded. Roberre told me the training initiative helped in an incident on Celeste, too. Did you know he ordered the drill into all Ranger training?"

"They're the fighting arm of the military and it is included in initial training."

"But not so much after initial training, or when at peace, or assigned space duty. Starbase Celeste's Admiral Otrika reported Colin Colend was found guilty of inciting and arranging riots. The Ranger squads there subdued them and pursued the investigation. They discovered who had arranged the attack on you, done at Vaughn's orders." He smiled. "One more nemesis eliminated. Colend remains in a brig, too, headed for the SSC prison on Constellation along with Vaughn."

"It has given Tom a sense of sublime completion to deliver Ries Vaughn to Starbase Constellation and a life-prison term. I doubt Wakeman will give any credence to anyone representing or supporting the Alliance's biggest scoundrel."

"Nor will President Uebel. Not with all the media coverage that Sal Imada's journalistic submissions have inspired. Aswenna also informed me that all the Xanthean colonies are sending new initiates to Amber Circle, and others are coming to sit amid the sacred dronai hoping some will wish to travel back within them when they return to their own circles. Are you prepared for Aswenna's festival?"

"Festival?" She swore in a very Jet-like way.

"Yes, it has expanded from a celebratory gathering. Your Pilgrim Lines ships and crews are all in orbit here, as are many Alliance and Khajari representatives. Isobel and Vanessa are helping Margarete make plans."

"Margarete will be returning to Griff soon."

"Isobel and Vanessa go with her. And I understand Aswenna has given you a mission there. I'm thinking I might deserve a vacation, and Griff sounds great. In the meantime, I believe they have an outfit for you to wear. Since going groundside all three women have dronai now. Aswenna thinks your genome drew the dronai to them."

"Margarete isn't of my genome. If she has dronai, something else attracted them."

He hesitated. "It seems all three Dachs men have dronai, too."

"Morgan?"

"Yes, although Aswenna doubts his mind will ever fully recover. She claims he is more childlike than adult. They will care for him."

"Does he have memories of what he did?"

"Aswenna didn't say. She told me Vanessa had visited with her brother and introduced her daughter to them. Something she knows elated both Reed and Austin. She reports all three men work very hard helping the Xantheans in the physical rebuild of the community, but Morgan needs constant direction and help. Austin is very interested in developing crop-fields and has made several Xanthean friends."

"I am glad they are not estranged, but I never would have believed humans and Khajari would want to live with Xantheans, or vice-versa. Strange."

"Admiral Wakeman informed me the Alliance has ships delivering the new components for the Starbase Amber."

Jezlynn swore again.

He sighed. "Enjoy the peace and entertainment while you can."

She stretched and rose. "Now that I am no longer Elite or Meat, I'm looking forward to helping with a starbase's construction." She grinned at him. "And I'm extremely glad to be free of security."

Krayne only smiled and rose, pulling her up to face him. "Sutta has joined T-Omer's security contingent and will act as a joint Xanthean-Alliance security officer. Gunnerman, of course, has taken your position."

"Yes, I know. His authority will expand with the ship turning into a starbase. Jedrick has taken me out of many command situations while I was on leave. I seem to be somewhat out of the information loop. So Sutta will be stationed onboard." She shook her head. "So many changes."

Entering their quarters, Jezlynn found Jedrick in the care of his grandmothers. For so recent a dronai infection, she noted their changes. They all looked healthier and stood straighter. Isobel brought Jedrick to her. She smiled and moved her shirt to feed him. They watched in satisfaction.

"Never dreamed I would see this," Vanessa said, her eyes glowing with emotion. "My grandson, and with my daughter and great-granddaughter."

"We have had an outfit made for Aswenna's celebration," Isobel said.

"So Lu has informed me," Jezlynn said, smiling at them.

"All Isobel's work," Margarete said. "I've heard from my farm manager. You will have to work another date into your schedule."

"Henry and Illa?" she asked.

Margarete smiled at her. "You are so discerning. Yes. They are getting married. Guess what else? Some Xantheans might move to Griff. It seems your dronai, or some others, have been discovered on Griff, near my farm of all places."

"It seems," Lucian said from behind her, "remarkable changes have also been noted in Bear Barunoski and Gale Jaynes."

Lucian's mention of the two *Constant* crewmembers who worked on their own ship, the *Compelled Pilgrim*, one of the Pilgrim Lines ships, grabbed her attention.

He continued, "A doctor acquaintance of Rae's on Griff, who services Barunoski's life support equipment, reported that his organs and body functions seem to be regenerating, and Gale Jaynes's facial scars are drastically reduced. He felt both of their attitudes have turned optimistic."

"Aswenna said the dronai might leave anybody, though," Isobel said, "and might not join with another. They don't know why. They do seem to develop on certain planet surfaces."

"Good thing. I expect the growth of the Xanthean's zenfler will expand to Ezredin."

"Already has, and hopefully not disamine," Lucian added.

Two days later she stood in the docking bay holding Jedrick surrounded by Rangers, many of T-Omer's security, and just about everyone left on the embassy deck, or not needed for ship's duty. An array of baby paraphernalia was packed, waiting to be loaded on the shuttle. Along with the ship's other shuttles, the *Crusader* and *Delve* also were docked to take passengers groundside, although portions of each shuttle tended to disappear in the bay's background.

"You look beautiful," Ambassador Nohl said. "How many shuttles are going down?" He stopped and stood next to her with his wife, Zella, on his other side.

"I believe all the shuttles are going down."

Zella smiled at Jezlynn, saying, "Your fashion reflects your eye color. I understand Isobel had it made onboard the *Sentinel*?"

"Yes, she did, and their outfits, too, I believe," Jezlynn answered and thanked her, knowing Zella's part in the embassy's amenities. Needed, since more families were arriving to take up previous positions.

She felt too showy in the dress Isobel and Lu had selected. It was a combination of blue pants, tunic, and long jacket, not overly ornamented except for the sapphire buttons on the jacket. Lucian had demanded flat boots or shoes and Isobel complied with his demands. Jezlynn discovered aggravation came with family. Surprisingly, Vanessa had done her hair. When asked about any hair clips and accessories, Jezlynn showed her the ones Nael had designed. Vanessa was amazed at their ornamental design and smiled when she discovered they were also weapons, saying, "So ingenious," in obvious approval. She did an exceptional job with braids and curls.

"You know you were right." Nohl reclaimed her attention.

"About?"

"So was President Uebel. This mission needed you. What you wrangled out of everyone involved in negotiations was amazing. I would not have even thought of those aspects, let alone persuaded any other negotiators to agree."

"Well, I did have experience and knowledge, but you are over exaggerating. You are a skilled diplomat. Our success was based on a combined team who did outstanding work."

He smiled at her. "Your diplomatic skills grow."

"I was a trader. Every successful trader needs diplomatic skills. Zella, are you going to continue your yoga classes?"

"I never stopped but suspect now that the mission has been completed and the crew and embassy personnel are not so tied up in duty… more will attend."

Jezlynn watched as John Olson started guiding the waiting groups to various shuttles. All embassy personnel were shown to the *Crusader*. Soon Lucian had a hand on her arm, guiding her, Margarete, and her grandmothers to the *Delve*.

"That was a very interesting conversation," Margarete said. The three women continued talking trivia and demanding to share Jedrick-holding time.

Jezlynn rolled her eyes at Krayne. He squeezed her hand in support. In recognizing the expression as one of Jesse's, he felt both a pang of mourning and a bolt of optimism.

A group of Rangers and crew joined them on the *Delve*.

"Ribberdan and Rae are remaining onboard," Lu told his wife.

"Think something is up?"

He smiled. "I know so. They've asked me to perform a ceremony."

"About time; glad to hear it."

Vanessa handed Jedrick to Lucian, and he took his son in a practiced and comfortable hold. Jedrick's lips moved but he remained asleep.

Once landed, they emerged from the shuttle and walked to a newly constructed terminal. "They have completed a lot of work," Jezlynn said, looking around. The building was obviously reinforced, safe, but had Xanthean basic, almost primitive, simplicity in design. Jezlynn felt the same tingling she felt in the cave begin on the soles of her feet, but it didn't move any further. Ahjias and Sutta waited nearby. Ahjias asked to hold Jedrick, and Lucian immediately relinquished his son to settle into the Xanthean's arms. Jedrick opened his eyes but quickly closed them, seeming to sleep, which may have been due to the soothing song-like sound Ahjias emitted. Sutta looked pleased.

"What's up, partner?" Jezlynn asked, giving Sutta's arm one of Jet's gentle punches.

"You are whole. I am myself again. I serve."

"And he has agreed to be my mate," Ahjias said. "So, practicing my infant skills should prove beneficial."

Sutta spoke in clear Space Standard. "We will serve on the *Sentinel* now as Aswenna holds the Amber Circle, partner."

The other side of the terminal emerged into the new colony's buildings. They had been turned to more Xanthean in style and surround a large plant-lined circle with smaller stone-lined circles. Jesse assumed for Circle meditations. Some still sat in their meditation spot. She recognized Morgan Dachs as one of them. He looked at her but did not seem to recognize her and just closed his eyes to continue his meditation.

They walked around the circle and into the central structure. Aswenna waited and lead them into yet a larger outdoor circle behind the building. It was lined with what Jezlynn recognized as zenfler. Many people filled the circle holding drinks.

"I cannot say I look forward to staying on Ezredin, and I hope they are not going to serve me zenfler," she murmured to Lucian.

Aswenna answered. "Of course, but a very mild rendition, have no fears, Genitor. It means everyone will relax and enjoy our celebration of Xanthean renewal and peace in space travel, which we now will have authority to ensure." Her face contorted to a confident expression.

"Plus, only truth will be told?"

"Yes, Genitor. May I hold Jedrick?"

Ahjias handed her the small bundle of her son which Aswenna took with gentle care. "You leave for Griff soon," Aswenna said.

Margarete seemed unsurprised at the revered elder's information. "Yes, they will probably travel with me and stay for a short, or perhaps an extended, visit."

Aswenna did not give up her hold on Jedrick, and soon she and Lucian were separated as guests came to speak to them. Jezlynn watched other guests walk toward her, some showing unease. Austin Dachs came.

"I cannot thank you enough," he said.

"You like it here?"

"Best place I've ever been. Even Uncle Reed has found a new purpose. Plus, both of our reputations within the Alliance have changed." He looked at his uncle. "I do doubt that Uncle Reed wants to return, even with his change in status. The Corps has reviewed his files, and he is now receiving retirement."

"Well, if he wants, he might find a position on Starbase Amber." Austin smiled, nodded, and as he left, the Individual Rights Bureau representative Miz Silmyn approached her. With her came Jesse's old nemesis, Doctor Harper Inserra. Sutta stepped in front of them stopping their approach. Their determined expressions turned apprehensive. Lucian was just as quickly by her side.

"I only want a few words," Silmyn said.

At his captain's nod, Sutta stood aside. Silmyn smiled at Lucian, and then at her. "I am very glad to learn you have completely healed. The bureau wanted to explain our purpose to the Xantheans, and they have permitted us to open a hospital here to help cure disamine poisoning. The Individual Rights Bureau sent Doctor Inserra here to help. You must have noticed how the dronai treatment here has helped Morgan. We hope others can be helped."

"I have no say over what the Xantheans do, or who they allow on their new home world."

"They hold you in extreme respect," Silmyn said. "We have learned your body chemistry seems to have a drastic effect on this symbiotic lifeform and hoped you might help us."

Aswenna spoke from behind them. "No, you can have no access to the genitor. If you speak to her again, you will lose your permission.

The Amber Circle told you about the restrictions, and the most important one is that of the genitor."

Silmyn straightened. "I am sorry to have upset the genitor, Revered Elder." She glanced at Jezlynn. "I was not sure exactly who the genitor was. We are just passionate about our mission and finding help."

"I will not be available to the Individual Rights Bureau for anything. You may speak with the Xantheans, but I have many other duties and interests. Those prevent me from partaking in your plans here."

"My apologies. Please excuse us," Silmyn said, and she and Inserra quickly retreated.

Aswenna still held Jedrick.

When Jezlynn knew they could not hear, she said, "The past never leaves, does it?"

Lucian held her hand. "No, but that doesn't stop the future and what it can hold. Have you decided where you want to live?"

She felt peace. "With you. Wherever."

Meet Rhobin Lee Courtright

Born and raised in Michigan, Rhobin spent one year in Colorado and twenty years in Missouri raising her family and working as a business writer. She now lives back in Michigan on twenty acres near the small village. Always interested in science, history, nature, and art, her overactive imagination led her to speculate on life beyond Earth, and the 'what-ifs' of changes to humanity that soon turned into fantasy and science fiction novels. She writes about writing and her quirks of mind on her blog at www.rhobincourtright.com

Other Works From The Pen Of

Rhobin Lee Courtright

Aegis Series:

Magic Aegis - Centuries ago, the witch Chloe cast the Aegis spell, binding four men and their descendants to protect Kaereya. Now, when needed most, magic is lost.

Change - Her mother demanded two things of Tyna...that she never expose her true nature and that she never enter Cygna, the land of witches. Now, her mother is dead, and her sister has abandoned her.

Acceptance - Responsibility and duty drove mercenary Kissre to find her estranged sister in Cygna, the land of witches.

Legend's Cipher - What Bertok had not related when the bishop gave him this mission was his most buried secret—he possessed an unnatural ability.

Black Angel Series:

Rogue's Rules - Traitor, mutineer, deserter—slanderous words fixed to Ensign Jezlynn Chambers' name.

Loser's Game - Jezlynn has plied the pirates' trade but won't let anyone use the signature of the Black Angel to hide their crimes.

Devil's Due - Command ordered Jezlynn into the Space Service Corp, yet it is one thing to think you can accomplish a goal, another to achieve it.

Home World Series:

Home World Aginfeld - On technically advanced but feudal Aginfeld, Alix Risseu is held for theft...the sentence is death. Only Alix is innocent.

Nanite Warrior - Hearing herself claimed as wife, Xandra gave a weak laugh. "Bad luck just won't end, but this time, I'm sure yours is worse than mine, husband."

Dragoons' Journey - Brigit has moved constantly for years, now a message offers her freedom on Aginfeld, a place her enemy, the Colonial Pact, desperately wants.

Home World Reax - Maera escaped the future planned for her on Reax, so what could make her return? Learning of her home planet's devastation.

The Carolingians:

Constantine's Legacy - Leonard must learn to be the Frankish warrior his father Radulf, the Dux Provinciae, demands. His difficult training is nothing compared to the dangerous deceptions he discovers.

Letter to Our Readers

Enjoy this book?

You can make a difference

As an independent publisher, Wings ePress, Inc. does not have the financial clout of the large New York Publishers. We can't afford large magazine spreads or subway posters to tell people about our quality books.

But, we do have something much more effective and powerful than ads. We have a large base of loyal readers.

Honest Reviews help bring the attention of new readers to our books.

If you enjoyed this book, we would appreciate it if you would spend a few minutes posting a review on the site where you purchased this book or on the Wings ePress, Inc. webpages at: https://wingsepress.com/

Visit Our Website

For The Full Inventory
Of Quality Books:

Wings ePress.Inc
https://wingsepress.com/

Quality trade paperbacks and downloads
in multiple formats,
in genres ranging from light romantic comedy
to general fiction and horror.
Wings has something for every reader's taste.
Visit the website, then bookmark it.
We add new titles each month!

Wings ePress Inc.
3000 N. Rock Road
Newton, KS 67114